THE GREAT ACCEPTANCE

THE LIFE STORY OF

F. N. CHARRINGTON

BY
GUY THORNE

DEDICATION

TO THE POOR OF THE EAST END
AMONG WHOM MR. CHARRINGTON HAS
LABOURED SO LONG

Then shall the righteous man stand in great boldness before the face of such as have afflicted him, and made no account of his labours.

When they see it, they shall be troubled with terrible fear, and shall be amazed at the strangeness of his salvation, so far beyond all that they looked for.

And they repenting and groaning for anguish of spirit shall say within themselves, This was he whom we had sometimes in derision, and a proverb of reproach:

We fools counted his life madness, and his end to be without honour:

How is he numbered among the children of God, and his lot is among the saints!—Wisdom of Solomon.

CHAPTER I

THE GREAT ACCEPTANCE

In the year 1882 the most popular novelist of his day wrote as follows about the East End of London—

"Two millions of people, or thereabouts, live in the East End of London. That seems a good-sized population for an utterly unknown town. They have no institutions of their own to speak of, no public buildings of any importance, no municipality, no gentry, no carriages, no soldiers, no picture-galleries, no theatres, no opera,—they have nothing. It is the fashion to believe they are all paupers, which is a foolish and mischievous belief, as we shall presently see. Probably there is no such spectacle in the whole world as that of this immense, neglected, forgotten great city of East London. It is even neglected by its own citizens, who have never yet perceived their abandoned condition. They are Londoners, it is true, but they have no part or share in London; its wealth, its splendours, its honours, exist not for them. They see nothing of any splendours; even the Lord Mayor's Show goeth westward: the City lies between them and the greatness of England. They are beyond the wards, and cannot become aldermen; the rich London merchants go north and south and west; but they go not east. Nobody goes east, no one wants to see the place; no one is curious about the way of life in[2] the east. Books on London pass it over; it has little or no history; great men are not buried in its churchyards, which are not even ancient, and crowded by citizens as obscure as those who now breathe the upper air about them. If anything happens in the east, people at the other end have to stop and think before they can remember where the place may be."

It will be a somewhat startling reflection to many of us to realise that Sir Walter Besant wrote *All Sorts and Conditions of Men* thirty years ago, and it is more profitable to inquire how true the words I have just quoted are to-day. It is indubitable that a great improvement has taken place. The East End has been "exploited" by many other eminent writers, following in the footsteps of Sir Walter. It is no longer true in the main to say that the East End of London is wholly neglected: the pages of any decent book of reference will bear witness to the innumerable philanthropic and religious missions which have sprung up in the City of the Poor. Yet, to the average man and woman of some place and position, both in London and in the country, I venture to say that the East End is just as remote and visionary a place as Suez.

As an average man myself—perhaps, owing to my profession as a writer, having seen even more of life than the average man, and being endowed with a rather eager curiosity and liking for new scenes—I had never visited the East End, or been nearer to it than Liverpool Street Station, until the early part of the present year.

About the time of which I speak certain facts[3] came to my knowledge about the work that was being done by Frederick Nicholas Charrington, Honorary Superintendent of the Tower Hamlets Mission. It was in a casual conversation with one of the great experts on inebriety that I first even heard of Mr. Charrington's name. What I heard seemed rather extraordinary and out of the way. From what was said, I suspected that a strange personality, and one offering considerable interest to a novelist, was hidden away—at least, as far as I was concerned—in the East End of London.

It came to pass that from other sources I heard more of Mr. Charrington, almost immediately afterwards.

I suppose every one knows how, when they have met with some new word, some quotation, or name of a place, entirely fresh to them, they find it cropping up on every possible occasion. Now, this, of course, is not coincidence. It is merely that one's eyes have been opened.

I heard of the subject of this biography as conducting a work unique in its scope and methods among the great charitable organisations of London. I heard of him as being the owner of a sea-girt island not more than forty-five miles away from London! and some vague story of the sacrifice, made in his youth, of an enormous sum of money.

One does not hear of this sort of personality every day, and my curiosity was immediately excited. Then, as chance would have it—or who shall say that it was not some Higher Power than chance?—I made the acquaintance of Mr. Charrington, chiefly through a novel dealing with the[4] subject of intemperance which I had recently published.

It is not necessary to say more about the genesis of this book, save only that from all over the world the subject of it has constantly received requests from people of every class to write his own biography. Publishers have approached him also with the same proposal, but he has consistently declined. In the event Mr. Charrington has done me the honour to appoint me his biographer, and to place the fullest information as to his career in my possession.

I have made personal experience of the work in the East End. I have read through an enormous amount of documents, both printed and written. I have interviewed and had long conversations with friends and fellow-workers of Mr. Charrington, who have been associated with him for forty years. And finally, I have lived with the man himself, upon his island.

The first time that I ever went to the East End was upon a Sunday, after lunch. I was sitting in my club in St. James' Street. After breakfast, in the smoking-room I asked a man there how to get to the Great Assembly Hall in the Mile End Road. His reply, which was prompt and to the point, was, nevertheless, not exactly what I wanted. He said, "Why, take a taxi-cab, of course," but I discovered that he knew no more how to get to the place in question than I did. Shortly afterwards, in my bedroom, I spoke to the head valet—a very old and confidential servant of the club. He, at least, was able to give me more detailed directions, but added, "If I may say so, sir, you will have a rather unpleasant time of it[5] among as nasty a lot of ruffians as you'd find anywhere!"

What experiences I *did* have upon this first visit, and upon subsequent ones, will be related in their proper place in this picture of F. N. Charrington, but the remarks of both member and servant recalled very forcibly the passage I have printed from *All Sorts and Conditions of Men*.

It is, then, to the East End, and to a series of incidents so rich in drama, a time so breathlessly exciting, and at all times so strangely seen in a light which is not of this world, that readers of this memoir are coming with me. To many of them it will be as fresh and as intensely interesting as it has been to me, and, as Thackeray indulged in theatrical simile in the preface of *Vanity Fair*, let me also announce the ringing up of the curtain upon as soul-stirring a drama upon the boards of life in a city as, perhaps, it has ever been the lot of a man to write.

You shall see the wars of the Powers and Principalities of the air against the Angels of Light, you shall hear the menacing drums of the legions of Evil, and the clear, clarion calls of the soldiers of God. Nor shall there be wanting a pastoral interlude also, of a lonely Island of Rest, where summer breezes blow among the trees, and there is a murmur of many waters.

. . .

The Mile End Road, which is the great main thoroughfare through the East End—from the City of London west, to the vast glades of Epping Forest in Essex—has no more conspicuous an[6] object than the vast brewery of Messrs. Charrington & Head.

It stands up in the middle of the wide thoroughfare like some Gibraltar rising from the human tide at its feet. It is a huge pile of almost goblin masonry, with its colossal ladders, towers, and vast receptacles for malt. It is surrounded by a high wall, and covers an enormous expanse of ground. It hits the eye like a blow with its vastness, its suggestion of mighty, vested interests, solidity, and wealth. It dwarfs everything else in the neighbourhood.

On almost every public-house that one meets one reads in huge gilt letters the words, "CHARRINGTON & CO.'S ENTIRE." If you go off the main roads it is the same thing—every little public-house flaunts the same legend. From the mighty portals of the brewery, day by day throughout the year, a never-ending flood of alcohol is pouring, and in those enormous vats who shall say how many souls have been dissolved?

I quoted above from Sir Walter Besant's *All Sorts and Conditions of Men*. The quotation was more *à-propos* to commence this life than most people are aware. The story of "Miss Messenger," the heiress to the great East End brewery of "Messenger & Co." in the Mile End Road, and how she went to live among the struggling millions of the East, was inspired by the life story of Frederick N. Charrington. It was his career that, in the first instance, made it possible for Sir Walter to write one of the most popular novels of the last fifty years.

A great many people will remember the description[7] in chapter four, where the heiress of the brewery is taken over her own possession for the first time in her life.

It is a singularly vivid picture Sir Walter has given us, and one which is substantially true to-day.

"The walk from Stepney Green to Messenger and Marsden's Brewery is not far. You turn to the left if your house is on one side, and to the right if it is on the other; then you pass a little way down one street, and a little way, turning again to the left, up another—a direction which will guide you quite clearly. You then find yourself before a great gateway, the portals of which are closed; beside it is a smaller door, at which, in a little lodge, sits one who guards the entrance.

"Mr. Bunker nodded to the porter, and entered unchallenged. He led the way across a court to a sort of outer office.

"'Here,' he said, 'is the book for the visitors' names. We have them from all countries: great lords and ladies; foreign princes; and all the brewers from Germany and America, who come to get a wrinkle. Write your own name in it too. Something, let me tell you, to have your name in such noble company.'"

. . .

"'Ah! it's a shame for such a property to come to a girl—a girl of twenty-one. Thirteen acres it covers—think of that! Seven hundred people it employs, most of them married. Why, if it was only to see her own vats, you'd think she'd get off her luxurious pillows for once, and come here.'

"They entered a great hall, remarkable, at first, for a curious smell, not offensive, but strong and rather pungent. In it stood half-a-dozen enormous vats, closed by wooden slides, like shutters, and fitting tightly. A man standing by opened one[8] of these, and presently Angela was able to make out, through the volumes of steam, something bright going round, and a brown mess going with it.

"'That is hops. Hops for the biggest Brewery, the richest, in all England. And all belonging to a girl, who, likely enough, doesn't drink more than a pint and a half a day.'

.   .   .   .   .

"He led the way up-stairs into another great hall, where there was the grinding of machinery, and another smell, sweet and heavy.

"'This is where we crush the malt,' said Mr. Bunker—'see!' He stopped, and picked out of a box a great handful of the newly-crushed malt. 'I suppose you thought it was roasted. Roasting, young lady,' he added with severity, 'is for Stout, not for Ale.'

"Then he took her to another place, and showed her where the liquor stood to ferment; how it was cooled, how it passed from one vat to another, how it was stored and kept in vats; dwelling perpetually on the magnitude of the business, and the irony of fortune in conferring this great gift upon a girl.

"'I know now,' she interrupted, 'what the place smells like. It is fusel oil.' They were standing on a floor of open iron bars, above a row of long covered vats, within which the liquor was working and fermenting. Every now and then there would be a heaving of the surface, and a quantity of malt would then move suddenly over.

"'We are famous,' said Mr. Bunker, 'I say we, having been the confidential friend and adviser of the late Mr. Messenger, deceased; we are famous for our Stout; also for our Mild; and we are now reviving our Bitter, which we had partially neglected. We use the Artesian Well, which is four hundred feet deep, for our Stout, but the Company's[9] water for our Ales; and our water rate is two thousand pounds a year. The Artesian Well gives the Ale a grey colour, which people don't like. Come into this room now,'—it was another great hall covered with sacks. 'Hops again, Miss Kennedy; now, that little lot is worth ten thousand pounds—ten—thousand—think of that; and it is all spoiled by the rain, and has to be thrown away. We think nothing of losing ten thousand pounds here, nothing at all!'—he snapped his fingers—'it is a mere trifle to the girl who sits at home and takes the profits.'

.   .   .   .   .

"Then they went into more great halls, and up more stairs, and on to the roof, and saw more piles of sacks, more malt, and more hops. When they smelt the hops, it seemed as if their throats were tightened; when they smelt the fermentation, it seemed as if they were smelling fusel oil; when they smelt the plain crushed malt, it seemed as if they were getting swiftly, but sleepily, drunk. Everywhere and always the steam rolled backwards and forwards, and the grinding of the machinery went on, and the roaring of the furnaces; and the men went about to and fro at their work. They did not seem hard worked, nor were they pressed; their movements were leisurely, as if beer was not a thing to hurry; they were all rather pale of cheek, but fat and jolly, as if the beer was good and agreed with them. Some wore brown-paper caps, for it was a pretty draughty place; some went bareheaded, some wore the little round hat in fashion. And they went to another part, where men were rolling barrels about, as if they had been skittles, and here they saw vats holding three thousand barrels; and one thought of giant armies—say two hundred and fifty thousand thirsty Germans—beginning the Loot of London with one of these royal vats. And they went through stables, where[10] hundreds of horses were stalled at nights, each as big as an elephant, and much more useful.

.   .   .   .   .

"In one great room, where there was the biggest vat of all, a man brought them beer to taste; it was Messenger's Stout. Angela took her glass and put it to her lips with a strange emotion—she felt as if she would like a quiet place to sit down in and cry. The great place was hers—all hers—and this was the beer with which her mighty fortune had been made.

"'Is it?' she asked, looking at the heavy foam of the frothing stout; 'is this Messenger's Entire?'

THE BREWERY
(This photograph was taken during the year 1912. Frederick Charrington is the centre of the three small figures below)
[*To face p. 10.*]

"'This is not Entire,' he said. 'You see, there's fashions in beer, same as in clothes; once it was all Cooper, now you never hear of Cooper. Then it was all Half-an'-arf—you never hear of any one ordering Half-an'-arf now. Then it was stout. Nothing would go down but Stout, which I recommend myself, and find it nourishing. Next, Bitter came in, and honest Stout was despised; now, we're all for Mild. As for Entire, why, bless my soul! Entire went out before I was born. Why, it was the Entire that made the fortune of the first Messenger that was—a poor little brewery he had, more than a hundred years ago, in this very place, because it was cheap for rent. In those days they used to brew strong Ale, Old and Strong; Stout, same as now; and Twopenny, which was small beer. And because the Old Ale was too Strong, and the Stout too dear, and the Twopenny too weak, the people used to mix them all three together, and they called them "Three Threads"; and you may fancy the trouble it was for the pot-boys to go to one cask after another, all day long—because they had no beer engines then. Well, what did Mr. Messenger do? He brewed a beer as strong as the Three Threads, and he called it Messenger's Entire Three Threads, meaning that[11] here you had 'em all in one, and that's what made his fortune; and now, young lady, you've seen all I've got to show you, and we will go.'"

To a brewery identical with the one described in almost every respect, owning hundreds of tied public-houses, producing the revenue of a prince for its proprietors, Frederick Nicholas Charrington was heir.

He was born in the Bow Road, in the East End of London, on February 4, 1850, and is now, therefore, in the sixty-second year of his life.

A dear venerable old lady (Mrs. Pratt), still retained under Mr. Charrington's roof, well remembers his mother, a deeply religious woman, driving in a pony and chaise visiting the sick and needy, and relieving them according to their several necessities, for miles round the neighbourhood of the brewery. She always took with her a cordial which was made up in her own home, and for which there was a great demand from the poor, who regarded it as an infallible remedy for all kinds of diseases.

Mrs. Pratt remembers carrying "Master Fred" in her arms when he was about two years of age, and how excited he became when she took him to see a balloon passing over what was then known as Charrington's Park, open fields by which the brewery was then surrounded, but which have long since been built over.

She also remembers Master Fred at nine years of age, taking a bundle of bank notes from his father's table in the counting-house, and throwing them into the fire. When asked by his father why[12] he did so, he characteristically replied that "he wanted to see a blaze."

Surely the child was father to the man!

In all the great breweries of London the rule has been made, and is very generally adhered to, that the partners share and share alike, so that it must be explained that Mr. Charrington was not sole heir to the business. The revenues, however, are so enormous, that, roughly speaking, a million and a quarter pounds would have come to the boy who was born in 1850. Mr. Charrington's parents were members of the Church of England, and belonged to the Evangelical school of thought. Frederick was educated at Marlborough, but during his stay at the famous public school he was laid low by a fever, which necessitated his removal at the time. Subsequently he was entered at Brighton College, where he finished his school career. He lived the ordinary life of a boy born to great wealth, and, when school days were over, he was given the choice of proceeding to the University of Oxford or of Cambridge, whichever he preferred. A University life, however, offered no attractions to the young man's cast of mind. His first experience of the larger world of men and things was made upon the Continent. It must be remembered that, at this time, the tradition that it was necessary for every young man of position to make what was known as "the grand tour," had not yet died away. Travelling was then a most costly affair, and only possible to the rich. Sir Henry Lunn and Messrs. Cook and Sons had not, at that time, made the chief Continental cities practically suburbs of London. It was thought, and rightly thought,[13] that a Continental tour was in itself an education, and this was the means selected to widen the young man's mind. All his subsequent life Mr. Charrington has been a great traveller, and there are few parts of the world which he has not at one time or another visited, and where he has not been welcomed. So that this first foreign excursion must have been a time of great pleasure and enlightenment.

He was accompanied by the Rev. Thomas Scott, a clergyman, and had for his companion Mr. J. H. Buxton, another wealthy young brewer, who subsequently became chairman of the London Hospital. The lads visited the Paris Exhibition of 1867, and travelled through Switzerland and Italy.

Upon his return Frederick Charrington at once elected to learn the details of the great business which there was, at the time, every prospect of his superintending. He went to the smaller brewery of Messrs. Neville, Read & Co., who were brewers to the Queen at Windsor. There he shared rooms with a young curate, the Rev. John Stone, who, by the way, was the author of the two famous and beautiful hymns, "The Church's one Foundation," and "Weary of earth and laden with my sin."

The young man's pursuits, even at this time, were by no means those of his contemporaries. Although he had the command of large sums of money if he had wished, the pleasures of ordinary young men did not appeal to him. It is not to be understood that he was in any way a milksop. He was a good waterman upon the river, and at a time when young men of position did not indulge in cricket, football, and other field sports to anything[14] like the same extent that they do to-day, he was yet a fearless, skilful rider. There had always been many horses in his father's stables, and from his earliest youth Mr. Charrington had been an expert equestrian. In those days a young man so fond of horses, and so good a horseman, nine cases out of ten owned horses or took great interest in betting and the affairs of the turf, while an alternative was the driving of a four-in-hand coach, generally in the company of people of both sexes, neither desirable nor worthy for them to know.

Mr. Charrington did nothing of the sort. The attractions of the gilded youth of his adolescence passed him by without any appeal, and at the end of the twelve months' experience at Windsor, he entered his father's great brewery in the Mile End Road.

A rather interesting little episode in connection with Mr. Charrington's horsemanship might be mentioned here. One day, during his time at Windsor, he was riding a very spirited chestnut in a quiet and narrow lane in the environs of the town. Suddenly a groom upon horseback turned the corner, galloped up to him, and with a rude and overbearing manner ordered him to turn round and go away. Extremely surprised at the man's insolence, Mr. Charrington refused to do anything of the sort, and it seemed that almost a scrimmage was imminent.

The man then explained that the Queen was coming, and Mr. Charrington asked him why on earth he had not said so before. It was now too late. A carriage and pair, with outriders, came down[15] the road in the opposite direction, and Queen Victoria was seated within.

Mr. Charrington realised at once what was happening, although the man had given no reasons, and he backed his horse as well as he could into the hedge. The lane was very narrow, and there was hardly room for the carriage to pass. Mr. Charrington made his horse rear upon its hind legs and took off his hat as he did so. It was only by the display of the most magnificent horsemanship that he was able to keep his seat, and allow the chaise to pass, and her Majesty smiled and bowed very graciously as she went by.

Soon after this he accompanied his parents upon another Continental tour. Upon this occasion he met with Mr. William Rainsford, son of the Rev. Marcus Rainsford, of Belgrave Chapel. The two young men returned to England together, and Charrington invited his friend to stay with him at his father's house.

It was during this visit that Mr. Rainsford spoke to his friend about his soul, and plainly asked him if he knew whether he was saved.

The question struck Mr. Charrington as singularly unpleasant. It startled him, and seemed also in bad taste. He had lived a moral and decent life in every way, and, moreover, a definitely religious life. Such a point-blank question appeared unnecessary, and he protested against such a subject of discussion, referring to the pleasant time spent upon the Continent, and hinting that a reminiscent talk of their adventures would be far more *à-propos* at the moment. Mr. Rainsford, however, pressed the question home, and would[16] not be denied. Eventually he made his friend promise that the next time he was alone he would read the third chapter of the Gospel of St. John. The promise was kept, though the reader expected no new spiritual experience whatever.

As he opened the Bible an incident of the past struck him, and before reading he paused to recall it.

Upon one occasion whilst staying at Hastings he became friends with a Mr. Canning, who subsequently became Lord Garvagh. This young man was at the time at the watering place with his tutor, and when he first met Charrington had just come from hearing Lord Radstock preach. Fired with enthusiasm, he straightway told his new acquaintance the history of the meeting, and made a special reference to the third chapter of the Gospel according to St. John. He related that he believed that he was now a saved man. He definitely stated that conversion had taken place. Now to Mr. Charrington the whole thing was a riddle, and he thought it was at least indecorous for a youthful aristocrat to go and hear a Dissenter, even though that same Dissenter was a peer himself. Moreover, the word conversion presented no very special meaning to him, and was associated in his mind with suggestions of sudden hysteria, and no particularly lasting result. He did not know, as Mr. Harold Begbie has pointed out in his brilliant psychological studies of spiritual experiences, that conversion is in reality nothing of the sort. As Mr. Begbie says—

"... And these critics with their 'cortical susceptibilities' and 'explosions of nervous energy,'[17] limit their investigations of conversion to those examples of the miracle which become public property through the chronicles of revivalism. It is now a vulgar idea that conversions only follow upon the hysterical absurdities of professional revivalists. It would be fatal to religion if such were the case. No one, I think, could more detest the professional revivalist than myself, and than myself no one could more entirely doubt the lasting effect of the majority of the conversions accomplished by this means. I can see the need for revivalism, and I can see in the future a development of revivalism which will be of noble service to humanity; but I dislike the un-Christly character of this worked-up excitement and I am utterly uninterested by its result. Conversion, real conversion, is almost always the effect of individual lovingkindness, of personal and quiet love, of intercourse between a happy and an unhappy soul in the normal colloquies of friendship, and passionate seeking of the lost by those whose lives are inspired by unselfish love. It may possibly have its culminating point in a public meeting; the act of standing up and publicly declaring for righteousness may have tremendous effect; but even in such cases, such rare cases, the preparation has usually been long and difficult, secret and gradual.

"... Conversion is a quite common experience among ordinary men, is very often nothing more than a secret turning of the face towards God, a private decision to live a new life, a personal and wholly tranquil choice of the soul for Christ as its Master and Saviour. No priest appears to be[18] necessary, the excitements of the revivalist preacher are absent. In the privacy of its own soul, the spirit turns from evil and faces towards God."

As Mr. Charrington began to read the suggested portion of Scripture, he remembered this Mr. Canning and his allusion to exactly the same chapter, and it seemed a singular thing that two of his friends of a similar age should agree in giving a certain passage the same interpretation. The remembrance made him read the chapter with the very greatest care, and the words "Marvel not that I said unto ye, Ye must be born again," came to him with a singular force. And though, perhaps, he was unaware of it at the time, in looking back upon it, Mr. Charrington is convinced that this moment was the great turning-point in his life. There was no sudden conversion, let it be remembered—that is, using the word in its more widely accepted sense. It must not be lost sight of that Mr. Charrington had always lived a religious life. But, certainly, whatever name we may give to the spiritual change which passed over him at the moment, it was a real and lasting one.

I have in my possession a letter written by Mr. Charrington a good many years ago, describing the occurrence exactly as it happened, and, as I am allowed to quote, it may be as well to supplement my own account with Mr. Charrington's own words.

"To begin with, I was travelling on the Continent along the Riviera, or the South of France, and just before I returned from Cannes I met with my friend William Rainsford, the celebrated episcopal clergyman from New York. We travelled home[19] together to England, and when we got to London I invited him to come and stop at my father's house at Wimbledon. At the time I was living a very moral life, and not without some interest in eternal things, but my only belief and trust was in the Book of Common Prayer, and especially the statement, 'Wherein I was made a member of Christ, the Child of God, and an inheritor of the Kingdom of Heaven.' When we got to my father's home, to my great astonishment Rainsford suddenly said, 'I feel very guilty, we have travelled together all the way over the Continent, and enjoyed ourselves very much, but I have never spoken to you about your soul. The fact is, I am a Christian, but I have spent the winter in the South of France for my health, and I have been in very worldly society; but now that I have got back to old England, these things seem to rise in my mind, and I feel that I must ask you if you are saved.' I said, 'Really, Rainsford, we have had a very good time on the Continent, and I think it is a very great pity that you bring up such a debatable subject just now.' He said, 'I only will ask you to do one thing, and that is: when I am gone you will promise me to read through the third chapter of St. John's Gospel.' I promised him I would, and accordingly the next night, while smoking a pipe before I went to bed, I read the third chapter of St. John, and as I read it I thought to myself, 'This is a very curious thing: here are two men, my new friend Rainsford, and my old friend Lord Garvagh, both say the same thing, that they are "saved" '; and as I read the chapter, Light came into my soul, and as I came to the words, 'He that believeth on the Son hath[20] everlasting life' I realised that I, too, possessed the 'eternal life.'"

We are come, then, to a certain definite point in the life of this young man. As a result of what I have just described, he felt that he ought to be doing something to help others, to be setting his hand to some good works.

In its proper place, I shall tell of these first tentative efforts at work for Christ, and how they broadened out into such a magnificent life work. It is not in the scheme of this chapter, which I have headed "The Great Acceptance," to give details at present. It is sufficient to say that this early work prospered and became engrossing, and it gradually led up to the astounding event, almost without parallel, one fancies, which I am about to describe. Mr. Peters, a nephew of Mr. Cunard the great steamship owner, used to help Mr. Charrington in the ragged school for boys, conducted in a loft over a stable. One evening at this period Mr. Charrington was walking from the brewery to the horrible slum where the school was held.

He passed a horrid-looking little public-house, known as the "Rising Sun."

When I say a horrid little public-house, I speak from experience. There are dozens of varieties, from the magnificent bars of the West End, with their columns of marble, their gleaming glass and silver, rich carpets and sumptuous good taste, to the flaunting gin palaces or even the picturesque, flower-covered country inn, and there are mean little holes in back streets which are absolutely destitute of any personality whatever. I think, for my part, though it is pure personal opinion,[21] that I have never seen a more utterly unlovely alcohol shop than this same "Rising Sun." I went personally to look at it before writing this chapter. It lies in an appalling neighbourhood, where even the police patrol in couples, and it is about as hideous an erection as can be found anywhere in England.

Mr. Charrington, then, upon the memorable evening of which I speak, came up to this place. I quote his own words in the account of what occurred here.

"As I approached this public-house a poor woman, with two or three children dragging at her skirts, went up to the swing doors, and calling out to her husband inside, she said, 'Oh, Tom, do give me some money, the children are crying for bread.' At that the man came through the doorway. He made no reply in words. He looked at her for a moment, and then knocked her down into the gutter. Just then I looked up and saw my own name, CHARRINGTON, in huge gilt letters on the top of the public-house, and it suddenly flashed into my mind that that was only one case of dreadful misery and fiendish brutality in one of the several hundred public-houses that our firm possessed. I realised that there were probably numbers of similar cases arising from this one public-house alone. I thought, as if in a flash, that, whatever the actual statistics might have been, there was, at any rate, an appalling and incalculable amount of wretchedness and degradation caused by our enormous business. It was a crushing realisation, the most concrete, unavoidable object-lesson that a man could possibly have. What a frightful[22] responsibility for evil rested upon us! And then and there, without any hesitation, I said to myself—in reference to the sodden brute who had knocked his wife into the gutter—'Well, you have knocked your poor wife down, and with the same blow you have knocked me out of the brewery business.'

"I knew that I could never bear the awful responsibility of so much guilt upon my soul. I could not possibly allow myself to be a contributory cause, and I determined that, whatever the result, I would never enter the brewery again."

Mr. Charrington went to his father and announced his intention of absolutely giving up all share in the brewery. The opposition he met with may easily be imagined. Mr. Charrington senior was amazed and angry. The thing seemed the height of quixotic folly. It verged on madness, and had neither rhyme nor reason to the older man, himself, it must be remembered, a liberal, God-fearing Churchman of the Evangelical school, as well as one of the most successful men of business of his day.

The arguments used against Frederick's determination were all such as keen common sense and the logic of this world would naturally employ.

A VERY EARLY FAMILY GROUP
Mr. Charrington with his sisters, brothers, and governess
[*To face p. 22.*]

Mr. Charrington senior pointed out that he had been many years in business, and that during every day of them he had been studying the drink question. His interest in it was old, and at least as close and personal as his son's could possibly be after a mere casual ramble in the slums of the East End. It was to drink that Frederick Charrington owed the position to which he was born. It might be distasteful to the young man—though to the older it[23] was nothing of the sort—but whether it was agreeable or not, the plain fact was that beer had made Frederick Charrington one of the richest young men in England.

It was suggested to him that he had suffered a kind of first nausea, just as young surgeons are supposed to do when they first handle the knife—or, more general still, and as has been so well described by Sir Conan Doyle, medical students when they first see an operation. But because medical students suffered nausea, it was quite unlikely that operating or dissecting rooms were going to be done away with, and certainly breweries and public-houses would not be done away with though a million fanatics were to call for their suppression. For his own part, Mr. Charrington had made it his business to brew as good beer as could be brewed. His business was conducted with conspicuous regard to decency and order, but, at the same time, he entirely declined to be responsible for the actions of fools. He asked no man to drink more of his beer than was good for him. He was not in the least responsible for drunkenness. It was the drunkard himself who was responsible for it. To indulge in sweeping condemnation of the brewery because there were drunkards, was, so Mr. Charrington senior imagined, just as logical and reasonable as to condemn religion because it makes fanatics and maniacs.

In reply, the young man stated that his convictions were unaltered. It was a question between himself and his conscience, his conscience and the God whom he served. Nothing could possibly affect the issue.

[24]"My father," Mr. Charrington has told me, and I record our conversation here, "was terribly distressed. At first, I think, he was more angry and astonished than pained, but afterwards his distress was very great, and I would have done anything I could to alleviate it but continue to take money from the brewery. I do not want to go too much into this—your own father is alive, and you can imagine what a son's feelings were. Of course, my decision was a very heavy blow to the pride of the family. I am afraid I did not realise that sufficiently at the time, but I do now, and I see what pain my decision must have caused, although it was inevitable. After the first shock, however, my father was extremely kind to me, when he realised that I could not change. He certainly sympathised with my wish to do good among the poor, and he had always helped me in my early efforts among the very rough juvenile population, and himself paid for more suitable premises in which we could carry on the work.

"Shortly after my decision was made my poor father met with a very severe accident. He was thrown from his horse while out riding, and he never recovered. When he was upon his deathbed I was sent for, and what occurred between us at that solemn moment has always been a most precious memory to me. Several other members of the family were gathered round, but he said, 'You all go out of the room for a little time. Let Fred remain with me. He is the only one who knows about these things.'

"When we were left alone together, my father said, 'You are right, Fred. You have chosen the[25] better part, which will never be taken away.' We prayed together then, and the next morning he again said to me, 'After you prayed with me, my sleep was like an angel's slumbers.' Finally he whispered, 'I am afraid I have left you very badly off, but it is too late now.' Shortly afterwards he passed away."

Here is another picture in this astounding history of the Great Acceptance.

One day in February, 1873, the whole traffic of the Strand at a certain point was disorganised. Thousands upon thousands of people were gathered in the vicinity of Exeter Hall. Exeter Street itself was impassable. The Strand was blocked for many hundred yards. The crowd was composed of people from all parts of London and the suburbs, but it was obvious—as the *Daily Telegraph* remarked in its issue on the following morning—that many of the thousands present were East-enders. "Troops of the East End saints were seen wending their way to Exeter Hall"—was how the *Telegraph* was pleased to put it.

And what was the occasion which brought such an enormous crowd together? What spell was there over them all that they pressed onward in phalanx after phalanx to the doors of Exeter Hall? The fact had been noised abroad that the young ex-brewer had accepted the invitation of the Band of Hope Union to preside over their Annual Meeting, under the presidency of the Rev. Charles Garrett, the most famous Temperance reformer of his day.

No other man living than Mr. Charrington has ever caused the Strand to be blocked for hours. No such sight was ever seen before or has been[26] since. The interest created was universal. An eye-witness of the scene has told me that it will never be obliterated from his mind while life lasts. Here was a young man, only just entering his twenty-third year, called upon to preside over an immense meeting for which many of his seniors in the Temperance Cause thought it an honour to receive an invitation.

When the wishes of the Union were first conveyed to him, and the formal invitation made, it gave him food for deep thought. He had left the brewery, and the world's eyes were upon him. He shrank from the great ordeal which acceptance would mean. Still, he was not a man to turn his face from anything he considered to be his duty, and for the welfare of the cause he had at heart. He assented to the wishes of the committee.

"On the night in question," writes a friend who was with him, "Mr. Charrington and I started from Stepney Green and mounted one of the City omnibuses about 7 o'clock. In those days travelling by 'bus was an entirely different thing to what it has since become, and there was always an element of adventure, inasmuch as it was extremely problematical whether the vehicle would keep any sort of time, or even arrive at its destination at all!

"We arrived, however, at last, but it was with great difficulty that we managed to get into Exeter Hall, and had almost to fight our way through the crowd which was already gathered, and which had not then anything like the dimensions it afterwards assumed. The front of Exeter Hall was blocked on both sides of the roadway with police[27] drafted to keep the traffic through, and others who were keeping back the non-ticket holders. Shortly after this the task of keeping this great artery of London clear was finally left, and the traffic was diverted into the side streets. Dr. Newman Hall, one of the speakers who arrived late, sat next me on the platform, and he told me that he had been three-quarters of an hour getting into the building.

"When Mr. Charrington appeared the whole vast audience rose to its feet. The cheering was deafening, and the waving of hats and handkerchiefs continued for several minutes. Again, when he rose to speak the audience broke out into a most extraordinary demonstration of appreciation, and it was a long time before he could get a hearing, so great and electrical was the excitement. It was said that no such gathering had ever congregated at any meeting held in that historic building."

While the meeting was proceeding, large reinforcements of police had to be sent for, as the crowd outside could not be persuaded to go away, or convinced that it was impossible for them to get into the hall. The "Hall Full" placards placed outside were of no use whatever in making them disperse. There was an enormous desire to catch a glimpse of Frederick Charrington as he left the building. On that memorable night many hearts were uplifted in earnest prayer that the young man might be kept true to the profession he had made, and become pre-eminently useful in the service of Christ—prayers which have been so abundantly answered.

Such is the history of Frederick Charrington's[28] Great Acceptance, and it is as well to consider for a moment exactly what it means.

Mr. Charrington gave up, for the sake of conscience, the enormous sum of a million and a quarter. It is very difficult for ordinary people to realise what this sum means. In the first instance, it means about fifty thousand pounds a year—roughly a thousand pounds a week, or about a hundred and forty pounds a day. And yet the figures quite fail to convey the reality. For those who set store by honours and high places, a million and a quarter means a peerage, a singling out and setting above the vast majority of one's fellow-men. It ensures the adulation of almost every one. Plenty of people say, "I do not value the man for his possessions, but for himself," and such a remark may be made perfectly sincerely. But in point of actual fact, there are very few people who can listen to the *obiter dicta* of a millionaire without unconscious deference, and, for my part, without the least wish to be cynical, I have always thought what truth there is in a certain celebrated passage from "Vanity Fair" *à-propos* of the rich Miss Crawley.

"What a dignity," says Thackeray, "it gives an old lady, that balance at the bankers'! How tenderly we look at her faults if she is a relative (may every reader have a score of such), what a kind, good-natured old creature we find her! How the junior partner of Hobbs and Dobbs leads her smiling to the carriage with the lozenge upon it, and the fat, wheezy coachman. How, when she comes to pay us a visit, we generally find an opportunity of letting our friends know her station[29] in the world! We say (and with perfect truth) 'I wish I had Miss MacWhirter's signature to a cheque for five thousand pounds'.... Is it so, or is it not so?"

We must remember also that, while the millionaire of sense does not pay much attention to vulgar flattery, it is very pleasant to have people of charm, intellect, and position around one, and to be great among them. A million and a quarter, if a man has artistic tastes, enables him to buy the finest pictures, the most perfect pieces of statuary, the rarest and most beautiful of books evolved by the genius of mankind. If Mr. Pierpont Morgan, for example, had not a passion for beautiful things, he would certainly not own the greatest art collections that exist. But above all, a million and a quarter means Power—the most eagerly sought for, the most satisfying possession that this world has to offer.

All these things, and the list might be prolonged indefinitely, Frederick Charrington threw away.

You remember—"And behold, one came and said unto him, Good Master, what good thing shall I do that I may have eternal life?"

And again, "Jesus said unto him, if thou wilt be perfect, go and sell that thou hast and give to the poor, and thou shalt have treasure in Heaven: and come and follow Me.

"But when the young man heard that saying he went away sorrowful: for he had great possessions.

"Then said Jesus unto His disciples, Verily, I say unto you, that a rich man shall hardly enter into the Kingdom of Heaven."

[30]We all know the story of the rich young man, which has been referred to over and over again as the Great Refusal. In this book you read the true story of what I beg leave to call "The Great Acceptance."

Christ Jesus came to this young man, Frederick Charrington, with exactly the same appeal as to that other in Palestine so long ago.

The challenge has been given many, many times since the words of our Lord were first spoken, but how seldom has it been responded to! The rich man went away in sorrow, for he had great possessions. It was probably not only the loss of worldly wealth which troubled him. The sacrifice demanded of him involved far more than this, great as this indeed was. We must remember that the expenditure of vast amounts of money on philanthropic objects have often been made with very unworthy motives. There are to be found dozens of men and women—most people will have a case of their own in mind—who would, and do, gladly spend thousands in order that they may obtain a reputation of superior piety, and, in short, become what one might call social saints. They lay the flattering unction to their souls that they "are not as other men." But surely it was the concluding words of Jesus that were the most important, it was the last condition which demanded the greatest sacrifice of all—"Come and follow Me."

When Agrippa said, "Almost thou persuadest me to be a Christian"—if the words were not merely ironical, as some scholars will have it—he seems to have been convinced in his judgment of the truth of Christianity. The native King of Judæa makes no objection whatever to anything the prisoner Paul says. He neither disputes the statement he makes of his astonishing conversion, nor denies the inference he draws from it, that the Jesus he preached was indeed the Christ. But Agrippa stopped at "almost." He could not give up his darling vice, so sweet just then, such a Dead Sea apple afterwards. He could not abandon Berenice; he could not face the sneers and the scorn of the gilded gang which were his companions at Cæsar's court. There are many Agrippas still in the world; there are many young men of great possessions who are convinced that the words of our Lord are true, who will bear to hear the Gospel, even love to hear it, are often deeply affected by it, and seem to themselves and others on the very point of being won over to it—honest, candid men, who are neither afraid nor ashamed to avow their feelings.

And yet, day by day, the Great Refusal is made.

I must not linger upon this starting-point in Frederick Charrington's career, fascinating as the discussion of it is.

How many others are there who have made this Great Acceptance? What sort of young man was this who started out upon life with such a record? As we go further we shall see.

CHAPTER II
BEGINNINGS

There is a certain passage at the end of the "Apostles," by Ernest Renan, which has always seemed to me to be one of singularly penetrating beauty.

Translated, it runs as follows: "I am impatient to tell again that unparalleled epic, to depict those roads stretching infinitely from Asia to Europe, along which they sowed the seed of the Gospel, those waves over which they fared so often under conditions so diverse. The great Christian Odyssey is about to begin. Already the Apostolic barque has shaken forth her sails; the wind is blowing, and aspires for naught save to bear upon its wings words of Jesus."

I am reminded of this passage now, as I begin to tell of Frederick Charrington's life work for Christ. The Great Acceptance has been made, the journey is about to begin. The soldier has girded on his sword and is marching to battle.

Among the first work which the young man undertook was that of helping in a night-school under the direction of the Rev. Joseph Bardsley, then Rector of Stepney. During his work among the very rough he heard of something of the same sort which was being carried on by two young men in the neighbourhood, and not far from the night-school itself. One was Mr. Hugh Campbell, junior, the other Mr. E. H. Kerwin, who has been secretary of the Tower Hamlets Mission ever since its inception, and one of Mr. Charrington's most loyal helpers.

Mr. Campbell and Mr. Kerwin conducted their Evangelistic work in a hayloft over a stable. It was all the shelter that they had, it was all they could afford, and yet from Mr. Charrington's association with it has sprung a mission so wide-reaching in its effects, so world-embracing in the influence that has radiated from it, that we may well marvel at such results from a beginning so humble.

Not long ago I was telling the story of these early days to a lady whose life has been passed in works of charity. She smiled when I spoke of the little hayloft, and she said, "The Light of the World streamed forth from the manger at Bethlehem."

One evening Mr. Charrington visited his new friends and made personal experience of their efforts.

He found the entrance to the stable guarded by a small boy, who showed him up a terribly rickety staircase of open boards to a long room lighted with cheap paraffin lamps which hung from the rafters.

There was a platform, none too elaborately constructed, at one end of the loft, and the floor was covered with rude benches.

The odour of the stable below ascended in all its pristine richness and mingled with the smell of the crude oil lamps, while the atmosphere was still further complicated by the fact that the roof of [34] the hayloft was a low one, and the ventilation almost non-existent.

Yet, on that night, with a congregation of the roughest and most untaught lads to be found in that part of the East End, in such unpropitious surroundings, the guest nevertheless heard addresses to the lads about the love of Christ for them, which made a lasting impression on his mind.

As he stood at the end of the hall and watched, something must have come to him to tell of the mighty work that, under God's blessing, he himself was destined to do in the future. New and unaccustomed as was the scene, strange as some of the methods must have been to him, yet, at that moment, some hinting, some prophetic vision, came to him. He had arrived at last upon the field. He was present at a mere skirmish with the forces of evil, but it was a foretaste of the great battle to come. He had arrived at the front.

He has told me that as he watched and listened he thought, "This is far more like real work for the Lord than my own more secular night-school work," and when the service was nearly over, as the lads sang—

Shall we gather at the river,Where bright angel feet have trod;With its crystal tide for everFlowing by the throne of God?

such an impression was made upon his mind that within another night or two he was again present at the service. He proposed at once that he should join forces with his friends, and brought immediately a fresh and burning enthusiasm, a fierce energy, a daring originality, which almost at once [35] began to alter the whole character of the little mission.

The difficulties, the discouragements, were enormous. The neighbours who surrounded this oasis in the desert were entirely unsympathetic. They scoffed and jeered at the whole thing. Hard words, however, break no bones—there are few men living who believe more thoroughly in the adage than Mr. Charrington—but hard words were not the only thing that the young missioners had to endure.

The man from whom the stable loft was rented was a burly, ruffianly fellow, who, when under the influence of drink, would do his best to upset the meetings.

Once this man burst into the room with an explosion of horrible oaths. He was in a fury, his face was livid with hate, and with every circumstance of violent speech, he bawled out that his poor horse, who had to work hard for its living all day long, could not sleep on account of the noise made by the lads singing hymns!

This ferocious, but singularly ineffectual person, on another occasion stood at the foot of the staircase leading to the loft with a horrible bulldog by his side, daring his tenants to approach the scene of their devotions.

But little circumstances like these had no effect whatever upon the work. Every form of opposition was only like the call of a linnet in a hedge as a regiment of soldiers marches down the road.

Boy after boy came thronging to the standard which the friends had unfurled, and the hayloft became far too small for the purpose. At this moment the Rector of Stepney very kindly placed [36] his schoolroom at the disposal of the three Evangelists. This kindly act, however, was not productive of much success. The lads who attended the meetings were of such a low character—I quote the opinion of the parents of the day-scholars who attended the schools—that the day work began to be seriously interfered with, and "respectable" people complained.

To overcome this difficulty, and perhaps not a very unreasonable opposition on the part of the parents of the day-scholars, a capacious workshop was next taken at Hertford Place, and fitted up by Mr. Charrington's father, at a cost of three hundred pounds, as a mission hall for boys. Another room was rented in Heath Street, Stepney, and this was for girls. In both these halls religious services were held nightly by Mr. Charrington and his friends. There is a brief account in my possession of what was being done at this period, which Mr. Charrington wrote a little later.

He said—

"These premises in Hertford Place, situated at the back of the building represented in our engraving, were secured in May 1870, and fitted up as a school and mission room for boys. Here we had accommodation for over three hundred lads, and the rooms were soon filled with some of the most troublesome roughs of the neighbourhood, including a number of boys known as 'The Mile End Gang,' who had long been a trouble to the police. This gang was soon broken up, in consequence of several of its members, including their leader, professing conversion. An interesting incident occurred soon after this. A number of lads from Whitechapel,[37] known as the 'Kate Street Gang,' or 'The Forty Thieves,' all of whom were by their own rules convicted thieves, came down one Sunday night, with thick sticks up their sleeves to fight our boys; but after our gaining their confidence, and assuring them that we were not in connection with the police, they were induced to enter the building and join in the boys' Sunday evening service.

"After we had continued these meetings for some time, many of the parents expressed a wish to attend them. At first we could not see our way to accede to their request, but after a time they became so pressing that we agreed to hold a service for them at the close of the boys' meeting. These services soon became so crowded that we had to seek a larger building.

"We started a Boys' Home, which was an outcome of the work among the lads. Often after a service boys would come and plead for their companions, who were without home or shelter for the night. This led to our taking a small house in the court in which we were working, and fitting it up for their accommodation. The numbers so increased, however, that we had to take another cottage, and finally, with the aid of kind friends, we purchased a building, which was previously a beer-bottling warehouse.

"In connection with the Home was a savings bank, which gave the boys the opportunity of putting by their spare money. Many instances could be given of the good resulting from the training in this home. Many of our lads were sent to Great Yarmouth, where, through the agency of the Rev. Mr. Nicholson, they were employed on the[38] fishing smacks. Through the kindness of Lord Polwarth, with whom I stayed at his place on the borders of Scotland, several lads were sent to Scotland, and gave the greatest satisfaction. A boy came to us direct from prison. After a time he was sent to Yarmouth. A few months afterwards he had a holiday, and called to see the Master of the House. The first thing he said was, 'I have come to pay you what I owe, and to thank you for enabling me to make a fresh start in life.' The Home was exclusively for boys who were willing to maintain themselves by their own industry. Over 1000 boys received the benefits it affords. Many of them were orphans."

Frederick Charrington had by this time definitely given up his huge inheritance, had left a luxurious home, and had taken a house in Stepney Green. In one of a series of long talks with Mr. T. Richardson, Registrar of the Eastern Telegraph Company, his life-long friend and helper, I have gathered some curious and amusing details about the life lived in Stepney by the young Evangelist.

"In his early days," Mr. Richardson told me, "Mr. Charrington's one idea was for self-denial—personal asceticism."

This early ideal he has persisted in throughout his life. Like other workers for God in different fields, he has chosen celibacy as his lot, in order to give his whole time and all his interests to his work.

LOOKING OUT UPON LIFE
Frederick Charrington at the commencement of his evangelistic career
[To face p. 38.

"He took a house in the East End," Mr. Richardson continued, "near the brewery, and in furnishing it went in for self-denial with an almost monkish enthusiasm. Although it is many years ago, I remember it all perfectly well. He had only a[39] table and one or two chairs, and when there was nothing else to sit upon, an empty packing-case did as well as anything else. He had no carpet at all. One day his mother came to see him, and was dreadfully distressed to see him living like this. Expostulations on the part of Frederick were in vain, and Mrs. Charrington drove immediately to the biggest furnisher's in the City of London and told them to take no denial, but to go at once and furnish her son's house properly.

"He was red-hot and full of enthusiasm. I remember we had been out to a meeting together one night, and somewhere about one or two o'clock in the morning we found ourselves sitting on a costermonger's barrow in a blind alley. Charrington clutched me by the arm and almost shook me. 'We must do something,' he said, 'we must do something to call attention to this cursed liquor traffic. We must get a gang of men armed with cudgels and go and smash the fronts of the public-houses. We shall never do anything till we call attention to it!'"

I shall have much to say shortly of the beginnings of what is perhaps the greatest Temperance crusade that England has ever known, but meanwhile these little glimpses I am able to afford my readers of the quaint house in Stepney so many years ago are curiously interesting.

"Mr. Charrington's house,"—so Mr. Richardson told me—"was the house of call in the neighbourhood, and by strange coincidence, everybody went there about mealtimes! Once, when Mr. Marcus Rainsford was staying in what was locally nicknamed the 'Monastery,' a certain zealous and holy[40] man of God looked in. It was during the evening. Now, a peculiarity of the gentleman to whom I refer is, that when he goes anywhere, he never knows when it is time to leave. On the particular occasion that I remember, he stayed on and on until he missed the last omnibus that could take him to his home. He said to Mr. Charrington, 'You will have to put me up for the night.' Mr. Charrington told him that he hadn't a spare bed. Accordingly, Mr. ——, nothing daunted, replied that he would sleep with Mr. Rainsford if he didn't mind. Mr. Rainsford did not seem at all delighted at the prospect, and said he preferred to take his rest undisturbed as a rule, but that for one night, at any rate, he didn't mind.

"Accordingly, the matter was arranged thus, and in the morning Mr. —— got up first. There was a bathful of water in the bedroom, and the guest inquired if he could take his bath at once. Mr. Rainsford was still almost asleep, and mumbled some sort of an assent. When Mr. —— had completed his ablutions, he asked Mr. Rainsford where he should empty the water, and Rainsford, who was by no means awake yet, and who hated being disturbed, growled out that he could pour it out of the window. The too literal Mr. —— obeyed blindly, with the result that the bath-water descended in an unbroken stream upon the poor old housekeeper, who was breaking coal in the area below."

It must indeed have been a most curious establishment at Stepney Green! Comfort, as ordinary people know it, appears to have been entirely absent. The strangest characters foregathered[41] there, all day and all night the place hummed like a hive. Mr. Charrington, as will be seen later, has always had a fondness for strange pets. In the house at Stepney a monkey was added to the *entourage*, and shortly afterwards a well-known Evangelistic preacher, who must also, I beg leave to think, have been a considerable prig, called at the "Monastery." Mr. Charrington, who was smoking his inevitable pipe, introduced this person to the monkey. The

Evangelist threw back his head, rolled his eyes upwards, and lifted his hands. "Not very spiritual, Charrington," he said, "not very spiritual!" "I wonder if your tom-cat is very spiritual?" was Mr. Charrington's retort.

Mr. Mowll, who is now vicar of Christ Church, Brixton, a college friend of Keith Falconer, who frequently visited the house at Stepney Green, always went to bed very late indeed. One night he rigged up a figure of a man with cushions and an overcoat, put a hat on its head and a pipe in its mouth, and then went to bed, leaving all the gas burning. The next morning, when the housekeeper went into the room to dust it, the poor thing was frightened out of her life to find, as she thought, a strange man sitting there in the full glare of the gas. She was so upset that Mr. Mowll, a most ardent Temperance reformer, was perhaps rightly punished by having to fetch the old lady some brandy from the nearest public-house.

These incidents are all trivial enough, but I give them as illustrating the happy and boyish natures of the young men who found themselves together under the leadership of Mr. Charrington. When the bathroom tap was left on, and the whole house was[42] flooded, their equanimity was not disturbed. When there was no proper dinner, they ate bread and cheese. The vagaries of the housekeeper, the odd behaviour of the monkey, were all subjects for mirth. The moral of this sort of life is obvious enough. These men cared nothing for personal comfort or pleasure. Their life was lived in an unceasing warfare with the powers of evil. Their swords were always girded on—the rest was as nothing.

The late Earl of Kintore stayed for some little time at the East End house, and, as it unhappily turned out, just before his death. As he was leaving after his visit he shook his host's old housekeeper—whose name was Mrs. Pilgrim—by the hand and said, "Well, good-bye. You're a pilgrim and I'm a stranger, and we shall soon be at home." As a matter of fact the earl died suddenly only a fortnight afterwards.

I continue the record of the early beginnings of the great work that was to come, for it was now that the East End Conference Hall first came into being.

"About this time Mr. Charrington received a letter from the late Mr. Pemberton Barnes, who was said to own the largest number of houses of any one in the world (then nearly a stranger to him), stating that he held a site known as Carlton Square, which he was anxious to devote to a Christian work. He had originally intended it for the erection of a church, but being deterred by the rapid advances of Ritualism, of which he was an opponent, he resolved to build a mission hall instead. The result was the erection of the[43]present building, which seated 600 persons, and was opened on Friday, November 1, 1872.

"The following extract is from *The Christian* of that day.

"'Another very interesting movement has been inaugurated in the East End. On the 1st of this month a new and very elegant iron structure, capable of accommodating 600 people, was opened for public worship and evangelistic effort of various kinds. T. B. Smithies, Esq., editor of the *British Workman*, presided, and addresses were given by Revs. Jack Kennedy, H. Barton, Dr. Sharpe, Dr. Barnardo, and other friends. A statement of the circumstances which led to the erection was made by Mr. F. N. Charrington, the honorary superintendent, who said, some time ago, being anxious to establish a boy's lodging house, he asked Mr. Pemberton Barnes to devote an old house (situated in the East End, and belonging to him) to that purpose; but Mr. Barnes said he had, unfortunately, given it into the hands of the builders a week previously, and so the matter dropped. A short time ago, however, he had received a letter from that gentleman saying he was desirous of doing something for the Lord; he owned a square on which he proposed building a house with a small hall attached. Mr. Charrington visited him the next day, and Mr. Barnes agreed to build a hall in which the Gospel might be preached, and in which the work would be thoroughly unsectarian. The meetings held on the four Sunday evenings since the opening have been numerously attended, and not one has passed without distinct testimony of blessing received by[44] some of those present. With much regret we add that Mr. Pemberton Barnes, the kind friend to whom the East End of London is indebted for this addition to its means of evangelisation, died within a fortnight of its opening.'"

At this East End Conference Hall Mr. Charrington took up the question of adult baptism. His work there was in no sense at all sectarian, nor has it ever been so from those early days until the present moment—a point which I shall enlarge upon at some length when I come to the story of the Great Assembly Hall itself and my own experiences there.

At the same time, Mr. Charrington's own personal conviction was that a form of baptism by immersion was warranted by his interpretation of Scripture, and was a means for good. Mr. Richardson, in one of our conferences, has told me the following curious anecdote. There was a baptistry built in the new hall at Carlton Square, but there was no water laid on. Accordingly, Mr. Charrington sent to the great brewery in the Mile End Road and asked for a supply of wagons containing hogsheads of water to be sent to the hall. The request was immediately complied with, but there was considerable consternation among the neighbours of the new mission when they saw great brewery wagons delivering barrels at the hall—barrels which it certainly never occurred to them, contained nothing but harmless water.

In addition to this central hall, interesting work was also being done in Bethnal Green, where there was a building attached to the now rapidly growing mission in Bonner's Lane. The neighbourhood,[45] in 1875, was a singularly interesting one. It took its name from the fact that Bishop Bonner, of infamous memory, in the days of "Bloody Mary," had his palace in the immediate vicinity, and additional antiquarian interest was that the faith the then Bishop of London sought to extinguish was afterwards propagated in that very neighbourhood by the

French Protestants, who settled there in 1572. The descendants of these people occupied the neighbourhood at the time Mr. Charrington started work there, and extremely picturesque their lives and habits were. A record has been placed in my hands, and it tells of a day when green fields and trees made pleasant a quarter now a wilderness of bricks.

I read—

"I know an old inhabitant who has seen the changes of the last fifty years, and he told me that a man he knew kept a farm a few hundred yards from Bonner Lane. This man's great desire was to possess a hundred black cows. For years he tried to collect them, but never managed to collect more than ninety-nine. As soon as he made the number up to a hundred, one always died, or was lost; and the old man said to him, 'It always reminds me of the lost sheep in Scripture.' The neighbourhood is well known by the name of Twig Folly, and there is an inscription placed upon some houses built by a man who obtained his property in the following way. There was living there a man who made twig baskets. He was greatly troubled by the boys robbing him of his fruit. One day, seeing a boy in one of his fruit trees, he shouldered his gun and shot him. Fearing the [46] consequences, he made over all his property to a friend, on condition that he himself should have it back at the expiration of whatever punishment he might get. But when he came to claim his property, he found his friend not so faithful as he had anticipated; for, instead of delivering it up, he kept it. In building these houses with the proceeds of the property, the friend asked a neighbour what he should name them, and received the following reply: 'What could be better than to name them after the old twig basket maker, for his folly?' So it was named Twig Folly.

"The place is now inhabited by the working-classes. A few of the old silk weavers are still left, who carry on a small trade which cannot be very remunerative. In our hall for the last three months some happy hours have been spent by many who formerly could never be induced to enter any place of worship.

"The plan of the services has been as follows: Meeting on Sunday evenings at six o'clock, and going out with a band of good singers, we invite the people in; then small handbills are distributed, setting forth the order of the services, which consist of singing by a good choir formed for the purpose, and a short address; sometimes a few will tell their experiences. We have by this means been able to fill the hall. This has greatly encouraged us, for if we can obtain such a good congregation in the summer months, we may expect nothing less in the winter. But we are thankful that we can go further and say, that many who have lived without God, and been careless as to their future state, have been awakened and [47] converted. A man came in one Sunday, and stayed after the service to be spoken to. He said he was a prize-fighter, and on the Wednesday following he was to fight. But before he left that night, he delivered his will over to God, and determined by His grace to lead a new life and to keep away from the fight. He has been seen since, and we are thankful to say that he kept his word."

The work in Bonner Lane went on for some three years. After that the activities at the Central Hall demanded so much of the Evangelist's time that it was felt impossible to give the necessary supervision to the offshoot of the mission.

Mr. Charrington was therefore glad to leave this field of labour in the hands of the Rev. T. Bowman Stephenson, who purchased the Hall from the chief organisation and carried on the work himself, though still with friendly relations with the organisers of the chief mission.

How my readers feel about this record I shall never be able to know. I myself am impatient to proceed to a certain point where the immense drama of Frederick Charrington's evangelistic life may be said to commence. But in a life of this sort it is obviously necessary to continue the story of small beginnings.

Throughout all these accounts of what happened in those early days I see Mr. Charrington as the main force, the apostle. But I see him thus only in imagination, only in the light of what he afterwards did. His own memories of this period in his career are simply those of a man who remembers that he was always hard at work, was always [48] sacrificing himself, his money, and his time for the good of others. But the picturesqueness of the days which were to come so soon has somewhat obscured in my mind—and I know in his also—the intimate and personal point of view.

At the same time, as this life is written once and for all, the story of the beginnings must be faithfully told, and told in such detail as I can.

[49]

CHAPTER III
MORE BEGINNINGS

As I know him now, a marked characteristic of Charrington is his extreme love of the open air. He has built the largest mission hall in the world. I should be afraid to say how many erections of stone, wood, and brick owe their inception to his courage and his work. But, at the same time, the open air—under God's sky—has always appealed to a man with a mind as clear and simple as running water.

The idea came to him that, while he could get large congregations into his various missions, the great tide of human life must necessarily pass them by. In that vast area of misery known as the East End, the halls where the gospels were preached were indeed but insignificant milestones upon the hard and tortuous way to salvation.

Open-air meetings were begun at a time when Mr. and Mrs. Booth, who afterwards invented and started the Salvation Army, had certainly given a lead, but were absolutely new factors in the attempted reclamation of the masses. The great success of the indoor services had had one inevitable effect. Accommodation for the great crowds who thronged to hear the truths of the supreme philosophy which is called Christianity, became inadequate.

[50]As the work progressed, the originators, organised bands of converts, who entered with willing hearts into the service, held open-air meetings almost incessantly. Open-air work was immediately successful. Large audiences were attracted in Victoria Park on Sunday afternoons, and on the Mile End Waste on mornings, afternoons, and evenings. Services were even conducted in the common lodging houses.

In Victoria Park there was a band of devoted adherents to the Mission who secured an excellent position under the trees near the fountain given by the Baroness Burdett-Coutts.

On the Mile End Waste, on Sunday afternoon, at the close of the preacher's address, a very handsome young man came up to the speaker. A faded document, with all that pathos which attaches to the records of the past, is in my hands now. I read that this young man came up to the preacher, and taking him by the hand, said, "It is all true what you have said, but I am so unhappy! I have spent in waste and pleasure between two thousand and three thousand pounds, and I am ruined."

The Preacher had a long interview with this young man, and ultimately he persuaded him to decide for Christ. He came afterwards to one of the East London meetings, upon a Tuesday evening, a new man in soul, mind, and body.

The open-air work was not, however, confined entirely to services. The hoardings offered a great opportunity, and it was Mr. Charrington's idea that these possibilities of advertisement should be made use of. Large posters were prepared and[51] set up upon the walls of half-ruined buildings, the wooden palings which circumscribed the erection of new houses.

"CHRIST DIED FOR US," stared at the passer-by from every corner. I have in my possession a wood-block drawing which represents one of the hoardings of that period, covered with messages of religion. I cannot reproduce it here, as there are other and more important illustrations which must have a place in this biography. But the texts which blazed out on a callous and only half-believing world were ones that must have indeed arrested the faltering one, have turned the eyes, if not to God, at least to a consideration of the fact that there was a God, who watched unceasingly over His children.

"I am the Light of the World." "I am the Way, the Truth, and the Life." "He that believeth on the Son hath Everlasting Life." "Fools make a mock of sin."

It is now necessary to mention another offshoot of the Central Organisation, known as the "Oxford Street Hall." The Oxford Street to which I refer is not the Oxford Street of fashion, or of De Quincey. It was a "street in the East."

This Branch of the Mission was opened in August, 1874. The Hall was used previously as a school and for other purposes, and being situated in a street leading from a main thoroughfare to a territory of working-men's dwellings, was admirably suited to mission purposes.

The house was accessible from the Hall, and was occupied by the missioner in charge of the work. There were no paid labourers; those who helped[52] were all engaged in daily toil, and were chiefly converts from the Central Hall. The experiences of the first were somewhat peculiar. Their efforts taught the workers the real wants of the neighbourhood, and being cemented by brotherly love, which abounded among them, they settled down with a doggedness of purpose that bore great fruit.

This Branch of the Mission was carried on there for some years, until the new site was secured and the Assembly Hall erected in Mile End Road. This being but a short distance from the Oxford Street Hall, and the lease of that building having nearly expired, the work was transferred to the Great Assembly Hall. The hall in Oxford Street was afterwards pulled down by the landlord, and a dwelling-house erected in its place.

It soon became necessary to "move on" from the Conference Hall. The place was too small for the enormous work which was now being done, and of which it was the centre, so that a more important site became imperative.

It was not long before a piece of ground in the Mile End Road, at the corner of White Horse Lane, was chosen—a spot that had hitherto been anything but an ornament to the neighbourhood. The largest portion of it had been used for years by travelling showmen with wax-works, merry-go-rounds, penny theatres, and every variety of exhibition. The local authorities considered that a great boon had been conferred upon the neighbourhood, and especially the police, who expressed their thanks when Mr. Charrington bought this land and removed the dilapidated buildings which stood there; while the respectable inhabitants[53] hailed with delight the demolishing of the old place which had afforded facilities for persons of the lowest character.

It was a splendid situation, and the Hon. Elizabeth Waldegrave, sister of Lord Radstock, kindly paid the rent, besides giving much of her time and energy to the work. Here a tent was erected and evangelistic services were conducted every night with great success during two whole summers.

The speakers were chiefly soldiers of the Guards, who came all the way from the West End barracks, many of them walking the whole way there and back (a distance of ten miles) on purpose to preach the Gospel night after night.

These soldiers were, of course, very far from eloquent, but they were terribly in earnest, and even their rough, but heart-felt words had a tremendous influence with the people they addressed. One can imagine well how these splendid, scarlet-coated men, in the full height of physical power, virile and disciplined, must have swayed the minds of those to whom they appealed.

Charrington's close association with these soldiers came about owing to a visit that he paid to a Mr. Fry, an Irish solicitor, at whose house on Dublin Bay Mrs. Charrington stayed.

His old friend Mr. Richardson has told me of this particular visit, and to what it subsequently led.

Mr. Fry had a little daughter, a young girl of seventeen, who took a great interest in the soldiers. One morning she asked Mr. Charrington to accompany her round the barracks. He complied, and[54] she showed him everything. At the conclusion of their tour, she said to him, "Mr. Charrington, all these soldiers are soon coming to London, where they will have a great many temptations to drink, etc. I wish you would be so kind as to try and do something for them when they are there." He promised that he would. When he got back to the East End, he went to the barracks to which they had been transferred, and asked them all to come to the Hall. The soldiers came in their busbies and scarlet uniforms, and as they were all over six feet high, they formed a magnificent group on the platform. He set them all to work, and they gave their testimonies. They could not, of course, speak well, but just the recital of their experiences was far more effective than the oration of the greatest speaker. They also used to accompany Mr. Charrington's procession through the streets, and were known as "Charrington's Bodyguard." They made a scarlet ring round him, and their great height made it very effective indeed. One man was over six feet four inches high, and was broad in proportion. He used to preach, saying, "Well, dear friends, I cannot preach. I never have preached. But I can tell you that if you don't give up the drink and turn to God you will be damned. Give up the drink! I cannot preach, but I can tell you that I was a drunkard myself, but I turned to God, and was saved. Give up the drink!" Several of these men afterwards became missionaries and preachers—notably Mr. W. R. Lane of the Free Church Council.

The great tent was set up upon a waste piece of land on the 21st of May, 1876. The inaugural[55] meeting was very largely attended, and Mr. Samuel Morley, the millionaire M.P., who, till the very day of his death, was one of the most generous supporters of Mr. Charrington's great work, was in the chair. He spoke as follows—

"I am here at the request of Mr. Charrington and other friends, at least to have the satisfaction of showing my earnest sympathy with the work which is to be carried on by them. The presence of several clergymen around me evidences that it is fully understood that in holding tent services there is no attempt to draw from existing congregations, but rather to reach those classes of which chapel and church know but little; it is wanted to get at the masses of the people. Born in London, bred, and brought up in the midst of that kingdom—for such London is—I have arrived at a conclusion that makes me anxious to co-operate with those who are seeking to lift up the masses of the people from the degraded condition in which they are now living. I fear that more than one million of the population of London never enter a place of worship, and if on the morning of any Lord's day there was a desire to attend a place of worship on the part of those who could go on the Sabbath, there would be needed 800,000 more sittings than are at present provided. That is proof positive of the neglect of public worship, which can be viewed by Christians only with deep grief and pain. I state this to stimulate to effort, not merely clergymen and other Christian workers, but all classes. I would quote from the Bishop of Lichfield, who said that immorality and drunkenness were destroying our nation. Well-to-do people who mix but little with the lower classes can have no conception of the condition in which they are now living. I would advise that, instead of suggesting[56] and inquiring as to what others should do, they should set about to find what, as Christians, they themselves should do. In the erection of this tent, you have raised a standard declaring the observance of the Lord's day. You can do this on physical grounds. The weekly day of rest is not only desirable, but necessary, and for that besides we have the authority of the Scriptures, and our great national boast and thankfulness is that England has an open Bible. Mr. Forster, addressing the children at the Crystal Palace on a late occasion, said that in every circumstance of life, whether of joy or sorrow, the Bible would be a boon to them. To this I would add that it not merely helps us amidst the joys and sorrows of this life, but it tells us what awaits us in the next. It tells—and this is the foundation-stone of this movement—it tells us that 'God so loved the world that He gave His only begotten Son, that whosoever believeth in Him should not perish, but have everlasting life.' This will be the basis of the utterances which will be delivered from this platform. Believing this, I desire to offer to my Christian friends—who, I am assured, have no idea of advancing a sect, or preaching a particular doctrine—my most earnest and heartfelt sympathy in their enterprise."

Such an inspiriting speech as this, from a man so well known and of such high place, who was a life long friend of Frederick Charrington, was the happiest augury for the success of this new departure.

Success it was, and in the highest degree, but everything to which Frederick Charrington has put his hand has been a success. Already my readers will be wondering at the ceaseless activity of this still very young man and his band of devoted[57] workers. They are, however, as nothing to what is to follow.

"Rescue bands" were organised at this time.

The various mission halls, and the great tent were in full swing. Upon the hoardings of bare spaces of the East End the texts of Holy Scripture were seen on all sides, interspersed with advertisements of Christian literature, and advertisements of forthcoming meetings.

Crowds of people were daily gathered round these stations, eagerly reading the words of life. On Sunday mornings working men, taking their weekly stroll, men who had never opened a Bible in their lives, would stop to read the parable of the Prodigal Son. In the dead of night the poor lost girl, as she passed along to her via dolorosa, was startled to see the familiar text which she had learnt as a child in the Sunday schools. The guardians of law and order on their solitary beats at night turned the lights of their lantern upon the hoardings, and in the darkness and the silence of the night read the story of Christ's love for them—the profligate returning from scenes of revelry was arrested for the moment by the words "Prepare to meet thy God!" Such a revival, at such a time, was absolutely unknown. A great light, growing larger and larger every moment, began to shine in upon the dark places of the East End. It was as though some great lighthouse of God had been built by living hands, growing rapidly, like some building in a fairy story, and flooding this part of London with radiance. And in the height of the tower, directing the unflagging rays of hope, was Frederick Nicholas Charrington.

[58]The Rescue bands which he organised and accompanied himself, penetrated to the lowest, and often most dangerous, neighbourhoods. London has changed since those days, and not, perhaps, in the direction of the picturesque, and the earnest workers for Christ moved among the strangest scenes imaginable. Space will not allow me the pleasant task of recalling some of those vanished scenes, but I may make a passing reference to one environment which certainly holds the imagination.

When the Huguenot refugees fled from the persecutions of their enemies to the peace and security of Spitalfields, they obtained a living by weaving, and Bethnal Green and Spitalfields were the recognised headquarters of this branch of industry. Machinery had done much to cripple the trade, but had not yet entirely destroyed it. The prices, however, paid to the weavers in this locality were barely remunerative, and a great amount of poverty existed. In Club-row and thereabouts, the upper windows of the houses were of that long, arched pattern which was sufficient evidence to show that these tenements were occupied by weavers, as they were built to admit as much light as possible. The connection between silk-weaving and bird-selling is not very clear, nor is it obvious how the ground floors of the weavers' houses were transformed into bird shops. But then every other shop, at least, engaged to provide for the wants of the "Fancy," whether it required poultry, pigeons, or small birds, not to mention rabbits, dogs, rats, guinea-pigs, mice, hedgehogs, and goats. An extensive trade was driven in these and other objects of interest to fanciers, but the[59] great Bird Fair, when business is at its full height, was reserved for Sunday morning.

A member of the principal Rescue band, that worked in Bird Fair, wrote—

"One bright Sunday morning we passed down Sclater Street as the fair was commencing. The glad sunlight was flooding the streets, searching every nook and cranny, and putting new life into the caged prisoners, so that they poured forth their hearts in song. A strange contrast, the sweet heavenly music of the country, and the pent-up, confined surroundings presented. At any rate, so it appeared to us; but the 'Fancy,' which was disporting itself in great numbers, clad in a variety of garments, usually with a blue-checked neckcloth, and a short pipe between its teeth, had eyes alone for lark, linnet, or chaffinch, and naught else. The 'Fancy' seemed to repeat itself every way one turned. Here was a man with a cage enveloped in a black handkerchief under his arm, and there another—his counterpart in every particular. They differed only in this, that they were variously laden; one had under his arm a cage, whilst another had a fowl, and another a dog; but cages and dogs seemed to be the most numerous, the former being more in favour than the latter. These men and their cages are inseparable. Walk in the park, they are there; walk into the country, they are there; go to their homes, they are there. Give a man his cage and his pipe, and he is content."

And again—

"The work in Bird Fair is especially interesting. As we entered one of the largest of these houses, we found scores of men congregated in the side-parlour,[60] and as soon as we could distinguish the objects on the other side of the room through the dense clouds of tobacco smoke with which it was filled, we saw that every available mantel-shelf or ledge was filled up with small bird-cages, each containing its little captive. A man just then came into the room, calling out, 'No. 6 and No. 2, are you ready?' from which we conjectured that a raffle or bird club was being carried on. They looked at us somewhat surprised, but civilly received the invitations to be present at the services in Lusby's Music Hall in the evening. We found another house where none but dog fanciers assembled. Ferocious looking bulldogs (carefully muzzled), and delicately reared little pug dogs were seated on their owners' laps, or squatted on the ground at their feet. Here, with the exception of one man whose language was not very choice, we received a kind welcome; and after we had visited the room at the back, the landlord, to our great astonishment, invited us to come round one Sunday evening and talk to the men in the parlour. We almost thought that this was a joke on his part, but on paying him another call on the following Sunday morning and asking him if he really meant what he said, he replied, 'Come to-night.' Accordingly, the same evening we sent off two members of the Rescue band to hold a service at the time appointed. They found a number waiting for their visit, and in a few minutes had forty of these men seated with the landlord in their midst. They talked to them for over an hour of what the Lord had done for them, and what He is willing to do if they would only[61] come to Him. At the close of the meeting there were many requests for them to come again on the following Sunday, and the publican said on leaving that they might come as often as they liked. As they passed the bar, those who had not come into the meeting explained to them which of the bull-dogs would fight, and which would not, etc., etc.; and as they patted the dogs on the head, they got a word with their owners about their own souls."

Support poured in to the multifarious activities of the mission from all sides.

The young Earl and Countess of Aberdeen attended, and were warmly interested. The great Lord Shaftesbury, for many years one of Mr. Charrington's most intimate friends, was also among those highly-placed Englishmen and women who gave their unwavering support.

Mr. Samuel Morley, M.P., has already been mentioned, and one of the richest men in England, Mr. T. A. Denny, was a magnificently generous subscriber, and never ceased in his unflagging patronage of the work. It was Mr. Denny who generously bore nearly all the pecuniary burden of opening a certain East End music hall on Sunday nights—a music hall which will be seen, as the story of Mr. Charrington's career advances, to have had a most extraordinary place and influence in his life.

The music hall crusade was Mr. Charrington's idea, and it proved an inestimable blessing to the population among whom he worked, hundreds being reached there who could never otherwise be brought within the sound of the gospel.

At the Foresters' Music Hall, the famous[62] Evangelist, Mr. Sankey, consented to sing, and for three years the most enthusiastic meetings were held there.

Both the Hon. Jon. Keith-Falconer and Lord Mount-Temple addressed the congregation. One service in this hall was broken up by the loud roarings of some caged lions who were to be shown there on the next night. The audience was terrified and refused to stay, despite Mr. Charrington's assurance that there was no danger. The great beasts were only separated from the Evangelist by the drop curtain, and the experience must certainly have been very unpleasant and nerve-shaking—though Frederick Charrington does not rejoice in "nerves."

Lusby's Music Hall, the place of amusement to which I first referred, and which was the largest music hall in the East End, was opened for several seasons.

Work was begun there on a night in November, 1877. The crowd was so great that it extended beyond the tram-lines, which were seventy feet from the entrance, while before the doors were opened the line itself was invaded, and the police had to regulate the crowd in order to let the trams pass through it.

The hour of this first service was seven o'clock, but at half-past six there was not a single vacant seat in the building, and wherever standing room could be found, it was immediately occupied. Madame Antoinette Stirling came down and sang "O rest in the Lord."

I wish especially to insist on the fact, ample record of which is in my possession, that these[63] music hall services on Sunday nights were *continuously* crowded. People who would not have even gone into the great tent or the ordinary mission halls were to be found in the transformed haunts of their ignoble week-day pleasures, and the souls that were led to the foot of the Cross were incalculable.

In connection with Lusby's Music Hall, in particular, I cannot refrain from recalling at least one case of very special interest.

A poor man, a dock labourer, who had not attended a service of any kind for several years, entered the hall one Sunday evening when Mr. Joseph Weatherley was the preacher. The sinner's need and the Saviour's power to save him were clearly set before the people, and the man that night rested his soul on the finished work of God. The next day, while at work in the dock, he fell down a ship's hold, and was carried to the London Hospital very much injured. The nurse (a Christian woman), under whose care he was placed, saw that he was dying and spoke to him of Jesus. She found him happy in the assurance of sins forgiven, and on asking how long he had been a child of God, he replied, "Last Sunday night, through the preaching in Lusby's Music Hall." He died rejoicing.

I shall have so much to say of Lusby's Music Hall in a forthcoming part of this book that I will not attempt, in this place, any word-picture of the services there.

In connection with another establishment of the same kind, and, if possible, much lower and more disreputable than the usual thing, I am able[64] to reconstruct a typical scene of the many that occurred there when Mr. Charrington and his friends turned it for one night in each week from a place of sin and corruption to a stronghold of our Lord.

Wilton's Music Hall, or, as it was affectionately called by its habitués, "The Mahogany Bar," was a music hall opening on a quiet square notorious as the Ratcliff Highway, then regarded as the most disreputable street of its kind in the whole world. Ratcliff Highway—has it not obtained an evil immortality in the words of innumerable songs which are minor classics in their way?—was the resort of the lowest characters of all nations, the very scum of the earth. It was here that "Poor Jack" fell a prey to the vilest harpies in Christendom, it was a den of prostitution, vice, drunkenness and crime, tenanted by fiends in human form, who made their unholy gains out of the passionate outbursts of the misguided sailors, who, by their orgies, their desperate affrays, and frightful excesses, did so much to confer its evil notoriety upon the street.

One Saturday night, Mr. Charrington and a friend, armed with handbills announcing that Wilton's Music Hall was to be opened on Sunday and that seats were free, turned into Leman Street, en route for some of the lowest drinking, dancing, and singing saloons that East London could boast.

They entered fifty public-houses and singing saloons of the worst type. There was a sink of iniquity known as "The Paddy's Goose." "The Gun Boat," "The Jolly Sailor" and "The Kettledrum" were hardly any better.

|65|Hardly any middle-aged women were to be seen, seafaring men, from the apprentice to the mate, from the nigger to the English tar, men of all stamps, sizes, nations, and colours; girls with shawl-covered heads, usually in parties of three and four, under the supervision of horrible old hags, made up the crowd that thronged these dens. Elbowing their way through a group of sailors and wretched girls gathered at the door of one of the establishments, and brushing past one or two ragged little urchins who were peeping in at the chinks, wishing, perhaps, to catch a glimpse of the comparative comfort within, they entered those swinging portals, which move so easily inwards, but with so much difficulty outwards. They found themselves in a large and crowded drinking saloon. With the reflection that "the righteous shall be bold as a Lion," they met the stare of the many eyes turned upon them with a rather painful composure. The landlord, a sporting-looking character, received them with evident astonishment and curiosity.

He was soon acquainted with their mission—"Would he kindly allow a bill or two to be placed upon his counter?" Appealed to in this fashion, he could not refuse. In one case, such was the obliging condescension, yet amazing incongruity, exhibited, that the monarch of the bar declared that "he would do anything to help the cause."

The company were soon supplied with notices, and acknowledged them with varying degrees of politeness. Some hardly looked at them, while others criticised them narrowly. "Ah! it's not for the like o' me," exclaimed one man, with the|66| marks of many a tempest upon his brow. "Take it away, it only adds to my sins." "What! the Mahogany Bar opened on a Sunday!" objected a would-be wit, "No, no; we'd go there to-night, but on Sunday——" And the speaker concluded his sentence with a well-affected pretence at remonstrance.

The opening service was on Sunday. For the first time within the "Mahogany Bar" Music Hall, God's praises were sung on February 24, 1877. Never before had the cry "Stand up, stand up for Jesus" rung from its benches, and never before, perhaps, had the Spirit of God descended in mighty power, breaking the hard heart, subduing the rebellious will, and making light to shine even in the stronghold of Satan. Most encouraging it was to find that, notwithstanding the service had been only scantily advertised by posters, and by the bills alluded to, the hall was at seven o'clock very fairly filled, and filled, too, by those same individuals that the Rescue party had addressed the night before. Such a congregation was rarely seen in those early days. Seafaring men were there in scores; and the girls of loose character they had brought with them—"the sailors' women," as they were known, almost entirely composed the audience.

Mr. Charrington conducted, and Mr. J. Manton Smith preached. Considering they were on their good behaviour, and evidently felt the restraint of silence during the prayers to be irksome, the people were much quieter than was expected. The sailors, however, sat with their arms round the girls who accompanied them as if it were quite|67| the right thing to do—otherwise they remained quiet and listened most attentively to the preacher.

Mr. Smith led the singing upon his silver cornet. In the course of the service he also sang a solo. Often hearts are touched by holy music when all else fails. His address was founded upon the words "Nothing to pay," and it was delivered in language understood by the people, as was really shown by the attention he gained.

Mr. Smith related an effective anecdote of five poor castaway fishermen, who had lost their smack and were tossing about in a boat without oars, upon a raging sea, and far from land. A vessel drew near to them. The captain—who related the incident to him—sighted them. He backed and made for them, but failed. Despairing cries ascended from the forlorn; they thought they were to be left to their fate. He backed again to the oarless boat, and gradually drew nearer. Upon the vessel there was a stoker—a huge man of immense strength. As the little boat rose upon the ocean and dashed against the vessel's side, the stoker stretched forward, and just as it was receding, caught hold of one of the poor fishermen and pulled him on board. He was saved in an instant. "And," said Mr. Smith, "that's just how Jesus saved me."

Before the service was over, six sailors were observed to follow one another out of the hall with the tears running down their cheeks, and trembling with emotion. It was not long before other cases were made apparent. God had sent down his Spirit as a witness that souls can be saved even in the Tempter's sanctuary. One brave fellow went|68| out of the hall rejoicing in the possession of the pearl of great price which he had that night found, but which in his wanderings all over the world he had hitherto failed to discover.

Every day in the week, and on every Sunday, the work of rescue and of salvation was continued without cessation. The light burned brighter and brighter. Mr. Charrington and his friends indeed seemed to be under the special guidance of the Holy Spirit. There was never the slightest diminution of energy or force. The white-hot fervour was maintained.

The young man who had given up an imperial fortune, who had renounced a life of luxury, for the hardest asceticism and constant warfare, never flagged for a moment.

One of his friends, who was associated with him at that time, said to me a few days ago, "Mr. Charrington has always been as fearless as a lion, both physically and morally. He would go, entirely unprotected, into districts where policemen only went in twos and threes. He never had any hesitation in speech. He was by no means a great orator, but once 'wind him up' and he would go on for ever. Dogged determination has always been characteristic of him in everything. He has an almost bull-dog tenacity of purpose, and will of iron.

"I remember, as illustrating Mr. Charrington's physical fearlessness, that one night a policeman had very foolishly gone alone into a low public-house in a back slum with a most sinister reputation to arrest two men. There was an immediate uproar, and a fight. Mr. Charrington happened[69] to be passing, on one of his errands of mercy, and saw what was happening. He realised in a moment that the policeman had no possible chance against the crowd of low characters in the public-house. He dashed in and asked if the constable required help. The man was being hard pressed, and reinforcement was indeed a godsend to him. 'All right,' Charrington said, 'You take one prisoner and I will take the other.' How Charrington and the policeman managed it, I don't pretend to say, but they collared their men. There was a furious fight, the women especially assaulting Mr. Charrington with great violence, scratching, kicking, and beating him on the head with umbrellas. The prisoners were eventually got outside, and other policemen came to the rescue, but when Mr. Charrington turned up at the hall he was hardly recognisable. His hat was smashed in, his clothes were in tatters, and he was fearfully kicked and bruised.

"He would stick at nothing in the work he had set himself to do. In his efforts in the cause of Temperance one of the greatest difficulties he had to contend with was that the police of those days, in the part of the East End where he worked, were themselves often heavy drinkers. The majority of them had regular houses in the neighbourhood where they would go and get drink when on duty.

"Mr. Charrington saw that it was essential that this should be stopped. It struck at the whole root of his campaign, and he determined that he would put an end to it if he could.

"One night he watched the doors of a certain[70] public-house. He saw a policeman come up to it, the door opened and a hand shot out with a can of beer. He had already started a definite campaign against drink being given to the police when on duty, and, at that moment, the policeman, who was just about to drink, looked round and saw Mr. Charrington, whom he recognised immediately. He dropped the can of beer upon the pavement, took to his heels and ran as hard as he could go. As an illustration of the tenacity and "downrightness" of Charrington, I may tell you that he gave chase, and after an almost interminable pursuit through dark and badly lighted streets, chaste and sober living told, and he caught his man.

"The policeman was utterly cowed, and begged Mr. Charrington not to report him.

"'Very well,' his captor answered, 'I won't report you if you will give me your word of honour to come to the hall to-morrow and sign the pledge.' The man replied, 'Well, sir, I am engaged to a very nice young lady indeed. She has always been on at me to give up the drink. And if you will let me off this time, I promise you faithfully that I will come round in the morning and do as you wish.'

"The next morning the man kept his word. He signed the pledge, and, what is more, never broke it. His whole life was changed from that day, and he became a regular worshipper at Mr. Charrington's services. And in connection with this side of Charrington's work—which resulted in purifying the morals of the East End police—I should like you to make a note of the fact that Mr. Charrington *never reported a policeman*. From first to last this never happened. He went about his work of[71]reclamation and purifying in his own way. It was entirely a case of individual discovery and remonstrance. He certainly visited headquarters and complained about the police generally, while he drew attention to the existing state of things in the Press. But never, from first to last, did he mention any individual. Then as now, he was always a thorough sportsman."

Such a little picture as this does more, by means of concrete instances, to explain Mr. Charrington's methods than pages of explanation could do.

I confess I laughed when I heard this story. I was sitting in the drawing-room at Rivermere with the gentleman who told it me, and I was still laughing when Mr. Charrington came in.

"I would give five pounds to see you chasing a policeman through London, now," I said to him. "There is something, to my mind, irresistibly funny in the idea."

He joined in my laughter—"Oh, I can tell you something funnier than that," he said with a chuckle, and for an hour or more there came a flow of reminiscences, all told with that merry smile, in that low, deprecating voice, which nevertheless bubbles with quiet humour, which is so marked a characteristic of my friend.

Throughout this life I have carefully avoided, as far as in me lies, the phraseology and methods of many biographers of great religious workers. I was told to write this story of Frederick Charrington just as I wished. I was given a free hand, indeed, I may even say that the reason why I *was* chosen for the work was because, that in many religious matters I take a diametrically opposite view to that[72] of Mr. Charrington and his friends, and have never been associated with any evangelistic movements.

I have rather hesitated, therefore, as to whether I should include—at this stage—any account of the numerous conversions which occurred at the time of which I am writing. I have in my possession an astonishing series of records, bearing witness to the spiritual value of Mr. Charrington's unceasing warfare for our Lord. The unrecorded conversions of this period, are, of course, countless. After some consideration I have decided to include a few instances, taken at random from the material I have.

It will be remembered that the words in which these instances are recorded are not my own, but are the *ipsissima verba* of one of Mr. Charrington's helpers, to whose lot it fell to record them.

Mr. M——: "I used to work for a bad master—the devil. I went to the Foresters' Music Hall—just out of curiosity—and thank God! my curiosity was satisfied, but not in the way I anticipated; for that night God laid hold on my soul and saved me. Mr. Manton Smith was preaching, and the words seemed all for me. I stayed to the after meeting, but no one came and spoke to me. God was working mightily in my soul, for the tears came stealing down my cheeks. I was just going out when Mr. Charrington took hold of me and spoke to me of Christ. And bless God he did! for if he had not, I don't know where I might have been to-night. Ever since then I have been doing all I can for my fellow-sinners."

Mr. F—— said: "I have much to thank God for, especially that He ever led me into this hall.[73] I came in here swearing on the first night it was opened. Mr. Charrington was praying, and in the course of the prayer he said, "Where will these spend their eternity?" The thought was an awful one, and it affected me much; and it took something to affect me, for I have been an awful bad 'un. I came next night. The words I heard had not left me; I heard them ringing in my ears over and over again. For twenty-five years I worshipped a wooden god. I went to confession, and I cannot tell you what I did; but, praise God! He led me away from the Romish Church, and brought me into His fold, and now I enjoy the glorious liberty of a child of God. There are many in this hall to-night who, with me, can bless God that ever this building was erected."

Mr. B——: "When I was in the world, my greatest pastime was skittles. I have gone into the skittle ground at seven o'clock in the morning, and not left it till late at night. I often lost all my money, and, of course, my poor wife used to suffer. One night I had no money, and I wanted some to go to my usual place with. My wife said to me, 'Now, look here; if you will go and hear Charley Inglis at Mr. Charrington's Tent, I'll give you some money for skittling.' I said, 'Alright. I'll go and hear Charley Inglis, or Charley Irish, if you like. Anything to get money to satisfy my appetite.' After the service was over I thought, 'Well, he's a nice sort of chap enough, but I suppose he makes a good thing out of it, or else he wouldn't do it.' I was just off when Mr. Kerwin tapped me on the shoulder, and taking hold of my arm said, 'Are you safe for eternity?' and I believe I said, 'Yes.' I didn't care about any one talking to me, I wanted to be off; but he would not let me go, and that night, bless God! I gave my heart to Jesus, and ever since that I have been working for my master."

[74]Mr. B—— said: "I can remember when I was a little boy, my dad taking me to a camp meeting. He was a preacher among the Primitive Methodists. I remember him saying to me, 'Ah, my boy, you'll remember one day, if you become a child of God, how your father has prayed for you.' Bless God! he has remembered me, and in this very hall I found Christ. The day after, I went to work, and being in a little position I wondered whether I should speak to all my workpeople. I decided that I would not; not because I was ashamed to, but I thought it would be better to let my walk show that there was a change in me. I used to curse and swear at my men very much. One day I said to one of them 'Tommy, do you know I have been converted?' 'Ah,' he said, 'I thought there was something up, because there is such a change in you.'"

Mr. G——: "I have been a downright bad 'un. When I was about fourteen years of age, I ran away to sea. I never found out the worth of a mother until she was taken away; she died while I was in China. One night I came in here, being attracted by the notice that a convict was to preach. I sat and listened to what the preacher had to say, and the words spoken by Henry Holloway went home to my soul. After the meeting he came and spoke to me, and we went into the inquiry room together, and, praise God! I found peace that night. The next day I asked my wife to come, and she found the Lord, and now we are both on the same road."

We have progressed a good deal in statements of spiritual experiences since the above words were written, now nearly thirty years ago. We have, for example, an acute and brilliant intellect, like that of Mr. Harold Begbie, engaged upon the[75] scientific psychology of conversion—an accomplished literary man blessed with Christian insight. Nevertheless, these simple records in their crude wording do but state again the astonishing fact that the power of the Gospel can and does change the whole course of men's and women's lives; that a herald of Heaven, a man bearing news of the Lux Mundi, may have his labours blessed and inspired by thousands of such results as these.

Once more, as I survey this period of Mr. Charrington's life, and have, moreover, a knowledge of the more stirring and astonishing incidents to come, I am lost in amazement at the power of the man's personality.

We see him now, and the close of this chapter marks another definite period in his life, at the head, as the central person in an enormous and rapidly growing organisation accomplishing an incredible amount of good.

This organisation was already definitely styled "The Tower Hamlets Mission."

The collection of little villages which clustered round that great stronghold of the English kings. The Tower, had been swept away so utterly that no single trace remained. But the name still existed, and that Sahara of crowded, pestilential dwellings, of narrow streets, where vice and famine walked hand in hand, that unknown city of the lost, still retained the pleasant title of the "Tower Hamlets," with all its associations of village greens, sweet trees, and simple homesteads.

The mission, while it never advertised itself, was, nevertheless, looked upon by some of the most eminent Englishmen of that day as the most[76] noble, the most adequate effort ever made to Christianise the heathen of the East End and bring them to a knowledge of God.

It was a *quiet* work for God.

Not marked by noise, but by success alone;Not known by bustle, but by useful deeds,

Making no needless noise, yet ever working Hour after hour upon a needy world.

I do not intend here to quote lists of the celebrated people who were interested in Mr. Charrington and his work at this time. I do, however, want to emphasise the statement I have just made. And when I say that that great and good Lord Shaftesbury, whose name is honoured and revered in the history of our own times, and always will be so honoured and revered, was the principal supporter of Mr. Charrington, then I have said all that is necessary.

At one of the annual general meetings of the Tower Hamlets Mission, Lord Shaftesbury was present, who till the time of his death was president of the mission. He made a long and interesting speech. From that speech, duly reported and preserved, I quote the following passages. The Right Hon. The Earl of Shaftesbury said—

"It is necessary that if I should address you at all, I should do so at this moment, for I cannot stay with you much longer. I am afraid whatever I say will be scarcely audible. My voice is very weak to-night, and it is not in my power to throw it out to the end of the hall. I wish first to say that I feel very much the kind reception you give me,[77] and to assure you that if I failed in my attendance two years ago, it was not on account of any frail and feeble excuse, because I have never, I think, broken an engagement, except on a really good excuse. And I confess I am more astonished at the assembly I see before me on such a night as this, than that I should have kept my engagement who had the advantage of coming here in a carriage. But the presence in such numbers, and the enthusiasm you manifest, show to me that the cause is in your hearts, and that by God's blessing you duly appreciate the kindness and the mercies here prepared for you. (Cheers.) For many years I have been in the habit of coming to Whitechapel, and many people say to me, 'Why do you go to Whitechapel so often?' My answer is, 'Because I always find very good people there; and if you knew Whitechapel as well as I know it, you would find there was a larger proportion of good people in Whitechapel than in an equal number of people in the West End of London.' I will tell you one thing which I like about Whitechapel people; I like their hearty, open manner, and the general enthusiasm of their demeanour; and I tell you fairly that you put me in mind of a large body of people with whom I was more conversant in earlier years than I am now, and my friend Bardsley here will bear testimony that the people of Whitechapel are, to my mind, more like the people of Lancashire than any other people in the metropolis. If you want to know what a Lancashire man is, look at our friend Bardsley on the right (laughter). He is descended from one of the noblest men I ever knew. His father was one of the grandest men I ever knew—a grand old patriarch, who has given some ten or eleven sons to the service of our Lord and Saviour Jesus Christ. I entirely concur with the sentiments of my friend Clifford, and I rejoice to see him here to-night, and may his life be long[78] spared to appear on this platform. What you heard from your friend Mr. Charrington and from Mr. Clifford is quite enough, and constitutes the strongest appeal I could well imagine to the wealthy and the powerful. What a manifestation of work is going on here day by day, night by night, and hour by hour! See the effects made for great ends, and apparently for small ends too: What we call a small end, when we have to do with the working classes, often constitutes the very turning point in the man's existence. The only way to assist a working man is to enable him to assist himself. Let me press on you seriously the immense advantages you enjoy compared with your forefathers. Time was, and not very long ago, when such a meeting as this would have been impossible, and you could not make such a thing intelligible to men's minds. Remember how this mighty city has grown up; and all the Church of England, and all the denominations, if they could be brought to be of one mind would be wholly inadequate to the great spiritual work of this metropolis. *Now I delight to see these lay agents come forward and, like your friend, Mr. Charrington, act as auxiliaries and subsidiaries to the efforts of the ordained ministers to preach the word of God.* It is a great blessing when you see how hundreds and thousands are brought to come in the spirit of freedom and choice, to hear the Word of God, who could never have been coerced by any system of ecclesiastical discipline which even the Pope might endeavour to institute. All these considerations should impress on you a sense of the deep obligations under which you are: first to God, and then to these men whom God has raised up to conduct these various missions, and to sustain all these manifold efforts to propagate the Gospel. I am certain that I am within the limit when I say that there are at least 400,000 persons at the present time in this metropolis who[79] would never have heard the Word of God but for the agency of such missions. Did these exist in former times? I recollect when we propounded nineteen years ago that the theatres should be opened for divine service on every successive Sunday, we were treated by some with scorn, by some with doubt (very sincere doubt), and by all with misgiving. What has been the result? Such gatherings as these. Thus the Gospel of God has been sounded out in the metropolis, and I, in going the rounds of our great cities in the dark hours of the night, have found that by such means as these many have come to know of the Gospel.

"The grand leading principle is to deal out to the hundreds and thousands of these districts a knowledge of the Lord Jesus Christ. And let me tell you how low people may fall, even as it were in the centre of religious light, unless that truth is brought home to them personally and individually. Some years ago, when our commissioners were making inquiry into the mines and collieries of this kingdom, one of the commissioners—a most excellent man, and very anxious about the religious welfare of the community—told me himself that in one of the largest colliery districts of England, he descended into a pit, and spoke to the man there—a hard-working man; and being anxious to know something of his religious state, said to him, 'Do you know Jesus Christ?' 'No,' was the reply; 'does he work on the bank, or in the pit?' Such was the state of a man in the middle of one of the most populous districts in England, in the mines and collieries, the centre of hundreds and thousands so utterly ignorant of the first elements of religion that he had never heard the name of the Saviour of mankind. But if none go forth to the highways and to the hedges to gather them in; if there be none to invite them to places such as these; none[80] to reveal to them the nature of sin and the fallen condition of man in his present state, they will certainly not learn it by intuition. Man has to preach the Gospel to man; and it is a sense of this duty that is occupying such men as Mr. Charrington and others in their endeavours to communicate to you the blessing God has so abundantly imparted to them. I am delighted to see such a meeting as this, because I see the enthusiasm with which you come: and when you joined in those hymns, I saw that you sang them from your hearts, that you knew what you were singing, and that the hymns were not merely exercises of music, but the expressions of true devotion. It is a mighty thing to have achieved such results in the wild and remote districts of the East of London, and would to God we had a hundred halls such as this! *where men of God should stand and daily preach the Word of God, and minister consolation to those who come.* Mr. Charrington has said that he desires a larger building, and so do you desire it, and so let every one desire it, and pray for it heartily, and do what in him lies to get it. Every person, I say, every woman, and every child may be a centre of influence. And recollect what that means. Your influence may be small, but if it be a centre it makes a little ring of itself, and these concentric rings one after another will at length cover the whole space of London, and will produce a feeling that will issue in the accomplishment of the prayer which Mr. Charrington has so devoutly pronounced. I trust you will have that building, and that it will be consecrated, as this one has been, to the knowledge of God and the salvation of souls. I am afraid I can say no more. I doubt whether you have heard what I have said. I heartily pray God that blessing may descend on you all, collectively and individually, in this great and important district of Stepney and Whitechapel."

[81]I have been tempted to give longer extracts than I at first intended.

Such words as these, however, definitely present the Tower Hamlets Mission of those days to your mind, and they also have a real historic value. I make no further apology for giving them.

They strike a note, however, which naturally leads me on to the next period in Mr. Charrington's life. They are most fitting to conclude this chapter, inasmuch as they definitely point to the movement which resulted in the building of the largest mission hall in the world, and establishing upon a firm and concrete basis the most successful unsectarian mission ever known.

Only the other day the papers announced the death of General Booth. The fame of that great leader of men and mighty warrior in God's cause has penetrated to the utmost corners of the earth. Yet, it was pointed out in a leading article in the *Daily Telegraph* that there were other organisations, no less wonderful in what they had accomplished, no less deserving of reverence and support, which nevertheless were hardly heard of—comparatively speaking—by the outside world.

Mr. Charrington's name was specially mentioned in this regard.

It is, perhaps, a whimsical fancy, but I like to think that—and Frederick Charrington has said as much to me—I have, in some sense, in this book, discovered him, from an unknown country. All this life he has worked for God, seeking no personal fame, no undue advertisement.

Comparisons very often lend themselves to the grotesque.

[82]I am no Stanley, but, be that as it may, I have found another Livingstone in a forest no less dark, impenetrable, and unknown, than that tropic gloom where the great journalist of the New York newspaper pressed the hand of the saintly missionary of Africa.

You are now to read three chapters which deal in detail with adventures in the cause of Christ as thrilling as anything in modern fiction. Afterwards we shall arrive at that glorious fruition of Mr. Charrington's work, which resulted in the building of the Great Assembly Hall.

But now—to the battles!

[83]

CHAPTER IV
DAVID AND JONATHAN

I suppose few eminent men of our time have been more blessed with friends than Frederick Charrington.

From the highest to the lowest he has had, and has, troops of devoted men and women who reverence and love him.

But there has been one friendship in his life which deserves to rank with the great friendships of the world, so uninterrupted, so firm and beautiful, was it. No life of the great evangelist would be complete without an account of his friendship with the late Hon. Ion Keith-Falconer, third son of the late Earl of Kintore.

This young man, who died at the untimely age of thirty-one, while engaged in whole-hearted missionary work at Aden, was one of the most remarkable intellects and personalities of his day. The beauty of his character, the ardour of his missionary zeal, his great learning, formed a combination rarely equalled. His life was one of true nobility and unselfishness. In its harmonious beauty, and the rich variety of its aspects, it was unique. That this man and Frederick Charrington should have been more than brothers to each other, is one of the most interesting and touching episodes in the latter's life.

[84]"I count all things but loss for Christ" was the essence of Keith-Falconer's career, and he found his truest inspiration, his greatest opportunity for doing good, in his friendship for Frederick Charrington. I have heard much of this association. Many things are almost too intimate to be recorded here. But with all the information placed at my disposal, and from the excellent *Memorials of the Hon. Ion Keith-Falconer*, published nearly thirty years ago by the Rev. Robert Sinker, D.D., librarian of Trinity College, Cambridge, I have been able to reconstruct much of a friendship passing the love of women, as firm, and true, as called forth from Lord Tennyson these noble words when Hallam died—

"Of those that, eye to eye, shall lookOn knowledge; under whose commandIs Earth and Earth's, and in their handIs Nature like an open book;

No longer half akin to brute,For all we thought and loved and did,And hoped, and suffer'd, is but seedOf what in them is flower and fruit.

Whereof the man, that with me trodThis planet, was a noble typeAppearing ere the times were ripe,That friend of mine who lives in God.

That God, which ever lives and loves,One God, one law, one elementAnd one far-off divine event,To which the whole creation moves."

Ion Grant Neville Keith-Falconer was born at Edinburgh on the 5th July, 1856.

His earlier years were spent at Keith Hall, varied by long visits to Brighton and elsewhere.[85] His childhood was quite uneventful, though, even in those early days, his mother afterwards spoke of his intense, and, as it were, innate truthfulness, and his unvarying thoughtfulness for others—not always prominent characteristics in children who may afterwards develop into the best of men.

At the age of eleven he was sent to the large preparatory school of Cheam in Surrey, where he gained a good many prizes, and seems to have been thoroughly happy.

In 1869, when thirteen years of age, Ion Keith-Falconer went to Harrow to compete for an Entrance Scholarship, which he was successful in obtaining.

In July 1873, I find the first reference to Frederick Charrington in a letter written by the young man of seventeen from Harrow. He had already made Mr. Charrington's acquaintance, who was six years his senior, in or about the year 1871, when Mr. Charrington was on a walking tour in Aberdeenshire, and was invited by Lord Kintore to Keith Hall. In later years, when Lord Kintore had passed to his rest in 1880, Keith-Falconer wrote to Mr. E. H. Kerwin, the secretary of the Tower Hamlets Mission: "It is pleasant to me to reflect that it was my father who first introduced me to Charrington and his work, and that he so cordially supported the Tower Hamlets Mission. I hope that his sudden departure may be a means of blessing to the careless, perhaps to some who heard him speak in the Great Assembly Hall."

The following is part of the letter I have referred to, written during the closing days of Keith-Falconer's life.

[86]"Charrington sent me a book yesterday which I have read. It is called *Following Fully* ... about a man who works among the cholera people in London, so hard that he at length succumbs and dies. But every page is full of Jesus Christ, so that I liked it. And I like Charrington, because he is quite devoted to Him, and has really given up all for His sake. I must go and do the same soon; how, I do not know."

There is another letter extant which was written from Mr. Charrington's house upon Stepney Green, towards the end of that same year.

It states that "after dinner we went the rounds to inspect the tent for preaching, and Charrington lent it to a little missionary to hold a midnight meeting in on Thursday. We also visited the Mission Hall, where they were making a pool for baptising people in.... In the evening a well-attended meeting at the tent; foul air. After the meeting the speakers were Dr. Sharpe, an old but very energetic and godly Scotchman, *broad accent*, a soldier from Wellington Barracks and Mr. Kerwin. We went to have some tea and then to the hospital to see a man supposed to be dying, but found to be recovering. I have lots to do here. I did not get to bed till nearly one o'clock, having been up nineteen hours. We visited the Boys' Homes, which I think a capital place. The dormitaries were perfect; the ventilation, cleanliness and comfort, could not have been better looked after."

At the end of the summer term of 1873, Keith-Falconer finally left Harrow, it being decided he should spend the last year before entering Cambridge with a tutor.

[87]Even at this early age, the friendship between the two young men had become fixed and immutable. The work in the East End to which Mr. Charrington was now so fully committed, and was carrying out with such success and blessing, was one which irresistibly appealed to Lord Kintore's son. The needs, spiritual and other, of that part of London were, and are, so great as to force attention from the most casual observer. And it was what Mr. Charrington had seen at the very beginning of his career, what he was one of the first evangelists to realise, that thoroughly coincided with Keith-Falconer's frame of mind. Charrington made it as the very basis of his work, that all attempts should proceed uniformly throughout on what he justly felt was the true principle of civilising by Christianising. Mr. Charrington has never been one of those—and was not then—who start with the idea that the religious life comes more readily when the material conditions of life are improved. He knew, of course, that there would often be great material need, but in such cases he saw his duty as a teacher of the Gospel perfectly clear. He would not, of course, offer Christian teaching to men and women in such dire bodily need that they were unable to accept it, without making any effort to meet those needs. But, on the other hand,

he would not insist on first civilising in every possible way save by religion—to attempt to educate the masses by art, general education, and so forth—and then, and only then, allow religion to be brought to bear and come into their lives.

In due course Mr. Keith-Falconer proceeded to[88] Cambridge. A don of that University, speaking of him as he was at this period, and, indeed, he altered but little from this time to the end of his short life, says—

"His appearance at this time, his manner, his tastes, were all strikingly like what they were in later times. He had a remarkably tall, well-shaped figure, whose symmetry seemed to take off from his height of six feet three inches. Physically very strong he certainly was, in one sense, or his wonderful feats of athletic endeavour would have been impossible. Yet, for all those feats, which were partly due, no doubt, to the sustaining power of a strong will, he could not really be called robust.

"His kindly voice and genial smile will live in the recollection of his friends; like good Bishop Hacket of Lichfield, he might have taken as his motto, 'Serve God and be cheerful.' Side by side, however, with his geniality, there was in Keith-Falconer at all times the most perfect and, so to speak, transparent simplicity. Never was a character more free from any alloy of insincerity or meanness. No undertone of veiled unkindness, or jealousy, or selfishness, found place in his conversation. From the most absolute truthfulness he would never waver; his frank, open speech was genuine, the unmixed outcome of his feelings.

"A certain slight, very slight, deafness in one ear made him at times seem absent to those who did not know this, and unknowingly had sat or walked on the wrong side.

"A characteristic habit of his seemed now and then to give a certain degree of irrelevance in his remarks. Sometimes, when in conversation on a topic which interested him, he would, after remaining silent for a short time, join again in the conversation with a remark not altogether germane[89] to the point at issue. He had been following his own train of thought suggested by some passing remark, and after working out the idea on his own lines, as far as it would go, made his comment on the result. Yet whenever the conversation had to do with the interests or needs of those to whom he was speaking, no one could throw himself more completely, heart and mind, into the matter. Talk for talking's sake he cordially abhorred, that talk which is simply made as though silence were necessarily a bad thing in itself.

"This interest in widely different topics of conversation was not, however, simply the result of mingled good-nature and courtesy, a mere complaisance, where it was but a careless good-nature that saved the courtesy from hollowness. Far from it. No one who knew Keith-Falconer well, needs to be told how thoroughly, how constantly, and in what varying ways, he could make the business or cause of another his own; whether it were a friend in need of help, from the most trifling to the most momentous matters, or the absolute stranger whom apparent chance had sent across his path.

"Still, with all this, his kindliness was by no means one lacking in its proper counterpoise of discretion; his strong, clear-headed, Scotch common-sense was constantly manifest, even in his schemes of beneficence. Yet even thus it must be remembered that his was a character in which the warm heart was guided in its action by the clear head, not one in which the clear head did but allow itself to be swayed more or less by the loving heart. Love was the dominant power, discretion the corrective influence."

Mr. Charrington used to visit his friend at the University, and it was there, as Mr. Richardson has informed me, that the evangelist obtained a[90] nickname which stuck to him for a long time. Special open-air services used to be held upon "Parker's Piece" in the University city, and on one occasion Keith-Falconer got his "gyp," as the men-servants are called at Cambridge, to come and join in the meeting. At the close Mr. Charrington was in the habit of speaking to those who had attended, and in earnest expostulation with this man, not knowing who he was, he said to him, "Down on your knees." After that, Charrington was always known—in the University city, at any rate—as "Doyk."

DAVID AND JONATHAN
[To face p. 90.

In 1880 Mr. Keith-Falconer took a First Class in the Semitic Languages Tripos. During the whole of his University career, not only was he one of the most brilliant students of his time, but also a well-known sportsman. There was no namby-pamby Christian about this young scion of a great house. Everything he undertook he did well, and he became a leading bicycle racer in England, scoring innumerable successes at Cambridge, in the Inter-University meeting with Oxford, and defeating the professional champion of England by five yards. All this time, and I cannot give more than a mere outline of Keith-Falconer's career, inasmuch as it is unconnected with the Tower Hamlets Mission and Mr. Charrington, he was sitting for innumerable examinations, and building up a record of scholarship which still survives. Yet he was most actively connected with Mr. Charrington's work, and was, now very shortly, to be more a part of it than ever. With his friend he penetrated into the most miserable homes, he conducted many services, and, as will[91] be seen in further chapters, when the luridly exciting story of the *Battle of the Music Halls* is told, he was Mr. Charrington's right-hand man.

One story of the earlier period was told me recently.

At the close of one of the meetings a little boy was found sobbing. With some difficulty he was induced to tell his tale. It was simple. His widowed mother, his sisters and he, all lived in one room. Everything had been sold to buy bread except two white mice, the boy's pets. Through all their poverty they had kept those two white mice, but at last they, too, must go! With the proceeds he bought street songs, which he retailed on the "waste," and so obtained the means of getting more bread for his mother and sisters. Now they were completely destitute. The boy was accompanied home. Home! It was a wretched attic, in one of the most dilapidated houses. It was a miserably cold and dismal day. In the broken-down grate the dead embers of yesterday's fire remained. On the table, in a piece of newspaper, a few crumbs. The air was close and the smell insupportable. "My good woman," said Mr. Charrington, "why don't you open the window?" "Oh," she replied, "you would not say that if you had had nothing to eat, and had no fire to warm you." The family was relieved.

He was intimately connected with the first beginnings of that famous "feeding of the hungry," which has gone on under Mr. Charrington's auspices for so many years, and is still one of the great living facts of the East End of London.

[22]*A-propos* of this, Keith-Falconer wrote—

"During the hard times of the winter of 1879 (due to the long frost and depression of trade), a work was forced on our Mission which we had never contemplated taking up. The difficulties and dangers of wholesale charity are very great, and our desire has been to avoid them, except in cases of extreme circumstances. But the distress of that winter *was* extreme, and for many weeks we opened our halls and fed the literally starving multitudes with dry bread and cocoa. The austere distress began in December. Hundreds of men were waiting daily at the Docks in the hope (nearly always a disappointed hope) of a job. Starving men were found in several instances eating muddy orange-peel picked off the road.

"Our feeding became a very public matter, as there was much correspondence about it in the *Times*, the *Daily News*, the *Echo* and other leading papers, and many people came from long distances to see for themselves. The public supported us liberally with funds, and we were enabled to give no less than twenty thousand meals from January 1st to February 14th, besides which we assisted over three hundred families every week in their homes. We look back to the time as one of very great blessing."

Of this feeding I propose to give as graphic a description as I can in its proper place, for I have attended at it myself, but I must pass on now to the time when the young Professor—for Keith-Falconer was shortly afterwards appointed examiner in the very Tripos where he had so distinguished himself—threw his whole heart and soul into the project for building the present Great Assembly Hall.

[23]For a time had come when Mr. Charrington's success had become so enormous, the whole machine so gigantic, that it was necessary to erect a huge building commensurate with the needs of the mission. Keith-Falconer was an invaluable helper. It is true that the great mass of work devolving on Mr. Charrington required that there should be also a secretary living in the midst of affairs and devoting his whole attention to the work. Still, Mr. Keith-Falconer's post was far from being a nominal one. In writing a business letter he was exceedingly business-like; his facts were put in the clearest and most methodical way. A letter from him asking for a subscription was no effusive appeal; it was a quiet, sensible statement of facts, written by a scholar and a master of English, all the more telling because the writer had shown himself to take all possible pains to do justice to his case.

An enormous sum of money was necessary, and at this juncture Mr. Keith-Falconer made a direct appeal for help in the form of a pamphlet.

This appeal, as his biographer points out, was so characteristic of the writer, so thoroughly earnest, entertaining, as it did, no doubt that the money would be forthcoming, and—as was his way in such things—so quaintly methodical, that I give it here in full. It is certainly one of the many historic documents in the archives of Mr. Charrington's life work.

"We now appeal for funds in order to erect a new and larger hall.

"The present one is altogether unsuitable.

[24](*a*) It is far too small. On Sunday nights hundreds are turned away for want of room. When, during two successive winters, the adjacent Lusby's Music Hall (one of the largest in London) was opened on Sunday nights simultaneously with our own hall, the united congregation usually amounted to 5000 persons. These facts tend to show that if we had a building sufficiently large, we could gather as many persons as the human voice can reach.

(*b*) It is a temporary structure, which by the Metropolitan Buildings Act must come down sooner or later.

(*c*) The corrugated iron is becoming dilapidated, and lets in the rain, so that rows of umbrellas are often put up during the service.

(*d*) The cold is intense.

(*e*) The acoustic properties are inferior.

"Please add to this that our site is the very best in all East London. It ought surely to be utilised to the fullest extent. The present building only half covers it.

"We have got the site, and we have got the people. May we not have a hall to accommodate them? The willingness to hear is very remarkable, and it is distressing to see hundreds and thousands turned away for want of mere room.

"The guarantees which the public have that the work is a proper one, and that the new hall will be properly used, are:—

1. The testimony of trustworthy persons who are acquainted with the mission. Mr.[95] Spurgeon has written a warm letter. Lord Shaftesbury is an old friend of, and worker in, the mission. He has delivered several addresses in the hall. The late Lord Kintore was a warm and constant friend of the work. Mr. R. C. L. Bevan has both promised £2000 and consented to act as treasurer.

2. A trust deed has been drawn up and signed, transferring the property to Trustees,—namely: F. A. Bevan, Esq.; Richard Cory Esq.; Frederick N. Charrington, Esq.; Hon. Ion Keith-Falconer; James Mathieson, Esq.; Samuel Morley, M.P.; Hon. Hamilton Tollemache; Joseph Weatherly, Esq.—and specifying the objects for which it is to be used.

"It may be objected that the East End ought to supply its own wants. This is impossible. The population of the East End consists of the working classes, who, though they furnish the sinews of wealth which resides elsewhere, are poor themselves. Thus the East End has a double right to look outside for help. It is poor and cannot help itself adequately, and the wealthy are responsible for the well-being of their servants, the toiling thousands through whose labour they derive their incomes.

"The character of our Mission is evangelistic, unsectarian and sober. I say sober, because of late years some have despaired of reaching the masses except by using certain unseemly and sensational methods. Our work is an emphatic[96] protest against this practice, and a standing disproof of its necessity.

"Finally, the building for which we plead will cost £20,000, a small sum indeed when we consider what amounts many are willing to spend on their own comforts and pleasures. This sum will not only build a suitable Hall, but a Frontage in addition, embracing a coffee palace, and a book saloon for the sale of pure literature. The site has already been paid for."

A beautiful letter was written by Keith-Falconer to a private friend during this period of his friendship with Mr. Charrington. It was written from the house at Stepney Green, to which I have already referred in an earlier part of the book. Nothing could more adequately show the young man's personal spirituality, and also his enthusiastic love for the friend whose own pure and self-sacrificing life was such an example to his own.

"Stepney Green.

"It is overwhelming to think of the vastness of the harvest-field, when compared with the indolence, indifference and unwillingness on the part of the most so-called Christians, to become, even in a moderate degree, labourers in the same. I take the rebuke to myself.... To enjoy the blessings and happiness God gives, and never to stretch out a helping hand to the poor and wicked, is a most horrible thing. When we come to die, it will be awful for us, if we have to look back on a life spent purely on self, but—believe me—if we are to spend our lives otherwise, we must make up our minds to be thought 'odd' and 'eccentric' and 'unsocial' and to be sneered at and avoided.

[97]"For instance, how 'odd' and 'unsocial' of my heroic friend (Mr. Charrington) to live in this dirty, smoky East End all the year round, and instead of dining out with his friends and relations, to go night after night to minister to the poor and wretched!... But I like to live with him and to watch the workings of the mighty hand of God and to catch a spark of the fire of zeal which burns within him, in order that I may be moved to greater willingness and earnestness in the noblest cause which can occupy the thoughts of a man. This is immeasurably better than spending my afternoons in calling on people, my evenings in dinners and balls, and my mornings in bed.... The usual centre is Self, the proper centre is God. If, therefore, one lives for God, one is out of centre or eccentric, with regard to the people who do not."

In 1884 Mr. Keith-Falconer was married at Trinity Church, Cannes, to Miss Gwendoline Bevan, daughter of Mr. R. C. L. Bevan, of Trent Park, Hertfordshire. Mr. Charrington was present upon this occasion, and acted as "best man" to his friend.

In 1885, together with his young wife, he sailed for Aden, resolving to take up missionary work there, being peculiarly fitted for it owing to his intimate acquaintance with Oriental languages. I am not going to expatiate upon his life and work there. I am writing the biography of his friend. In 1887 he passed away, and was reverently laid to rest in the wild and dreary cemetery there, far from home and those he loved, yet among those for whom he laboured, and for whom he counted no loss too great, if only he might win them for Christ.

[98]I may quote, perhaps, those words from *The Pilgrim's Progress*, which describe the death of Valiant-for-Truth.

"'My sword I give to him that shall succeed me in my pilgrimage, and my courage and skill to him that can get it. My marks and scars I carry with me, to be a witness for me, that I have fought His battles, Who will now be my Rewarder.'... So he passed over, and all the trumpets sounded for him on the other side."

The loss to the Tower Hamlets Mission was incalculable, and it is pathetically expressed on a certain page of *The Record*, Mr. Charrington's official organ.

Mr. Edwin H. Kerwin wrote:—

"Another faithful soldier of Jesus Christ has fallen at his post—the post of danger and honour. Those of us who knew him are weighed down with sorrow to think we shall hear his voice no more. We loved him from the first time we ever saw him. My thoughts go back to the year 1873, when, as a young man of seventeen, his beloved father, the late Earl of Kintore, brought his son and interested him in Mr. Charrington's work. From that date until the day of his death he was devoted to the Tower Hamlets Mission. Amid his arduous studies at Cambridge he delighted to break away from them for a day, and run up to Mile End. In a letter before me, dated

July 1880, and written to me while his beloved father was lying dead, he says, 'It is pleasant to me to reflect that it was my father who first introduced me to Charrington and his work, and that he so cordially supported the Mission. I hope that his sudden departure may be the means of blessing to the careless, perhaps to some who heard him speak in the Assembly Hall.'[99] How strange that the son should also be struck down suddenly! May the prayer he breathed at his father's death become a reality in his own sudden departure. In another letter, written to me in 1879, in answer to one I had addressed to him respecting some young men who had been impressed with an address he had given at Mile End, he said: 'I was so thankful about those five young men. The best of this work is that so few of the conversions are directly traceable to any particular person; we all help.'

"About ten years ago he was staying at Mr. Charrington's residence. I picked up his Bible, and found written upon the fly-leaf this motto—

'Henceforth, Lord, I wish to be Wholly given up to Thee, That in life and walk I may Glorify Thee day by day.'

"Surely those who were acquainted with him can testify that he carried this out!

"His brilliant achievements at the University of Cambridge, his linguistic proficiency, together with his exceptional abilities, were all devoted to the cause of Christ. He worked hard in the interests of purity and temperance. He often spent nights with Mr. Charrington in watching the music halls. I shall never forget the night when Mr. Charrington was taken off by the police, falsely accused of disturbance outside Lusby's Music Hall. I was not there, but, hearing of the incident, I went off to the police station, and, on nearing it, saw a large crowd. In the dark I could see one tall man standing in the centre, head and shoulders above every one else, and perfectly white; this was Falconer, who had been covered with flour by the frequenters of the music hall. He gave evidence on this occasion, and it is within the recollection of many that he was entered to run on this very[100] day in the University Champion Bicycle Race; also the stir he made in the sporting world by telegraphing to the course—he was staying with Mr. Charrington on Stepney Green at the time, and Mr. Charrington suggested it—the following words: 'The race is safe with Dodds. I have made up my mind not to run, having started in the race spoken of in Hebrews, chap. xii, verses 1, 2.'

"He also gave evidence at Clerkenwell Sessions against the character of Lusby's Music Hall. While at Cambridge he interested himself in evangelistic work, and he was mainly instrumental in converting the Theatre into a Mission. Through his efforts the building was purchased, and ever since the work has been carried on with great success. It is with melancholy interest that I turn to the notes of the conference on the evangelisation of the world held at the Great Assembly Hall in May last year, and read his grand speech on the work he and his devoted young wife had commenced in Aden; and when I peruse his still grander oration given before the Free Church Assembly in Scotland in the same month, it impresses upon me how great is his loss to the Church of God. He wound up that memorable speech with an appeal which it will be well for all to take heed to. He said: 'There must be some who, having the cause of Christ at heart, have ample independent means, and are not fettered by genuine home ties. Perhaps you are content with giving annual subscriptions and occasional donations and taking a weekly class? Why not give yourselves—money, time, and all—to the foreign field? Ought you not to consider seriously what your duty is? The heathen are in darkness and we are asleep. By subscribing money, sitting on committees, speaking at meetings, and praying for missions, you think you are doing the most you can to spread the Gospel abroad. Not so.[101] By going yourself you will produce a tenfold more powerful effect. You have wealth snugly invested in the Funds; you are strong and healthy; you are at liberty to live where you like, and occupy yourself as you like. While vast continents are shrouded in almost utter darkness, and hundreds of millions suffer the horrors of heathenism of Islam, the burden of proof lies upon you to show that the circumstances in which God has placed you were meant by Him to keep you out of the mission field.' What force, what irresistible urgency, does his death give to this solemn appeal for dedication to the service of the kingdom of Christ!

"He was a proficient phonographic shorthand writer. He was a firm friend of the tonic sol-fa system, and took the matriculation certificate. He provided a scholarship that bears his name at the Tonic Sol-Fa College. His work on earth has ceased; he has now gone to his reward. Though we feel that we can ill spare him, yet we will not grudge him the well-earned repose he is now enjoying. He rests from his labours, and his works do follow him. He is a witness still that the spirit of heroism and martyrdom is not extinct, and while men who love their lives lose them, a man who gives his life for the Lord's sake, 'keeps it to life eternal.'

"The great Assembly Hall was crowded to its utmost extent the Sunday after the news reached England of the death of the Hon. Ion Keith-Falconer. The announcements of a funeral service brought friends from all parts.

"The platform was tastefully decorated in crape, and in the centre facing the congregation, was displayed Mr. E. Clifford's life-like portrait of the deceased gentleman, which he had kindly lent for the occasion. Many of the late Mr. Falconer's personal friends were present on the platform, including his brother-in-law, Mr. Granville Smith, Mr. F. N. Charrington, Hon. Superintendent of[102] the Mission, Mr. E. H. Kerwin, Secretary, Mr. C. H. Warry, and others. Mr. W. R. Lane was the preacher. Upon the occupants of the platform taking their places, and in response to the invitation of Mr. F. N. Charrington, the organist of the hall, Mr. Day Winter, played the Dead March in *Saul*, the audience rising and remaining standing until its conclusion. A special service of hymns was used upon the occasion, and distributed to the congregation upon entering the building. They were taken in the order named.

'Let saints on earth in concert sing,With those whose work is done;For all the servants of our King,In heaven and earth are one.'

"'Home at last, thy labour done,' 'The Son of God goes forth to war,' and 'For ever with the Lord.'

"During the evening the choir also sang McGranahan's anthem, 'I am the Resurrection and the Life.' Mr. F. N. Charrington, who presided, made many touching references to the deceased gentleman, and his well-known sympathy with the work carried on by the Tower Hamlets Mission, notably his donation of £2000 towards the building fund of the hall in which they were then meeting. He also made references to his brilliant achievements at the University of Cambridge, his linguistic proficiency, etc. Yet in spite of the undoubted future which was in store for him in England, had he (Mr. Falconer) devoted his exceptional abilities to his own land, fired with missionary zeal, and at the bidding of the voice of God, he devoted his all to His cause, and proceeded to sacrifice his future prospects to the welfare of his brethren in lands beyond the sea. To this noble self-abnegation had he devoted his life, and as truly as any of old was he a martyr to his faith, for it was in the discharge[103] of his self-imposed duties as a missionary that he contracted the fever which terminated a life that was all but limitless in its possibilities.

"'He rests from his labours, and his works do follow him.' Although inscrutable were God's ways, yet they could bow to His ruling and say, 'Thy will be done.' He had but gone before. Mr. G. H. Warry led the congregation again in prayer, and after the singing of one of the hymns mentioned above, Mr. E. H. Kerwin spoke, and then read the appropriate Scripture to be found in 1 Corinthians, chap. xv, commencing at the 26th verse. Mr. W. Lane followed with a very earnest and solemn address."

Of Mr. Charrington's private loss what can I say here? I think those who have followed me thus far will realise what a crushing blow it was. I am loth to intrude upon the sanctities of private grief: I can only say that from my conversations with the surviving member of that happy, Christian brotherhood, I know that the loss is, even to-day, after so many years, as fresh and keen as ever.

And I know that not one of the least of my friend's hopes and anticipations is that of once more meeting in Heaven the man he loved so well on earth.

[104]
CHAPTER V
THE BATTLE OF THE MUSIC HALLS

There was a time when the name "Charrington" was, for quite a considerable period, a household word in England.

The reason for this was not because the public had suddenly awakened to the fact that among them was a man who had given up all that makes life dear to ordinary people, who lived a remote and buried life in the far East End, denying himself everything, and working for Christ among folk as sordid and savage as those to be found in any distant land, but because this same "Charrington" had presumed—actually presumed!—to interfere with the immoral pleasures of London.

I have called this chapter THE BATTLE OF THE MUSIC HALLS, and well, I think, does the title epitomise the story I have to tell.

It is a dual story. It shows Frederick Charrington himself going into the gravest personal danger, and fighting the most tremendous of fights with a few devoted adherents, and it also tells of efforts made in the newly-constituted forum which was to rule the destinies of London—the London County Council.

I will begin with the "Battle of the Music Halls" proper.

In connection with Mr. Charrington's campaign[105] against the music-halls of the East End, and one in particular, one of the most sensational law cases upon record held the public mind for a considerable time.

I shall shortly quote from those legal proceedings, shall draw upon a store of drama, unequalled in the history of Evangelism.

And, as an introduction, I shall tell certain facts of the inner history of this affair which have never yet been published, and which I have wrung from Mr. Charrington, with his reluctant consent to use them.

Let me begin, then.

Mr. Charrington's attention was first called to the question of music halls by something that a poor man, to whom he was speaking one day, said to him.

This poor fellow was in great distress of mind, and in the course of the conversation, he was asked if he was a married man.

His reply was, "No; those reptiles at —— ruined my wife."

The man mentioned the name of a certain music hall, and his earnestness of demeanour, his profound sorrow, gave Mr. Charrington food for thought. He had known, of course, that the music halls of those days were centres of evil. Now he came to think that the evil might be even greater than he had previously imagined.

It must be remembered that I am writing of a time quite remote from the present.

I know little of the music halls of to-day, though once or twice I have watched a spectacle of shifting colour and extraordinary grace, accompanied by [106] lovely music, at a certain palace of amusement in the West End.

I know nothing more than this—personally—but, from inquiries, I am well aware that the music halls of to-day are very much improved for the better. And, as I read in my daily paper that His Majesty the King, accompanied by his court, has witnessed a performance at the chief music hall of London, it seems obvious that these places are nothing like what they used to be. So, in reading of this Homeric contest made by Frederick Charrington, you must transport yourselves into the past, and realise that I am speaking of old days.

While Mr. Charrington's attention was being drawn to the music halls of the East End—by the incident previously referred to—an American friend of his came into his house one evening, and said, in great agitation, "I have just seen a horrible thing. I was passing the door of a music hall when a man, with a girl upon his arm, was just entering the gates. I saw a woman, evidently his wife—for she had a wedding ring on her finger, and recognised him at once—rush up to this man and cry out, 'Oh, John, whom have you got there?' The man hesitated for a moment, and as he did so, the girl left his arm and rushed inside the place.

"The man turned his head, looked at his wife with an evil expression, and then hurried in after his companion. The poor wife naturally attempted to follow them both, but the man in uniform at the door stretched out both his arms and stopped her, saying, 'Oh, no, we don't want you in here.'"

[107]This new incident stirred Mr. Charrington's indignation afresh, and he thought, "If this is a fair sample, these places ought to be called music *hells* instead of music halls."

He determined to see for himself whether this was an isolated case or not. Further investigations proved that it was not so, as I shall shortly show.

He soon found out what the character of these places really was, but, believing that most people were ignorant of their horrible character, he began active steps immediately.

The first thing he did was to see what powers the law could enforce in cases of the kind. He found that the law *was* quite strong enough to deal with them, as a clause existed to the effect that *any person could be dealt with who harboured prostitutes*, for the purpose of prostitution or not.

This, Mr. Charrington thought, was quite enough, and after he had done all he could, by personal influence, to deter respectable people from going to a certain notorious East End hall, in due course he opposed the license at the Quarter Sessions at Clerkenwell.

This, however, had but little result. Although in one year he actually proved by witnesses prostitution to be going on in three parts of the premises of the hall in question. To his horror and amazement, the magistrates (with a few noble exceptions) allowed the license to continue, although every minister of religion in East London, including the Bishop of Bedford, and 1800 respectable inhabitants, signed the protest against the house as "the nightly resort of prostitutes."

[108]Mr. Charrington's worst fears as to the evil results of music halls were one morning more than confirmed by reading in the *Daily News*—

"On Saturday morning a young medical student named R—— shot himself with a revolver while at a house in Brompton Crescent, Fulham Road, where he had passed the night. It appears that he met a female outside the Pavilion Music Hall on Friday night, and accompanied her to her home. In the morning, during her absence to get some tea for him, the report of firearms was heard. Police constable S——, of the B. Division, was called in, and found the deceased lying on the bed, bleeding from the forehead, with a six-chambered revolver fully loaded under his leg, with the exception of one which had recently been discharged. Dr. R—— saw the man soon afterwards and found life extinct. A letter was found upon the deceased addressed to his mother in Mildmay Park, Islington. The deceased was about twenty years of age, and was a pupil to Dr. L——, of Kensington."

Now the mother of this unhappy young man had been previously asked to assist him financially in his campaign against the music halls. She was the only person Mr. Charrington *had* ever asked to help him. She was a very wealthy woman, but nevertheless she refused utterly!

Mr. Charrington's mind was made up. A definite campaign was determined on, and the determination resulted in a battle which, for its sheer fearlessness, audacity, and far-reaching consequences, is probably unexampled in the chronicles of missionary effort in England.

In order that the personal testimony of Mr. [109] Charrington may be supplemented by public words, I quote what *Punch* said in one of its issues at that period.

"It is, however, in the disgraceful scenes enacted in the drinking-bars and saloons attached to these halls that the greatest evils exist—evils which cannot fail of exercising a fatal influence upon the frequenters of these places, of both sexes, who, in the first instance, go to hear a song, but become initiated in vice and immorality, rendered more easy and dangerous by the seductive influences by which they are surrounded. The more respectable the hall, the more prominent is this feature. These saloons are filled by men about town of all ages and conditions, with and without characters. There may be seen the young and inexperienced clerk, the heartless skittle-sharp and blackleg, the patrician *roué* and the plebeian fancy-man. This mixed crowd of folly and vice keep up a continued chattering, composed of obscene and vulgar repartees, to the great annoyance of the decent tradesman or working man who, accompanied by his wife or sweetheart, may have visited the hall with the delusive hope of hearing some good singing, but whose ears are thus polluted with vulgarity and slang. It is this sort of thing that has driven, and is driving, the respectable portion of society from these halls; and it is to provide attraction for the more spicy patrons that comic ladies and other sensation performances have been introduced. In these saloons the scenes that used to be enacted in the lobbies and saloons of theatres are reproduced, even in a worse and more offensive form."

The first definite step that Mr. Charrington took was to write a tract, which he caused to be disseminated very largely.

|110|I give extracts from it here. It is not a great literary effort by any means—Frederick Charrington's life has been far too strenuous for any dilettante toying with words. But it is, at any rate, a direct and forcible appeal, written in language which those for whose ears it was destined were well able to understand.

There was a picture in this tract—which I have before me as I write. The art of reproduction in those days was in its infancy. The thing is a rude wood-cut, of what we should think to-day appalling crudity. And yet, the picture had its effect, no less than the strong words which accompanied it.

I see, in faded ink, a young man, whose state of indecision is well shown by the almost impossible puerility of his face. On one side of him there is a very concrete devil, as horned and horrible as those creations of the monkish mind in the middle ages which adorned—or defaced—the pages of missals. The devil is offering this young man the sinful pleasures of the world—the sinful pleasures being shown in a few crude symbols—a large tankard, dice, and cards!

Upon the other side is an Angel of light, pointing to the Crown of Life, and to that happiness which "hath the promise of the life that now is, as well as that which is to come."

In our time such a thing would be laughed at. In those days it was doubtless as good as many other efforts of its kind. Be that as it may, who shall laugh or sneer at an earnest and well-meant effort to engage the thoughts of the passer-by?

Engage the thoughts of the passer-by it certainly did—and the accompanying words, from which I|111| make extracts, were read all over the East End of the Metropolis.

"This is a picture of you, reader. The devil is striving on one side to lead you down to Hell, by the alluring temptations of sinful indulgence. The Holy Spirit on the other side is striving with your heart and conscience to lead you up to Heaven; and God, by His word, is now saying, 'Choose ye this day whom ye will serve.' Nothing will avail you but an entire change of heart, or conversion. Our Lord says to you, 'Except a man be born again, he cannot see the kingdom of God' (John iii. 3); and again in verse five he says, 'Ye cannot enter into the Kingdom of God.' You can go to the theatre or music hall, and there your eyes can gaze upon the indecent dance, and there you can hear the filthy song, but unless you are born again, you can never see the glories of Heaven, and you will never hear the song of the redeemed. You may enter the swinging doors of the public-house, and take the intoxicating cup as you stand in the way of sinners; you may enter that house (which is the way to Hell, leading down to the chambers of death), but unless you are born again, you will never enter through the pearly gates of the city, and you will never meet with loved ones gone before. In conclusion, 'the wages of sin is death; but the gift of God is Eternal Life through Jesus Christ our Lord.' God grant that you may accept the gift instead of earning the wages; 'that as ye have yielded your members servants unto uncleanness and to iniquity unto iniquity; even so now yield your members servants unto holiness.'

"A time is coming when God will say, 'He which is filthy, let him be filthy still; and he that is holy, let him be holy still,' but 'Now is the accepted time, now is the day of salvation.'

|112|"'Faith cometh by hearing, and hearing by the word of God' (Romans x. 17), therefore come and hear the Gospel at the great Assembly Hall, Mile End Road, open every evening."

Thus the tract, which already began to create considerable interest, and to agitate the neighbourhood in no small way.

Like a good general, Frederick Charrington followed up one blow with another. He collected all his forces, and night after night outside Lusby's Music Hall he was found distributing tracts, with his friend Keith-Falconer and other helpers.

He stood at the very door of this music hall, and took every possible opportunity of entering into conversation with such people as responded to his tentative advances. Many and many a man and woman, who were going to this place with nothing but sensual and material thoughts, were given pause by the proffer of a tract, or, more often still, by a few earnest words from the young evangelist and his helpers.

The scenes at this time—outside the flaring front of the music hall—were extraordinary. I do not propose to enter into many details, simply because they will be well seen in the legal evidence which is to follow. It is sufficient to say that the proprietors of the hall brought an action against Mr. Charrington, and the records of that *cause célèbre* tell their own story.

But there are certain incidents, as I said in an earlier part of this chapter, which have never before been made public, and which I had some difficulty in obtaining my friend's permission to record.

|113|This Lusby's Music Hall was, without doubt, a sink of iniquity. It was notorious in the locality, but it also spread its evil tentacles westwards. The well-to-do, foolish, and drunken young "bloods" of the period—I believe "masher" was their designation at the time—used to drive down in cabs from Piccadilly and haunt

Lusby's in pursuit of the girls of the East End. It was a new sensation. It provided an evening's amusement quite out of the common.

One night during Mr. Charrington's campaign, five young men arrived from the West End in evening dress. As they were entering the music hall, Mr. Charrington and his friends spoke to them in no uncertain way. I have been told—and I feel quite sure—that the remonstrances addressed to them were made in the most quiet, gentlemanly, and unobtrusive manner. At any rate, these people were horribly enraged. There are two things you must not do if you wish to be popular with worldly men. You must not wound any man's vanity, and you must not interfere with his guilty pleasures.

Charrington and Ion Keith-Falconer, both of them men of breeding and position themselves, hit these young aristocrats from Piccadilly too hard. A remonstrance from some earnest but illiterate tub-thumper might have been passed by with a light laugh, or at most a sneer. In this case an evil and malignant anger was aroused. These young men were again accosted, and their resentment was thereby heightened to fever heat.

With faces flushed with drink, their eyes blazing[114] with anger, they advanced to the young evangelist, loudly expressing their determination to "do for him."

Then occurred, in an instant, one of the most pathetic and dramatic things of which I have ever heard.

Several wretched girls, who had been with these young men, plying their dreadful trade and hoping to reap a richer reward than usual, turned round upon their patrons.

They made a ring round Frederick Charrington, snarling like tigresses, and using—so Mr. Charrington has told me—the most appalling and awful language it is possible to conceive.

They told the young men from the West End that they would tear them to pieces rather than that they should touch a single hair of Mr. Charrington's head.

It all occurred out in the public street, and only a Zola could describe the occurrence as it really happened. What I myself have heard from Mr. Charrington is horrible enough. These poor women must indeed at that moment have been inspired by something beyond their knowledge or understanding.

There is good in all of us. The latent good in these poor creatures was stirred into activity, and they defended the man whom they believed was doing his best to spoil their business and ruin their trade, with the ferocity of wolves, and the shrieking courage of the hyena at bay.

In the result, the young aristocrats were so taken aback that they grew pallid with shame and fear. All thoughts of aggression left them, and they[115] simply turned tail and fled away down the flaring thoroughfare of the Mile End Road.

They went back to their own place and concocted a scheme together—a scheme which was to result in the "outing" of Frederick Charrington.

They engaged several low-class pugilists, sent them down to Lusby's Music Hall in cabs, with the direction to thrash Charrington within an inch of his life. They were to do him all possible bodily harm which stopped short of actually killing him, and were each promised a five pound note for the work.

These hired bullies went into the music hall and stood at the door. They drank sufficiently to loosen their tongues, and the manager of the hall heard, through one of his satellites, what was on foot. The manager, a shrewd business man, at once saw that, if these fellows were allowed to carry out their dastardly plan, such an uprising and stir of public opinion would take place, that the hall would be swept out of existence. He deputed an emissary to treat these prize-fighters with champagne. This was done with such success that they became helpless for any evil purpose, and were put into cabs and sent back home.

Mr. Charrington knew nothing of this organised attempt until some time afterwards.

All these incidents made it imperative for the proprietors of the music hall to take some action if they were to keep the place open.

The armies of Christ were at their very doors, they must needs defend their stronghold by every means in their power.

In the High Court of Justice, Chancery Division,[116] on February 12, 1885, before Mr. Justice Chitty, the case of CROWDER *versus* CHARRINGTON was called.

"Mr. Ince, Q.C., and Mr. Francis Turner, instructed by Messrs. Peckham, Maitland and Peckham, appeared for the plaintiffs, and Mr. Romer, Q.C., with whom was Mr. Charles Mitchell, instructed by Messrs. Shaen, Roscoe, Henderson and Co., appeared for the defendant.

"This action was brought by Messrs. Crowder and Payne, the owners of Lusby's Tavern and Music Hall, in the Mile End Road, to restrain the defendant, Mr. Charrington, who is carrying on a Mission Hall about a hundred yards from plaintiffs' premises, from annoying them in their business, and from making representations, by the distribution of tracts or otherwise, to the plaintiffs' injury."

It is impossible to give more than certain extracts from these celebrated proceedings, which are even now not forgotten. I must at least print the testimony of two girls, who had been rescued by Mr. Charrington from the dreadful life that they were leading. They were rescued by him and placed in good situations. Their past life, with all its shame and horror, seemed quite obliterated. No one, in their new surroundings, had the slightest idea of what they had been. But when Mr. Charrington was engaged in the lawsuit, both these girls came forward and voluntarily gave testimony—surely one of the noblest instances of gratitude, that rarest of qualities, upon record!

One girl deposed as follows—

"I am nearly twenty-one years of age. I remember[117] being taken to the hall one night in 1880. A young man took me. I had drink given me at the bar of a public house. I had more than was good for me. The young man then took me away and seduced me. After that I attended the hall habitually.

"Sometimes I used to go by myself, and sometimes with other girls. I used to go there for the purpose of prostitution.

"A great many other girls used to go there as well for the same purpose. I have often met young men there, and taken them to houses of ill-fame. I sometimes have returned to the hall. Sometimes I had to pay for re-admission, but not always.

"Prostitutes were in the habit of drinking at the bars; they had been in the habit of being treated at the bar. They frequently used to be there in considerable numbers, and often got tipsy.

"The men at the hall door never objected to my going into it, and I never saw other prostitutes objected to. I have now left that life. In 1881 I went into a home maintained by Lady ——. I am now in domestic service and am leading a virtuous life.

"I used to attend the hall every night. I used to get my living by attending the hall. I never walked the streets. I had been living a modest life up to then. I have often been intoxicated in the music hall itself. I used as a rule to hang about the bars."

The other young woman who had been rescued, also came forward and bore her testimony—

She said she first went to —— on Christmas Eve, 1880, with a young man, and had too much to drink[118] at the bar there, was taken away to a house and seduced. She afterwards led an immoral life, and frequented the music hall for the purposes of prostitution. Going in unaccompanied by anybody, she used to get men in the hall to go home with her. Many other girls attended it in the same way. She was treated there by men. On one occasion was present in a box in the music hall when an act of prostitution was committed, and knew another girl who had done the same thing. After taking men out of the hall she would go back again the same evening, and was on these occasions readmitted without payment. Other prostitutes were allowed to do the same. They were passed in by the man in uniform at the gate. Was never refused admission to the hall, and did not know of other prostitutes being stopped. Mentioned as attending the place, the keeper of the brothel to which she used to take men. She led that life for a twelvemonth, constantly attending at the music hall, except for about two months. Eventually she was persuaded by Mr. Charrington to enter a home. She had since lived a moral life, and was now a domestic servant.

CHARRINGTON'S MORAL MICROSCOPE
A cartoon during the Music Hall Campaign
[To face p. 118.

Henry Ward Beecher describes the bitter experience of such an one, in the following words—

"That one who gazed out at the window, calling for her mother and weeping, was right tenderly and purely bred. She has been baptised twice—once to God and once to the Devil. She sought this place in the very vestments of God's House. 'Call not on thy mother! she is a saint in Heaven, and cannot hear thee.' Yet, all night long she dreams of home and childhood, and wakes to sigh and[119] weep; and between her sobs she cries, 'Mother! Mother!'"

And well may he exclaim—

"Oh, Prince of torment! if thou hast transforming power, give some relief to this once innocent child, whom another has corrupted! Let thy deepest damnation seize him who brought her hither! Let his coronation be upon the very mount of torment, and the rain of fiery hail be his salutation! He shall be crowned by thorns poisoned and anguish-bearing; and every woe beat upon him, and every wave of hell roll over the first risings of baffled hope. Thy guilty thoughts and guilty deeds shall flit after thee with bows which never break, and quivers for ever emptying but never exhausted. If Satan hath one dart more poisoned than another; if God hath one bolt more transfixing and blasting than another; if there be one hideous spirit more unrelenting than others; they shall be thine, most execrable wretch, 'who led her to forsake the guide of her youth, and to abandon the covenant of her God.'"

I think I cannot do better now than give my readers the evidence Mr. Charrington gave before Mr. Justice Chitty during the case.

"I am the Hon. Superintendent of the Tower Hamlets Mission, Mile End Road. The Mission-house is about twenty or thirty houses off the music hall. I am a guardian of the poor, and also a vestryman. I have been Hon. Superintendent since the year 1869, and have devoted the whole of that time to missionary work in the East End. I made considerable sacrifices on leaving the brewery, in order to devote myself[120] to the work of the Mission. Since 1880 I have, amongst other things, distributed tracts, etc., and endeavoured to persuade people not to go to the music halls, and have also endeavoured to rescue prostitutes from their evil courses. My efforts have not been solely confined to the music halls. The three tracts produced were amongst others I have given away. My ground for persuading people not to go to the music hall was because I found it was the nightly resort of prostitutes. I have watched the hall from the year 1880 up to the time of the fire, and also to a certain extent since the fire. I used to go down night after night as a rule, from about eleven o'clock till nearly one o'clock in the morning. I occasionally went earlier in the evening when the people were going into the hall. I used especially to speak to and remonstrate with prostitutes who used to go in and out of the house. I used to use an expression when I first went there, that the place literally swarmed with prostitutes. Numbers of prostitutes went into the hall unattended by men. I have seen brothel-keepers going night after night into the house with their women with them. I may mention especially a woman named Becky Hart. I have seen her with two and three poor young girls. She was a most notorious brothel-keeper, living in the Canal Road, Mile End Road. Another well-known brothel-keeper with her girls was also there nightly. She was known by the name of Fraser; no one could mistake her, she being excessively stout. There were also two or three other brothel-keepers, whom I knew very well by sight, who used to go to the hall[121] regularly, and also take their girls with them. Two of these brothel-keepers, a man and his wife, kept a house in Cleveland Street, the very next turning to the music hall. They used to go backwards and forwards continually during the evening, from the brothel in Cleveland Street. This brothel-keeper was thrown out of the hall one night, very drunk, and I caught him in my arms to prevent him from falling on the pavement. He then said to me, 'It's a great shame to treat me in this way, for I bring my girls here constantly.' I used to see him and his girls going into the hall night after night, and the girls leaving it after with men. I persuaded the man and his wife to give up the brothel. I have been requested by the man to visit one of the girls when she was dying. I have seen them night after night go out from the music hall with customers, sometimes with respectable-looking, well-dressed men, apparently from the West End of London, the girls having previously gone into the hall with their keepers. I have seen them go to the cabs that usually stand in a rank outside the hall. I have heard them tell the cabmen to drive to well-known brothel-houses. I have sent messengers to follow them to the houses for my own satisfaction, because I wanted to know positively if they did drive to the brothels. I have seen a girl do this kind of thing twice during a night. I have seen that on more than one occasion. I have seen them get into cabs; I have heard the cabmen ask them where to drive to. I have said to the cabmen, 'You know where you are going to drive them to. You know perfectly well, cabman, the brothel to which they are[122] attached. You live by these wretched women's trade.' I have seen numbers of women come out of the halls drunk. I have seen them when they have been drunk behaving in a most disgraceful way, and using the foulest language. On one occasion I saw three prostitutes take away with them from the hall three seafaring men, apparently captains or mates of vessels. They tried to get into a four-wheeled cab—all six of them. While they were getting into the cab I remonstrated with them, and told them they were ruining themselves, body and soul, going with such women to such places. I made use of the words, 'her house is the way to Hell, going down to the chambers of death.' One of the three men said, 'I think I will be out of this.' Another one said, 'It is getting rather hot for us.' They seemed to agree that what I said was true, and the result was that they got out of the cab. The three women, when the men walked away, turned round on one another, and fought together on the pavement, in front of the hall. I went into the midst of them, separated them, and persuaded them to leave off fighting. They were using all the time most filthy language, and causing a crowd to assemble. On another occasion I saw four prostitutes bringing down from the hall a particularly gentlemanly-looking young man, not only evidently a gentleman, but a well-bred one. He undoubtedly belonged to a good family in the West End. He was a little drunk. Those four prostitutes were half pulling and half dragging him from the hall to one of the cabs standing, as usual, in front of the hall. He struggled and tried to release himself[123] from the grasp of the women. I appealed to a policeman to rescue the man. I said to the policeman, 'This is simply highway robbery,' the man being taken off by force. I tried my best to rescue him when the police declined to interfere. There were plenty of prostitutes' bullies about the hall. These bullies used to frequent the hall nightly. They were unfortunately too strong for me, and the result was that the women took the young man off with them in a cab. I could multiply these instances, which were constantly occurring night after night. I have seen brothel-keepers come out with gentlemen, they having gone in alone. I have seen them standing on a pavement persuading men to go home with girls, and at the same time I have been persuading them not to do so. On one occasion a seafaring man, apparently a captain or mate of a vessel, came out of the hall so very drunk that he was incapable of taking care of himself. Two prostitutes came out with him partly holding him up and partly dragging him along. They got him half-way across the pavement towards the cabs in front of the hall. The cabmen, I found, as a rule, were only too anxious to help the prostitutes and their customers. The cabman, in this instance, came and helped the prostitutes, partly by pushing and partly by persuasion, to get the man into the cab. I managed to stop him just before he got to the cab, and endeavoured to persuade him not to go with the women. The cabman and the women tried in the meantime to persuade the man to go with them, the man hesitating. I then appealed to a policeman who was standing near apparently on duty, to interfere. I called his attention to the[124] fact that the man was helplessly drunk, wearing a gold chain, and no doubt having money in his pocket. I said to the policeman, 'This is simply highway robbery.' The policeman refused to interfere at all, and the result was that the two women, aided by the cabman, took the man away. I said to the women and the cabman, 'I'll run after you and get two policemen who will do their duty.' The cabman drove his horse as fast as he could. I ran after him till I came up to two policemen on duty a little farther up the road. I appealed to them, and they did their duty, saying to the women, 'You get out of this or we'll give you a night's lodging.' They said to the cabman, 'You had better mind what you are about.' Signals were then passed between the prostitutes and the cabman, which proved to me that the cabman was only going round another street to meet them again. I pursued the cab, followed by bullies from the hall. I outran the bullies, overtook the cab, and succeeded in getting the man out of the cab. I have seen prostitutes stopped going into the hall, but that was not during the first eighteen months or two years I worked outside the hall. After about that time a number of prostitutes came round me one night outside the hall and said I was stopping them from getting a living. I have seen prostitutes turned back from the hall on one occasion, after about eighteen months from the time I had commenced working. The prostitutes said to me, 'It is through you we are being turned out of the hall, and are prevented from getting our living in consequence, and you know we are getting our living there.' Great disorder arose outside[125] the hall when prostitutes came out drunk; upon several occasions disorder took place. On one particular occasion a prostitute came out drunk, marched up and down in front of the house, shouting and causing a great disturbance. She said, 'It is by the likes of us that Crowder and Payne get their living.' After the time I have spoken of the prostitutes seemed to go in and out of the hall as they liked. I used to take a number of tracts with me when I went outside the hall. I used to offer them to people going in and out of the hall and to passers-by on the pavement. If people refused to take the tract offered I allowed them to pass on. Sometimes, however, they would enter into conversation with me. I then used to draw them aside to the waste ground between the road and the pavement. My doing this did not cause a disturbance nor a mob to assemble. There were occasions, however, on which disturbances took place; one occasion when flour was thrown over me by some person from the direction of the hall; on another occasion human filth was thrown on me from an upper window of the hall. I have been assaulted on a great many occasions by roughs from the music hall, prostitutes' bullies being amongst them. On one occasion one of the roughs followed me and assaulted me. I gave him into custody and he was sentenced to three weeks' imprisonment. That was in June, 1883. I did not know the man who assaulted me. These assaults caused mobs to assemble. I remember in October, 1883, I was assaulted and driven across the road. The disturbance arose from an angry mob of roughs coming out of the hall and surrounding me. They asked[126] me what I meant by trying to ruin the music hall, by taking away its licence. That, of course, caused a large number of people to crowd together and look on. I appealed in vain to the police who were there for protection, but I did not get it. They said, 'If you like it you can get mobbed.' I walked across the road and asked for protection at the station house. I did nothing on that occasion to cause the disturbance. It is not true that whenever I was in front of the hall disturbances took place. I have been there scores and scores of nights alone distributing tracts, and no disturbance has taken place. Disturbances have not been caused by my missionary work. The largest number of friends who ever accompanied me was eighteen, and out of that number there would be two or three ladies. All these friends used to be engaged in the missionary work. The average number accompanying me was about three or four. Only on about twelve to twenty occasions a dozen or more persons were with me. In one year I went to the hall about a hundred nights. I have rescued several of the prostitutes who used to regularly frequent the hall. It is not true that I and my friends have ever tried to form a barrier round the door of the hall to prevent people from going into it. It was in consequence of the manager of the hall inciting the mob to assault me that a barrier was formed round the door of the hall. I have never stopped any person going into the hall by physical force. I have never followed a person across the threshold of the hall. I have seen officials connected with the hall incite people to attack me. A door-keeper named Young has done[127] so. The manager, Mr. Friend, on one particular occasion said to the mob, 'Halloa, boys, make a row,' but they did not appear to be very responsive. He has incited the people to attack me on more than one occasion. He often stood in the entrance hall cursing and swearing at me, and at times he would address the people from the hall. On one occasion he said to a man, 'He is a very good advertisement for the house.' He has used very foul and abusive language towards me. On one occasion he so lost control of himself that the passers-by stood still and looked at him in amazement. The wife of the shop-keeper next door has also used foul language towards me. Mr. Friend's action has caused great crowds to assemble. I am bound to say I have, as a rule, had great sympathy from the crowd. Working men would say, 'Go it, Charrington, and put an end to that den of iniquity.' Mr. Crowder has assaulted me, and has also incited others to assault me. Mr. Crowder used to walk beside me pushing me about, and causing a crowd to assemble. On one occasion he stood on the box-seat of a carriage and incited a mob against me, and on another he used a most horrible and foul expression towards me, which I would not like to repeat. On a Monday night in particular the roughs did rush out of the hall at a signal from Mr. Crowder, and surrounded me. Crowder then said, 'Police, take him up for obstructing the thoroughfare.' I managed to get away from the roughs on to the waste ground near the pavement. I said to the police, 'I am not obstructing the thoroughfare.' Crowder, however, gave me into custody, and Mr. Friend signed[128] the charge sheet. I was locked up all night, and the following morning the magistrate dismissed the charge, observing that an action would lie against the people who had given me into custody for false imprisonment. I have been frequently threatened by roughs. From the waste ground I have addressed people, but not from the pavement. None of these addresses caused the pavement to be blocked. I have spoken to a number of girls whom I have known to be prostitutes, urging them to abandon their course of life. I have never called them by such a name; I used to call them by their Christian names, because I knew most of them. I have never called a woman a —— because she would not take a tract. I have never said that none but prostitutes went into the hall, but I said that numbers of them went there. I was here when Mr. Payne's father gave his evidence. I have said to him, 'You ought to be ashamed of yourself to bring a young girl to such a place,' or words to that effect. I meant just the opposite to what Mr. Payne implied, because I could see that the young girl was respectable. I said nothing on that occasion that could be construed into an imputation on the girl's character. I heard Piggott give his evidence. On several occasions he has threatened me. He seemed to be always at the hall; in fact, he made it a custom to be there. He told me he supplied plaintiff with wine and spirits. On one occasion he followed me about with an oak stick. He shook it in my face and swore he would do for me if he followed me all over London. He was so excited that I feared every moment he would drop down in a fit. I have said that the hall[129] is the way to hell, because there were so many prostitutes attending it. I have never said that it was hell itself. I deny that anything I have done has caused a riot or disturbance. M——, H——, and C—— are three girls who gave evidence for me on a motion for injunction: C—— is not now in this country. These girls used to attend the music hall; they were prostitutes. I rescued them from that life."

Mr. Charrington then left the box, having been in it four hours and a half.

It is interesting, as throwing a light upon the character of Frederick Charrington, and the way in which his efforts were viewed by the most astute legal intellect of that day, to paraphrase the words of the judge who decided the issue of the case. I simply use those sentences from the bench which refer to the personal character of Mr. Charrington.

"The plaintiffs have, for some years past, carried on the business of a music hall, in the Mile End Road, the music hall being commonly known as Lusby's Music Hall. The defendant is a gentleman, the son of a well-known brewer, who has apparently given up a lucrative position in the brewery for the purpose of devoting himself to missionary work, and he has established a missionary hall in the neighbourhood.

"The question before me, then, is one of fact. Unquestionably on several occasions, when the defendant has been present, considerable disturbance has been caused by the crowds which have assembled. The evidence is, that these crowds have been brought together, not by the acts of the defendant, but by the conduct of the[130] plaintiffs themselves, and their agents, and other persons connected immediately with the music hall.

"Lusby's Music Hall is, as I have said, situated in the Mile End Road; and there is a paved footway in front of it of some thirty feet or so in breadth, and then, between the paved footway and the carriage-road, there is a piece of ground which some of the witnesses described as waste ground, and others as roughly paved, of about ten feet or so in breadth.

"The other witnesses, of whom Mr. Rainsford, who is a clergyman, I will select as an example, spoke also to the defendant's demeanour. His demeanour on these occasions is quiet and gentlemanly and courteous; and one of the plaintiff's witnesses, Mr. Dale, spoke of him, in cross-examination, in similar terms. Sometimes the person to whom he offers a tract responds with a sharp word, but on the evidence, as it stands, there is no ground for saying that the offering of the tract brings him into any angry or noisy altercation with any person to whom he is offering it, even those who have rejected it. He said, about one-third of the times that he has been there (he has been there on numerous occasions), he has been alone, and sometimes he goes with two or three friends, who are also engaged in missionary work, and occasionally, he said as many as from twelve to eighteen. Mr. Grenfell, whom I have already mentioned, spoke of him as having a *remarkable ascendancy over the persons whom he met on this pathway*; sometimes he also was accompanied by ladies.

"In my opinion, as the result of the evidence,[131] all these persons conducted themselves in an orderly manner. They do not, as was alleged on the part of the plaintiffs, and particularly by the plaintiff Crowder, in his evidence, form a 'living barricade,' nor do they cause, in my opinion, any obstruction to the highway.

"Now, the defendant says that plaintiffs and their servants, and particularly their manager, have been the real cause of such disturbances as have arisen. The principal offender is Mr. Friend, the manager, whose testimony I cannot rely upon. Young stands on a level with him. Young was the doorkeeper, and was not called as a witness. Mr. Crowder and Mr. Payne have certainly, each of them, taken some part in creating the disturbances, though in a less degree than Friend and Young. Now, the witness Howes, who also gave his testimony, amongst other witnesses, described what was done by some of these persons whom I have named. They walk up and down with Mr. Charrington. I should say that his beat, or his patrol, if I may use such a term, appears to be a distance of about thirty yards each way from the music hall; and they not only walk up and down with him, but, according to Howes, they tread on his heels, and a mob accompanies them as they go.

"Mr. Mason, the shorthand writer, who also gave his evidence admirably, was a witness to the same effect. As Mr. Kerwin, another witness for the defendant, said (and I believe him rather than the plaintiffs' witnesses on this point), if Mr. Charrington had been left to himself, there would have been no crowd and no disturbance. What[132] they said is this: I mean, what Friend particularly does, and Young also; they try to incite the passers-by, and those persons who are coming from the music hall are irritated. Well, it is said, it is natural they are irritated; I have no doubt, and it is a fair observation to make, that they are, to some extent, naturally incited against him. They look upon this as a crusade against the music hall; but they have gone far beyond, in my opinion, what they were justified in doing. They called on the mob to shout, and, on several occasions, certainly, Friend has tried to incite them, by saying, 'Halloa, boys, halloa!'

"They assail him with foul and filthy language and they have cursed him and they have sworn at him; they have assailed him with flour and with pease-pudding; they have knocked his hat off; they have kicked him, and the roughs from the hall have certainly made a dead set upon him. On one occasion he was assaulted, and the man was committed to prison for three months. They have actually, some of them, thrown human filth from the windows. On one occasion, particularly, there was a violent attack made upon him; that is, in October 1883, and I am satisfied that that was an organised attack. He was driven across the road, and had to seek refuge in a police section house on the opposite side. On one occasion they gave him in charge, and the magistrate dismissed the case, making, I am satisfied on the result of the evidence, observations which showed that the charge was wholly groundless. Mr. Piggott, who was a witness for the plaintiffs (and who denied what I am about to state, but I think he was in[133] error; I think Mr. Piggott was an excitable man, and a strong partisan), threatened him with a stick. Besides this, the defendant has been kicked.

"On one occasion, Friend endeavoured to incite the mob in this way. The witness was delivering some tracts, when Friend called on the passers-by to assemble, and said, 'Come and see what this man is calling your wives—nothing but common whores.' The people followed him to a coffee house window, there were people in the street; he was then going to read a tract, and found it was not what he wanted. Friend, said the witness, and I am satisfied that he is right, caused the crowd. There is some truth indeed in that metaphorical description that Mr. Charrington in the witness box gave himself; he said he was no more responsible than a target that is shot at. They have maltreated his friends, or those who have assisted him. Alston, who looks a respectable witness, was hit in the face for calling attention to the man who had knocked in the hat of one of his friends, and the man Young, the doorkeeper, actually committed the indignity of spitting in his face. Kerwin, another respectable witness, was butted in the stomach. Mr. Rainsford, the clergyman, was threatened to have a knife put into him, and Mr. Grenfell himself was mobbed."

These are hard and definite records.

But you must picture to yourselves Frederick Charrington and Ion Keith-Falconer accompanied by their friends, night after night—in all weathers—conducting their campaign amid the jeers and obloquy of the mob.

Often, from the upper windows of the music hall[134] they were drenched with flour, red ochre, and even more horrible things than these.

But Frederick Charrington stood there undaunted. His physical courage was supreme. His moral courage was even greater than that. He was determined upon the work which God had set him—he did not flinch nor falter.

What he must have endured I only faintly hint at. It is not my design to draw a lurid picture of that ascetic abnegation, that utter throwing away of all that makes life sweet, which was his cheerful, daily portion.

But I remember an old Cornish woman, whom I met on a wild, heath-covered moor upon a windy Sunday afternoon, when we were both leaving a little granite meeting-house, where a rugged, moorland farmer had spoken of his spiritual experience, and his fresh-cheeked daughters and their friends had sung hymns to the accompaniment of an harmonium, hymns which were drowned by the rushing mighty winds.

The old lady, whom I helped over the rough tussocks of grass—she is dead now, and, I am sure, in Heaven—turned to me, coughing and spluttering, when we had for a moment some shelter from the wind.

"Ah!" she said, referring to the words of the preacher, "Jesus belonged to have a brave, bad time! 'Twas a bitter nailing, sir, 'twas a bitter nailing!"

That is the note—that is the right note in which, I think, we ought to revere in memory those strenuous days when Frederick Charrington dared everything for the Lord.

[135]
CHAPTER VI
THE FIGHT ON THE LONDON COUNTY COUNCIL

The personal campaign against Lusby's Music Hall, the astounding details of which are found in the preceding chapter to this, was complemented by Mr. Charrington's work upon the London County Council, to which we find him elected as member for Mile End.

Some one has told me that after Mr. Charrington was returned to London's local Parliament, one of his congregation at the Great Assembly Hall remarked that he ought to be known from henceforth as "the member for Religion." Certainly, Mr. Charrington immediately recommenced his efforts to purify London, and these attempts—upon such a public stage—made his name known to almost every one in England in a very short space of time.

It was during the London Licensing Sessions that the world at large first heard of him. It was his efforts to make the Empire, the Aquarium, and other places of amusement, fit for the patronage of the ordinary man or woman, that called down upon his head a tempest of scorn, a tornado of obloquy, and induced the congratulation, the prayers, of thousands of Christian men and women who thought with him.

[136]We have seen him endure personal violence of the most vindictive kind, as he stood fighting for his convictions, outside the music halls of the East End. We are to see him now, no less calm and dignified, enduring the insults of the press, and the angry opposition of his colleagues upon the Council.

Here is a little study in contrasts!

Upon one occasion, during the battle in the East End, Mr. Charrington was arrested as causing an obstruction, and taken to the local police court, where he was confined all night in a cell. He had his Bible with him, and during the hours of his incarceration, he solaced himself with the word of God. In the morning, he was accosted by a fellow prisoner—as all the offenders of the night before were marshalled in the passage outside the cells.

"What are you in for?" said his new friend.

"Oh, I am in for a little affair in connection with Lusby's Music Hall," said Mr. Charrington with a smile.

The other chuckled. "Well, I never!" he said, "so am I! I sneaked a 'am from the bar of the same 'all."

There were others in that dismal company who recognised the young evangelist who had worked so earnestly among them for so long. He seized the opportunity. He prayed with these derelicts of the night, and ere they were ushered into the court to stand their hurried trials, they had all sung a hymn together, the police standing reverently by in complete sympathy with what Mr. Charrington did. The evangelist was liberated at[137] once, the magistrate remarking that the charge was perfectly unfounded, and that, if he wished, Mr. Charrington would have his legal remedy for false imprisonment. It is hardly necessary to say that the evangelist brought no action against the police or their instigators. Of all the men I have ever met, he has realised and applied the words of the Gospel to practical life. He has always turned the other cheek.

Here is one picture. Come with me now into the debating-room of the London County Council and see Frederick Charrington, well-dressed, well-groomed, strikingly handsome, and with the manner of the polished man of the world, quietly, but forcibly, combating the emissaries and paid supporters of vice.

I believe that this, his first prominent appearance in the London County Council, was the occasion of much surprise.

Although he had never advertised himself at all, his name was, of course, familiar to his colleagues. Buried in the East End as he was—and has always been—he was, nevertheless, not unknown by rumour. The assembled members of London's parliament expected to see an elderly, bearded man—the typical missionary among the poor. They saw, instead, a slim and debonair gentleman, aristocratic in appearance, and self-possessed in manner. Such shocks to preconceived notions are not nearly so rare as people suppose. A type—of this or that vocation—gets fixed in the public mind in some odd way. The reality is often startlingly opposed to the expected.

Every one who looks at the photograph of Mr.[138] Charrington in evening clothes, which I made him have specially taken for this book, will agree with what I say. Indeed, during his whole life in the East End, people who have never met him before, have called upon him for spiritual or material assistance, and have not left him without expressing their surprise and wonder at his personal appearance. A man once came to him who would hardly believe that he was "the" Mr. Charrington.

"I thought I was going to see an old bloke," he mumbled in clumsy apology, "you know, one of them old blokes with a white beard, seeing as I'd 'card of you for so many years."

So, when Frederick Charrington stood up to oppose the licenses of certain notorious music halls in the West End in the London County Council, his personal appearance and manner created a vast amount of surprise, and, if what I have heard is true—and I have no reason to doubt it—something of consternation also.

The Licensing Committee of the London County Council met in the Clerkenwell Sessions House, to consider applications for music, dancing, and theatre licenses. Mr. T. G. Fardell, Chairman of the Committee, presided, and there was a very full attendance of members.

The Sessions House had just been under the hands of painters and decorators. It looked quite bright and cheerful, but it proved quite inadequate for the accommodation of those people directly interested, and others who had gathered to hear Mr. Charrington give his evidence and endeavour to purge London of so much that he felt inimical to Christianity.

Photo Elliot & Fry
FREDERICK CHARRINGTON IN 1912
[To face p. 138.

[139]I have before me all the verbatim reports of that historic meeting. The fairest and most unbiased seems to me that of the *Daily Telegraph*, and it is from those columns that I reprint an epitome of what occurred. I see no better way of presenting the scene as vividly as possible than by doing this, but my readers must understand that I have only made extracts, as the whole proceedings are far too long to be incorporated in a book of this size.

And, moreover, I shall only print the record of Mr. Charrington's opposition to the licenses of music halls known by name, then and now, to the great mass of the public.

For months he had been obtaining evidence as to the character of these places, and also of similar and less famous ones. In a general picture, such as I wish to present, the cases of the less important halls must be eliminated. It is sufficient to say that the opposition to these minor licenses was as carefully considered, and as earnestly presented, as the objection to the others.

I will deal at once with the objection which Mr. Charrington made to the renewal of the licenses to the Empire Theatre of Varieties in Leicester Square. In order to make certain references in the report intelligible to the reader, I must say that one of Mr. Charrington's inspectors—a Mr. Frye—was a grocer by trade. Half the ribald press of London, for many days, constantly referred to this fact. "Mr. Charrington and his Grocer" became a byword in the columns of purely worldly newspapers. It was a cheap enough joke, and I entirely fail to see why a grocer should not be as efficient[140] a critic of morals as any one else. But if Mr. Frye had been a solicitor, a banker, or a vendor of smoked spectacles, through which to look at an eclipse, the comments would have been just the same.

Mr. George Edwardes applied for the renewal of the music and dancing license held by the Empire Theatre, Leicester Square.

Mr. Charrington: I oppose this license.

Mr. Forest Fulton, M.P., who appeared for the applicant, said no notice of opposition had been received.

The Chairman asked whether Mr. Edwardes would prefer to have the case adjourned.

Major Probyn: I think it exceedingly unfair to applicants not to have had notice of opposition. It is not at all in conformity with English ideas of fair play.

Mr. Beachcroft thought that as the option of having the case adjourned was given, there was no case of complaint.

The Chairman: The Theatres Committees were not aware of any opposition until this moment.

Mr. Forest Fulton said the difficulty of course was that they had no knowledge whatever of the nature of the complaint which was made, whether it was that they were harbouring prostitutes, or allowing indecent songs.

The Chairman observed that it was quite as inconvenient to the Committee as it was to the applicant.

Mr. Charrington said that the reason of his opposition was that the Empire was not only the resort of prostitutes, but that the prostitution was of a most dangerous character to those who went to the house. The license he had opposed previously affected the poor of the East End of London, whereas in this case the license was particularly[141] dangerous to young men of the better class. He was told on good authority that there might be seen in the hall young fellows from Oxford and Cambridge, who there saw vice and prostitution in its most attractive form. The prostitutes, who were often in evening dress, were to be found in the best parts of the house, and not, as in other music halls, in the cheaper seats. If the committee did not see their way to withdraw the license, he trusted that they might draw attention to the state of matters and so deter many from being inveigled into this place. It was also a frightful source of temptation to young women of the poorer classes. The evidence of his informant would show that the dresses of the performers were very indecent, especially in the ballet called "A Dream of Wealth." He opposed the licenses so that he might not again be accused of partiality in attacking poor places of entertainment only.

The Inspector Bartlett was then called.

Mr. Forest Fulton: Oh, this is the grocer again.

Witness, in answer to Mr. Charrington, said he visited the Empire, and thought that the dresses were very objectionable as they exposed the shapes of the performers very much. He thought them very indecent. That was in the ballet called "A Dream of Wealth."

Did you see any people who were disgusted besides yourself?—There was a lady sitting before me with her daughter, and I heard——

Mr. Forest Fulton: I believe I am in the presence of a judicial tribunal, and the statement of this witness as to what he heard somebody say who is not to be called is in defiance of the first principle of law and justice as administered in this country.

Mr. Charrington: Did other people show by their behaviour that they were disgusted? Did you not hear them?

The Chairman: Objection is taken to the question,[142] and we must be governed, as near as may be, by the practice in courts of law.

Mr. Forest Fulton said he objected from every point of view. The witness could give the impression upon his own mind, but not upon the minds of other people.

Witness: Some people went out.

Mr. Forest Fulton said the witness was not able to peer into the minds of other people. He said some people went out, but they might have gone out for fifty reasons.

Mr. Charrington: Have you not evidence that they said they were disgusted?

Witness: I only heard——

The Chairman: You must confine yourself as to what this witness saw that he thought of an objectionable character.

Mr. Charrington: Tell us what you saw, especially as to the indecency of the dresses.

Witness: My impression was that the dresses were indecent.

Mr. Charrington: I will ask what was the impression upon the audience, because I think that is important.

The Chairman: The witness has stated that he considered the dresses were objectionable, but he has not said why they were objectionable.

Mr. Forest Fulton: He said that the dresses were objectionable as disclosing the shapes of the performers.

MR. CHARRINGTON APPARENTLY SNUFFED OUT
A widely circulated cartoon during the Licensing Fight on the London County Council
[To face p. 142.

Replying to further questions by Mr. Charrington, witness said he found in the dress circle a number of prostitutes, respectably dressed, walking about in twos. They were very well-dressed indeed. In the dress circle he counted twenty or thirty. He did not see them in other parts of the house, but he saw one come downstairs, look about, and go up again. He was there about three hours. He did not see them drinking with gentlemen. He[143]went outside, and saw them go away in hansom cabs—some with gentlemen. He saw one come down with a decanter of brandy under her "harm," get into a hansom, and drive away with a gentleman. He believed she was a prostitute.

38

Cross-examined by Mr. Forest Fulton: I only once visited this place. I have been many times in a theatre. I have never seen a ballet at the theatre or the opera. I have seen ladies in evening dress at the theatre. There was nothing very different in this case from the ordinary evening dress worn by the people of this country as a matter of habit. I do not know that it is possible for any ballet to be performed without the performer wearing tights underneath the dress. I believe that it is the practice in every country in the world that where a ballet is being performed, tights are worn under the dress. That was what was done here.

The tights are worn under the short dresses?—They had long dresses, but they opened down the side.

What do you mean?—The dresses were drawn up at the sides.

You were shocked?—Not shocked, but I think it was indecent.

You thought it was indecent?—Yes.

But you were not shocked?—No.

In further cross-examination witness said he submitted his report to Mr. Charrington a few days ago. He did not do so sooner because he had several places to visit, and he was told to send in all his reports together, and Mr. Charrington had been out of town. This was his first visit to the Empire. He knew the women were prostitutes by their way of walking round. It was different from the way ordinary people walked, in respect that they walked in twos.

Do I understand you to ask the committee to [144] say that they were prostitutes because they walked in twos? And the manner they were going about, and, when they passed by people, the suggestions they made with their eyes.

Did they look at you?—I do not know as they did.

Did they look at you in the manner you have suggested?—I was hardly swell enough for that.

Did you see anything come of the looking?—No. I did not see that anybody took notice of them. I may say I saw one walk away and sit down beside a gentleman and get into conversation with him. That was the only case I observed. I cannot say I observed any of the undergraduates who have been spoken about. Beyond the case I have mentioned, I saw the women do nothing except walk about. The lady who went downstairs turned back. I cannot say if she saw me when she turned back. I cannot say if this is the reason she turned back. Nobody spoke to her. My impression was that she was a prostitute. She never solicited me—none of them ever did. The contents of the decanter the lady brought down might have been sherry: it might have been toast and water. I cannot say whether I said in my report that the decanter contained brandy. I saw the lady in the place earlier in the evening. She did not have the decanter then. She did not solicit anybody as far as I saw."

Several members of the Committee stating they did not wish any more of this class of evidence.

Mr. Charrington said he wished to call the responsible manager of the Empire.

Mr. George Edwardes was accordingly examined by Mr. Charrington, and stated that he was responsible manager of the Empire. They did not knowingly admit prostitutes to the Empire. They turned away ten or twelve every night. An inspector of police was stationed at the money-box to refuse them admission.

[145] If a member of the committee says he has been there, and has seen fifty or sixty prostitutes, you would say he was a liar?

The Chairman suggested that Mr. Charrington should not put such questions.

Mr. Charrington: If a gentleman went into the Empire and said there were seventy or eighty prostitutes there, you would say he must have made a mistake?

Mr. Edwardes: I should ask him to go with me and point them out. I deliberately say we do not admit women into the Empire if we know them to be prostitutes. The same applies to brothel-keepers and bullies. We keep a large staff of police and detectives to stop that.

Mr. Charrington: We know all about the police. We do not want any evidence from them. I do not think I need ask you any more. I shall, however, ask the police to come forward and swear, probably as usual.

Several members warmly protested against this as an insinuation against the police.

Inspector Burke was then called, and stated that the report to the Commissioner of Police was that the house was well conducted. He testified that, in his belief, every effort was made to keep out prostitutes. Prostitutes might be admitted, but they were women who were not known as such.

Mr. Davis, who said he was interested in the welfare of the people of London as any member of the Council, said he went there one Saturday night and found the place well conducted. He was not accosted there, although he was when he got into the street.

Mr. Charrington said his contention was not as to the behaviour of the prostitutes, but as to their presence.

Mr. Davis said it was the case that prostitutes were to be found at fashionable West End churches.

[146] The Chairman then announced that the Committee were in favour of recommending that the license be granted. He wished to say that the Committee generally did not agree with what had been said as to the evidence of the police, and that it was not just to say their evidence was untrustworthy.

In opposing the licenses at the London County Council of some of these more notorious music halls, Mr. Charrington, according to the regular procedure of the council, had to conduct the whole case himself without any legal training, and was not able to have a barrister to speak for him. On one occasion he had Sir Charles

Russell opposed to him, and also Mr. Grain, these eminent counsel representing the music halls. During the case in question some point arose in regard to one of the halls, and Mr. Charrington said to Sir Charles that the noise was so great on the other side that it drowned the counsel's voice and perhaps he did not hear correctly what Sir Charles had just said. But if he *had* said so-and-so, Mr. Charrington thought that he would find that he was misinformed. Sir Charles thereupon consulted his solicitor, and rising to his feet, bowed, and said, "That is so, Mr. Charrington." At the conclusion of the case Mr. Grain came over to Mr. Charrington and said, "I really must congratulate you, Mr. Charrington, on the way in which you have stood to your guns."

One can read this story, this official account of Frederick Charrington's noble efforts to rid London of what he firmly believed to be a plague-spot, from two points of view. But one can only come[147] to one conclusion about the earnestness of the man himself.

I am personally not very sympathetic to this effort of Charrington's, in those days. I think he would have been better advised to have realised that men and women cannot be made good by any Act of Parliament. Of the personal campaign outside Lusby's Music Hall I think very differently. He was then endeavouring to oppose the views and the solace of Religion to the forces of Evil.

No crowd encircled him about,He stood despised with two or three—But like a spring in summer drought,The word he uttered, quickened me.

Since then I tread the pilgrims' way,Still plodding on through sun and rain,But, like a star shines out that day,The day which saw me born again.

Here, he was making a well-meant endeavour to do something which the experience of life shows to be impossible. But whatever we may think of the method, one cannot but admire the courage which made this man hold himself up to public obloquy, misrepresentation, misunderstanding, in the way he did. I am writing the life of Frederick Charrington as it has occurred, and the more I engross myself with his splendid and fearless history, the more I admire the man himself. I am of another generation. Social circumstances have altered since the time of which I write. Other ideas occupy the public mind. But I do ask you, who read this book, to think with me, and to join with me, in an admiration for such a stern and[148] uncompromising fighter for what he believed to be the truth.

I have said that Mr. Charrington's name was bandied about among the sensual and the vulgar—all over England—as a term of reproach. It will be as well if I give some concrete instances of this. For one thing he was cruelly caricatured in all sorts of illustrated papers—many of the drawings quite passing the limits of legitimate fun; and at certain of the theatres grotesque and hideous figures were brought upon the scene designed to represent him and introduced to the audiences in that way. The opposition went as far as it dared. Of what was said *a vive voix* I can only surmise, but it can be estimated from the virulence and bitterness of the printed attacks made upon Mr. Charrington at this time.

The *Scots Observer*, for example—and the paper, as every one knows, was most brilliantly served by the best young literary blood of the day—wrote as follows—

"By the gracious condescension of the London County Council, that august body which includes all bright, particular stars of vestrydom and watches with maiden-auntish tenderness over the public morals, we are permitted for another year at least to expose ourselves to the perils of the music halls. But thankful as we are for thus much of mercy, to contemplate the future without apprehension is impossible. That bright band whose microscopic vision detects indecency on the chastest hoarding, has not at present the support of a compact majority. But the sentimentalists of all denominations are rallying round the chieftains of the fig-leaf, and when Mr. Charrington[149] and the great M'Dougall, scourge of the music-hall, are put in power, the fires of Smithfield will soon be set ablaze for all whose costume and deportment do not satisfy the modest County Council. Meanwhile, the defenders of virtue—in others—are crippled and helpless. They cannot hope to carry the citadel of vice at the first assault. They must perforce content themselves with enacting scenes which are nothing less than a national scandal. And the protagonist is Mr. Charrington's Grocer.

"This person has been suborned to do what he himself would call the 'Alls. His business is to seek out impropriety wherever it may be found. Mr. Charrington is himself far too good to pass the porches of sin. For him it is enough to shout in the doorway and distribute handbills. But his Grocer is made of sterner stuff. Did he not declare on oath that he was not easily shocked? He has been 'winked at' by 'bad characters' at the Popular Palace of Varieties. He has clamoured for recognition in the lounge of the Empire; but the 'lydies' of the West End Music Hall declined to waste a look upon him. 'He wasn't swell enough,' he complained. Of course he wasn't. Does the man not know his betters? However, he was quite sure the performance was indecent, because some people went out and the dresses were not what he was accustomed to see at Mile End. He is absolutely convinced that the 'lydies' who frequent the Empire are no better than they ought to be, and his reasons are ingenious, if not entirely conclusive. It is worth while to set them forth with some circumstance; (1) the 'lydies' were respectably dressed; (2) they wouldn't look at him; (3) they walked two and two; (4) one of their number was observed carrying a brandy-bottle under her 'harm'! A 'lydy' with a bottle under her 'harm' is likely to arouse suspicion,[150] and when she is accompanied by another 'lydy' (not a gentleman) her character is gone for ever. That Mr. Charrington should employ the service of the creature who wrote this testimony is not surprising: a fanatic is capable of anything. But when you read that the Grocer is now the accredited agent of the County

Council, you can only conclude that that respectable body has marked out the music hall for destruction, and devoutly believes that any stick is good enough to beat a dog withal.

"Reason does not seem to have played a conspicuous part in the deliberations of Mr. Charrington and his friends after the case of the Empire was cleared away from vice. War was declared against the Aquarium, because Mr. Coote, Cardinal Manning, and the faddists, have smelled out impropriety in a poster. The fact that posters are outside the jurisdiction of the Council was no bar to the discussion. The great M'Dougall observed, with a characteristic touch of Zolasim, that all was not well with Zæo's back. Another sensitive Councillor objects to snakes, and begged that Paula's portrait might be withdrawn. And finally the Council threatened (its action cannot be otherwise described) that if the directors did not suppress their posters, it would not renew their license. To impose this condition were *ultra vires*; but Mr. Charrington and his Grocer are the ultimate arbiters of morality, and we can but submit."

Thus the howl of the witty, the brilliant, yet the thoroughly irreligious.

The *Saturday Review* had its say in an article so stupid in its bitterness that I do not wish to quote it here. But I should not be giving a complete picture if I did not include one or two of the remarks made by the professedly anti-Christian[151] press—newspapers which owed their very existence to their pandering to vice. For example, an amusing print—long since fallen into oblivion—but, during its brief space of life, known as *Sporting Truth*, was pleased to remark as follows—

"The best censors of morals are the public, who are quite able to get along without the aid of the Council. We do not want to be made moral by a paternal Council any more than we wish to be made sober by Act of Parliament. And the sooner the Council turns itself to its own work—to the better drainage of the city, to the improvement of the water supply, and the thousand and one other urgent needs of this mighty town—the better we shall be pleased. And if they must have the spies and informers they appear to have so plentifully engaged—the Peeping Toms, the Paul Prys, the key-hole listeners, the dirty-minded, leprous beings they seem so pleased to patronise—the man who can never see a couple crossing a field but he scents immorality in the air, the lineal descendants of those revered elders in God who concealed themselves in order to descry Susannah's nakedness—if they must have these writhing, detestable *police de mœurs* in their employ, let them withdraw them from music halls, and send them to the sewers; and the quicker they are poisoned in that foul, mephitic atmosphere, the better for the business of the world."

This is enough.

It is necessary to have indicated the nature of the opposition to Mr. Charrington's work for the purification of the music halls, but it serves no good purpose to particularise further. Let me[152] rather turn to another side of the evangelist's fighting life. Let me tell, as I am impatient to tell, of his wonderful purity crusade, and its results. It is a terrible story, and shows Frederick Charrington, perhaps, in the greatest peril of his career, yet—as always—undaunted and unstayed.

[153]

CHAPTER VII
THE FIGHT FOR THE PURITY OF THE EAST END

In 1885, the late Mr. Stead, whose death this year in the "Titanic" suddenly closed so brilliant a career, startled the whole of England by the publication of his "Maiden Tribute" in the *Pall Mall Gazette*, of which he was editor at that time.

When the Criminal Law Amendment Bill was talked out just before the defeat of the Ministry it became necessary to rouse public attention to the necessity for legislation on this painful subject.

The evidence taken before the House of Lords Committee in 1882 was useful, but the facts were not up to date; members said things had changed since then, and the need for legislation had passed. It was necessary to bring information up to date, and that duty—albeit with some reluctance—Mr. Stead resolutely undertook. For four weeks, aided by two or three coadjutors of whose devotion and self-sacrifice, combined with a rare instinct for investigation and a singular personal fearlessness, he explored the London Inferno.

"It has been a strange and unexampled experience," he wrote. "For a month I have oscillated between the noblest and meanest of mankind, the saviours and destroyers of their race. London beneath the gas glare of its innumerable lamps became, not like Paris in 1793—'a naphtha-lighted[154] city of Dis'—but a resurrected and magnified City of the Plain, with the vices of Gomorrah, daring the vengeance of long-suffering Heaven. It seemed a strange inverted world, that in which I lived in those terrible weeks—the world of the streets and the brothel. It was the same, yet not the same, as the world of business and the world of politics. I heard much of the same people in the house of ill-fame as those of whom you hear in caucuses, in law courts, and on 'Change.' But all were judged by a different standard, and their relative importance was altogether changed. It was as if the position of our world had suddenly been altered, and you saw most of the planets and fixed stars in different combinations, so that at first it was difficult to recognise them. After a time the eye grows familiar with the foul and poisonous air, but at the best you wander in a Circe's isle, where the victims of the foul enchantress' wand meet you at every turn. But with a difference, for whereas the enchanted in olden times had the heads and the voices and the bristles of swine, while the heart of man was in them still, these have not put on in outward form the 'inglorious likeness of a beast,' but are in semblance as other men, while within there is only the heart of a beast—bestial, ferocious, and filthy beyond imagination of decent men.

"For days and nights it is as if I had suffered the penalties inflicted upon the lost souls of the Moslem hell, for I seemed to have to drink of the purulent matter that flows from the bodies of the damned. But the sojourn in this hell has not been fruitless. The facts which I and my coadjutors have verified I now place on record at once as a[155] revelation and a warning—a revelation of the system, and a warning to those who may be its victims. In the statement which follows I give no names and I omit addresses. My purpose was not to secure the punishment of criminals, but to lay bare the working of a great organisation of crime. But as a proof of good faith, I am prepared to substantiate the accuracy of every statement contained herein."

I can only paraphrase and hint at the nature of the burning pages which heralded the most awful revelations of London life ever presented to the public, revelations which ended in a revolution in the laws affecting immorality. And I must not stay to do more than pay a slight tribute of respect to the brave and courageous man who did so much for womenkind.

As some of my readers may be aware, in the earlier part of this year—1912—I had occasion in a public work of mine to pay a man whom I never saw, but with whom I had been in intimate correspondence about various social matters for a very considerable time, a tribute of respect I had long wished to make. One of the last letters, upon a subject affecting public thought, ever written by Mr. Stead was written to me—just before he made his final voyage in the Titanic.

I am telling here, for the first time, some of the secret history of that "Maiden Tribute" movement—for it was *to Mr. Charrington* that Mr. Stead came in the first instance in order to find out the truth of what was going on in the East End. Up to that time, Mr. Charrington, though, of course,[156] he had been painfully aware of many of the horrors that surrounded him, had been too occupied with his other campaigns, and his evangelistic work, to take sword in hand, himself, against this particular aspect of the immorality of the darkest portion of London.

Do not misunderstand me. You have just read of what Mr. Charrington, with the most fearless courage, did in the case of the Battle of the Music Halls. What I mean is that he had not yet begun the extraordinary campaign against the brothels of the East End, of which I have to tell in this chapter.

At any rate, he was able to respond to Mr. Stead's request, and it was he who first—if I may so use the word—"introduced" Mr. Stead to the erst-while ruffian of whom the editor of the *Pall Mall Gazette* goes on to speak.

It is of some historic interest, and I wish my readers to remember that it was Mr. Charrington who first put Mr. Stead upon the path which had such magnificent results.

The man of whom I speak, and who told Mr. Stead of the horrors that went on in the East End, was converted in the Great Assembly Hall by Mr. Charrington by means of that magnetic and spiritual power which he has on so many occasions wielded like a veritable Apostle. The fellow was led from the dark byways of unnamable infamy and brought to Jesus.

At the present moment of which I write, he is an active worker for Christ, and holds an official position in one of our great over-sea colonies, to which he was shipped by Mr. Charrington.

It was owing to this conversion that when[157] the late Mr. Stead came to Mr. Charrington for information, the evangelist was able to put him into communication with this man.

Mr. Stead used this man's revelations in his "Maiden Tribute of Modern Babylon," under the heading "Confessions of a Brothel-keeper." The statement was to the effect that the man had formerly kept a noted house of ill-fame near the Mile End Road, but was now endeavouring to start life afresh as an honest man. Mr. Stead saw both him and his wife, herself a notorious woman, whom he had married off the streets, where she had earned her living since an early age.

He gathered that the white slave traffic, more particularly in regard to very young girls, was in the most flourishing and lucrative position. He exposed all the details, the working of this infernal machinery, and all England was thrilled with horror. This man made it a part of his daily business to go away into the country, and to decoy girls from their parents for bad purposes. Among his patrons were many wealthy men who paid him large sums—monsters of iniquity, who stood at nothing to gratify their evil desires. The whole story is a systematic confession of a depravity which can hardly be equalled, and yet we see how, before the man was put into communication with Mr. Stead and confessed, Frederick Charrington was able to rescue even such an one as this, and bring him to Jesus!

I have quoted other testimonies elsewhere, but I think this is probably the most striking instance upon record of the exercise of Mr. Charrington's God-given power.

[158]Never was a more striking amplification of the saying, "It is never too late to mend." Never was a more extraordinary instance of the power of Jesus to cleanse and purify, than in the case of this man.

He owes everything, his whole chance of Eternal Life, his veritable salvation, to Frederick Charrington, through the working of the Holy Spirit.

If the evangelist in all his long career had done nothing else than this, even then, I beg leave to think, his career would have been a marvellous one.

Miracles still happen. This is one of them. I have gone into some of Mr. Stead's efforts in the furtherance of this bill for the protection of young girls. After his publication it was deemed advisable to further influence public opinion by holding a great demonstration in Hyde Park. A public meeting was accordingly held, at which the project was considered. At this meeting Mr. Charrington was unanimously elected chairman of the executive to carry out the necessary arrangements, Mr. Samuel Morley, M.P. acting as treasurer. Everything was organised successfully, and a gigantic meeting was held in Hyde Park, noted clergymen and ministers, leading laymen, and members of Parliament, presiding or speaking on the platforms erected for the occasion. Huge processions were formed and came from all parts of London. It must be remembered that this demonstration was for the furtherance of a bill for the protection of young girls, and, perhaps, the most noticeable and touching feature of the processions was the van-loads of quite young girls dressed solely in white. Mr. Charrington tells me that he will never forget[159] the effect this particular feature had on one of the opponents of the bill, who came out of one of the great clubs in Pall Mall, and who turned perfectly white as he saw these groups of innocent children.

In 1887, the state of the East End was still appalling. It was then that our "Valiant-for-Good" began a furious, God-inspired onslaught upon the dens of East London, which actually resulted in the closing of two hundred brothels and in purifying the East End to an extent that can hardly be realised by those who knew it in those days, and who know it now.

Alone, or occasionally accompanied by a friend or two, always unarmed, Charrington penetrated to the foulest sinks of iniquity.

He came this time as an avenger of Christ in the first instance. He came to reprove the blackest evil—he came with a sword in his hand to destroy it.

And destroy it he did.

I am told by those who remember that strenuous fight that the bullies, the keepers of evil houses, the horrible folk who battened upon shame, and enriched themselves with the wages of sin, feared Frederick Charrington as they feared no policeman, no inspector, no other living being.

They ran from him. They hid themselves like frightened birds at the mere rumour of his approach, as he marched alone among them.

His name actually excited the same sort of terror as the name of Napoleon excited in England in 1813. The blackest scoundrels in London trembled both at his footsteps and his name.

And it was not only that he came determined to[160] sweep them out of existence, to destroy their horrid trade, armed with all the powers of his organisation and the majesty of the law—the supine law which he himself had stirred to activity—it was that he came among them as a man of God, radiating the wrath of the Almighty against sinners, and by that mere force of personal magnetism which was actually testified to in a surprised court of law, insisting upon the fulfilment of his commands!

I am not going into too many details, but let me tell of one street alone which was purged and cleansed by the evangelist.

I think no more striking record than this could possibly be found.

"Lady Lake's Grove, Mile End, has long been notoriously the most disorderly and the most irreclaimable of any of the streets or roads of East London. A mere lane, running almost parallel with a portion of the Mile End Road, it contains about eight houses, while, near the middle of the Grove, and running off at right angles, is another but an infinitely smaller lane, only some four feet in width, known as Cottage Row, nearly the whole of the houses in which are devoted to the shelter of loose women, and what are colloquially known as their 'bullies.' These 'bullies' are men who, for the purpose of having some sort of a legal claim upon the proceeds of the shame of these women, either marry or live with them, or, when the earnings are small, take up the profession of thieves. For this latter purpose the houses in Cottage Row are peculiarly adapted; the whole property is somewhat like a rabbit-warren, communicating, as the houses do, with each other. The rooms[161] contained in each of the five houses in Cottage Row number but one or two, and it is in these rooms, crowded with women and children, that scenes of the grossest immorality frequently take place. The eight houses known as 22, 24, 26, 28, 30, 32, 34, and 36, Lady Lake's Grove, are but little better than those in Cottage Row. They contain about six rooms each, of the most dilapidated description, each of which are let off to one, two, three, and even four girls, and women of loose character, and at rents varying from four to six shillings for each person occupying the rooms. In none of these houses are there less than ten girls and women carrying on their nefarious trade, and in some there are as many as twenty. The scene on every night of the week at Lady Lake's Grove is one of the most unqualified bestiality, the women occupying the houses in the Grove being largely reinforced lately by those whose former haunts have been indicted. Worse than all, an extensive system of procuration has been carried on at some of these houses for a long time past, the agents of 'Continental houses' finding at the 'Grove' their largest and cheapest supply of 'goods.' Hitherto, owing to the fear of the 'bullies' who reside in the locality in large numbers, there have been none sufficiently courageous as to lodge information against the houses in the Grove, and it was reserved for Mr. F. N. Charrington, of the Great Assembly Hall, to take up the cudgels against the Grove. This he only did after long and careful personal inquiry had convinced him of the character of the houses. The summonses were taken out this week against the owners of the houses mentioned in the 'Grove'—amongst[162] them William and John Loman, Emma Breeson, and Charlotte Squire, together with the owners of the houses in Cottage Row—and were made returnable at the Thames Police Court yesterday afternoon. On the receipt of the summonses, however, the owners of all the houses in Cottage Row decided that the better policy would be to close their houses, which was at once done. The owners in Lady Lake's Grove, however, decided to hold out a little longer, and accordingly four of them waited until Wednesday to close their premises. The owners of the four houses, 22, 24, 26, and 28, a little more determined, perhaps, refused to close their houses even then.

"In the meantime, Mr. Charrington, to show that he was actuated by no animosity towards the girls and women themselves, determined to give them a breakfast on Thursday at one o'clock—the usual hour of breakfasting with these women. No formal invitations were issued, but on Thursday morning Mr. Charrington, accompanied by one or two of his fellow-workers, went into the 'Grove' and personally invited the women and the girls there to the breakfast. The reception accorded Mr. Charrington and his colleagues was by no means flattering—on the contrary, it was in the highest degree threatening. The women standing on the steps openly laughed at him, while the bullies hanging about began to close round them in a decidedly 'ugly' manner.

"The discreet appearance of a policeman's helmet at the further end of the 'Grove,' however, induced the bullies to move away to a respectable distance, while Mr. Charrington proceeded from house to[163] house, begging and entreating the women to come. The invitation was at first viewed with some amount of distrust, and open expressions of its being 'a plant' were frequently heard, but as Mr. Charrington proceeded to tell them that his only desire was to show that he was not their enemy, they began to get a little more confident, and finally, about twenty-five girls who had been plying their trade outside the four enclosed houses made their way to the hall—the majority of them confessing that their only object was 'to have a lark with Charrington.' Arrived at the small hall, they found two long tables laid out with piles of bread-and-butter and ham and beef, with two large coffee urns steaming at either end. Mr. Day-Winter was sitting at the organ at the time, and by a happy inspiration he proceeded to start the refrain 'For Auld Lang Syne.' The reception was somewhat different from what the women had expected, and after a brief pause of surprise they joined heartily in the refrain. And then they proceeded to attack the viands placed before them—an operation in which the latter suffered the greatest damage. It cannot honestly be said that the talk and the general remarks indulged in were of the most carefully chosen or elevating character, but, bad though it was, Mr. Charrington and his friends patiently bore it, nor ventured to protest when matters went considerably further, and the coarsest of jokes were cut. One satisfactory feature, however, there was, deserving of mention. The girls and women who had met Mr. Charrington that morning with expressions of open and undisguised hostility now began to see that he was[164] sincerely anxious for their welfare, and treated him accordingly. It was, perhaps, a mistake—though a well-intentioned one—to start the singing of hymns at the close of the meal; Sankey's solos and a very recent connection with disorderly houses do not always agree, especially at such short notice. Mr. Charrington saw at once that the attempt at reformation was too premature, and proceeded accordingly. He asked the girls whether they had any objection to leaving their names and addresses for the purpose of ascertaining whether something might be done for them in the future, and the information was furnished to the best of their ability, considering that some of them had no other names than 'nick' names, such as 'Aunt Sally.' And then they were asked if they had any objection to their photographs being taken in groups—a request to which they assented with even more avidity after they had extracted from Mr. Charrington a promise that they each should have a copy. They were rather rough and very coarse-speaking groups that were formed before the photographer's lens—groups in which every colour under the sun might have been found in a proximity at utter variance with all the prevailing laws of fashion—but taken they were. Then, while the photographer examined his proofs, Mr. Charrington and others questioned the girls as far as possible as to their future prospects, and, without a word of rebuke, asked them whether they intended to continue their present lives, or whether they really wished to become a little better. These inquiries had to be conducted in the quietest possible manner, for there was, among the women present, one who[165] owned a house in the 'Grove,' the girls in which had practically sold themselves to her, body and soul, and who seemed in no way disposed to allow them to be taken to a place where they were not likely to increase her shameful receipts. One such instance was that of a light-hearted Irish girl, who, on some pretext or other, ran round a corner to where a gentleman connected with one of the Refuges was standing, and, in a few excited words, told him that she was tired of the life she was leading; that she would see him a few days later, but that she must not be seen talking to him on any account. It was with sad hearts that the little party saw the girls troop out from the hall into their old haunts of vice."

These details are almost too dreadful for amplification, but I must conclude this story of Charrington's battle for purity with the extraordinary incident of a woman known as Mrs. Rose.

Mrs. Rose was a procuress and brothel-keeper of the worst description. She was told that Mr. Charrington had her name in his "black book," and was coming, as indeed he was, for the purpose of warning her that he was taking proceedings.

The woman was standing at the door of her house when the news of Mr. Charrington's approach was brought. She at once ran indoors, fell upon the floor, and died within the space of a very few minutes.

There are some who will say—and far be it from me to disagree with them—that terror of detection acting upon a weak heart caused this evil woman's sudden death. This is the way in which it might be scientifically accounted for. But, science, which[166] so often thinks itself the destroyer of religion, is, after all, only the handmaid—the unconscious handmaid—of the Unseen. It was surely the power of God, approaching

44

in the person of His servant, who "pressed God's lamp to his breast," that struck down this woman, as a terrible example to all the others?

It must be an august and terrible thing for a man to know that, filled with the power of the Holy Ghost, he was the medium of so sudden and awful a death.

During the Purity Crusade such dramatic instances were of constant occurrence. Two girls rescued by Mr. Charrington—who afterwards gave evidence in the Battle of the Music Halls case—were decoyed into a public-house known as the "Red Cow" which still exists quite close to the Great Assembly Hall, by the publican to whom the place belonged. They remained there all night. The man, who had previously publicly cursed Mr. Charrington in the most appalling way, took poison, and was found dead in his bed on the very next morning.

There was also a humorous side to all this strenuous campaign.

Mr. Charrington on one occasion set out to rescue a young girl who was being detained in a house of infamy. He was accompanied by two detectives disguised as water-inspectors. The girl was duly rescued, and upon the mantel-shelf of the principal room of this abominable house the evangelist discovered his own portrait. He was naturally considerably startled, but still more so when one of the detectives told him that there was not a house of this description in the East End which had not such a portrait.

The explanation, of course, is very simple. The keepers of these places wished to have a ready means of identifying the man who was breaking up a dreadful trade.

Altogether two hundred brothels were swept out of existence. The rescued girls were sent to the beautiful home provided for them by the liberality of Lady Ashburton. Souls and bodies were saved.

A man had come into dark places, in the words of St. Paul: "Giving no offence in anything, that the ministry be not blamed; but in all things approving yourselves as the ministers of God, in much patience, in afflictions, in necessities, in distresses, in stripes, in imprisonments, in tumults, in labours, in watchings, in fastings; by pureness, by knowledge, by long-suffering, by kindness, by the Holy Ghost, by love unfeigned, by the word of truth, by the power of God, by the armour of righteousness, on the right hand and on the left, by honour and dishonour, by evil report and good report; as deceivers, and yet true; as unknown, and yet well-known; as dying, and behold, we live; as chastened, and not killed; as sorrowful, yet always rejoicing; as poor, yet making many rich; as having nothing, and yet possessing all things."

CHAPTER VIII
FRUITION!

All the work of years, all the successes, the fact that Frederick Charrington had become an acknowledged leader—perhaps I should say "*the*" acknowledged leader of the armies of Christ in the East End of London—are now about to culminate in the erection of that last, and permanent, "Great Assembly Hall."

We have seen him in all his earlier periods. We approach the moment when his work for our Lord is to be consolidated in a concrete form. The huge machinery for good inspired by him, invented and directed by him, is to be centralised. A new temple of righteousness is to arise, built by hands indeed, but far more by prayer and self-sacrifice.

The present chapter marks a very definite stage in the career of which I am privileged and happy to write.

The subaltern has become a commander-in-chief, and a commander-in-chief who, for the first time, is about to have a commissariat.

The time has arrived when the words of the Wisdom of Solomon sound strangely true.

"Then shall the righteous man stand in great boldness before the face of such as have afflicted him, and made no account of his labours.

"When they see it, they will be troubled with terrible fear, and shall be amazed at the strangeness of his salvation, so far beyond all that they looked for.

"And they repenting and groaning for anguish of spirit shall say within themselves, This was he whom we had sometimes in derision and a proverb of reproach:

"We fools counted his life madness, and his end to be without honour:

"How is he numbered among the children of God, and his lot is among the saints!"

The foundation stones of the frontage of the *final* Great Assembly Hall were laid in November 1883, the Right Hon. the Earl of Shaftesbury, K.G., the president of the mission, taking the chair. Over five hundred ladies and gentlemen, including many of the local clergy and ministers, witnessed the ceremony, in which the venerable earl himself, Lady Blanche Keith-Falconer, Miss Cory of Cardiff, Mr. John Cory, Mr. George Williams, Mr. and Mrs. Frank Bevan, the late Lady Hobart, and others, took part.

The foundation stone of the great Mission Hall itself, which is the centre of the whole group of buildings, was laid by Her Grace the Duchess of Westminster, on July 4, 1885, and opened by John Cory, Esq., J.P., February 4, 1886.

I am anxious that readers of this book shall have a very complete picture in their minds of this centre of Mr. Charrington's work.

They must see it as it was then, from a contemporary's reminiscences; they must also see it as it was when, only three or four months ago, I, Mr.[170] Charrington's biographer, made a comprehensive experience of it.

Let the first chronicler, at the moment when the largest mission hall in the world was thrown open to view, speak before me.

"'Does it really hold five thousand people?' was a remark I overheard in the crowd which had gathered outside the entrances to the New Great Assembly Hall, on the day of the opening, the 4th of February, 1886. The doubter was soon set at rest upon that point by those who had had the advantage of a private view. A few days earlier I had availed myself of Mr. Charrington's invitation, and had noted the carpenters putting the finishing touches to the magnificent building which, like some Aladdin's palace, had risen in the space of ten months. I was prepared for surprises, but not such a surprise as the one here provided. The effect the first view of the hall produced upon the mind was one of amazement.

"Size, beauty, and simplicity, are its three great qualities. But, so true are the proportions, its vast capacity is not at once discoverable. It requires some little effort to impress upon the mind the idea that a ground-floor area, seventy feet wide by one hundred and thirty feet long, is very seldom secured unbroken. All the seats on the ground floor are movable, and not fixed as pews, so that when occasion requires, an extensive promenade under one roof can be in a few minutes commanded. And so again the large accommodation furnished by the two galleries is not immediately perceived, the curving lines of the architecture making no feature too prominent. The beauty of the proportion[171] subordinates every part of the building, and all unite in a pleasing effect.

"From two spots a capital view of the hall can be obtained. Standing in the centre of the uppermost gallery, looking towards the organ, the eye notes the depth, forty-four feet in the clear, from the flat ceiling to the parquet floor. The lines of the galleries converge upon the double platform, with the choir space behind it, and the organ recess, now concealed by the painted drop curtain. Placing oneself upon the upper platform, the width of the building can be seen at a glance, but not the length, the platform itself extending a good way outward. If the length but not the height is to be seen, the point for the spectator to station himself is at the entrance from the vestibule, or a sweeping perspective may be even obtained from the iron gate in the Mile End Road, the centre passage-way having an uninterrupted line from the pavement to the organ; few such buildings can boast as much.

"The illumination of the hall I heard frequently and favourably commented on. There are upwards of 130 windows, which, being glazed with yellow glass, admit a pleasant-toned light, whilst they wholly exclude any objectionable view. The bright orange, complemented by chocolate, of the decorations assists the aerial effect thus obtained, and there is an additional benefit secured by the adoption of ground glass windows. By shutting out external surroundings the hall is rendered self-contained. No mean neighbours, murky atmosphere, nor curling smoke distract the attention, which is left free to concentrate itself[172] upon the life within the building itself. In a word, it will be quite possible for a visitor to imagine himself far from the squalor of the East End of London, from the moment he enters the Great Assembly Hall.

"The windows, especially the clerestory windows over the galleries beneath the flat ceiling, breaking the line of the coved sides, serve also to enhance the pleasing effect produced by the graceful lines of the architecture.

"At night the artificial lighting is not less striking, a continuous row of gas jets following the outlines of the clerestory arches. A skilful arrangement of subsidiary lights destroys all shadows, and the effect is that of bright sunshine. An alternative system dispenses with the upper jets and substitutes a row at the level of the first gallery which is sufficient to give light to the ground area, when small meetings only are to be held.

"With regard to ventilation, the plan selected seems most effectual. Every part of the building is under separate control, and there are numerous cunning little contrivances which are simple and not patented, but which do their work extremely well.

"In an accoustical sense the hall is perfect. I am told that the flat panelled ceiling, which resembles in form that of the House of Commons, contributes to this result.

"I was curious to know the truth of the assertion that from every seat, and there are four thousand three hundred, a view of the speaker upon the upper platform could be gained. I found it a fact.

"Three prominent adjuncts of the hall remain to be described. The first is the great organ,[173] containing 2178 speaking pipes, erected at the cost of £1000 by Messrs. Bevington & Son. The natural steel colour of the pipes has been preserved. It is a very fine instrument, and is not dwarfed or spoilt by the platforms in front of it, nor hidden in the recess which it fills. This shell-shaped alcove acts as a sounding board.

"Over the great arch there are bas-reliefs representing groups of angels in the act of praise. From this arch falls the painted drop curtain, the subject of the picture thereon being the Feeding of the Five Thousand on the slopes of the Sea of Galilee. The curtain gives colour to the hall, and protects the organ when not in use.

"Under the choir platform there is a large inquiry room, a part of which is partitioned off to provide space for a gas engine to work the great organ.

"Another unusual feature is the octagonal Italian loggia or lobby, which intervenes between the frontage buildings and the hall. It is forty-four feet each way, by thirty-four feet high, and is lighted from the roof. The landings from two of the four great staircases, at each corner of the hall have exits into two galleries or balconies, looking down into the lobby.

"The warming of the building is by an improved hot-air method, and the exits for use in case of fire are ample."

The opening meeting, an occasion fraught with a significance that only Mr. Charrington and the thousands of friends who support his work can realise—for the outside world has known but little of the great work compared with its knowledge of[174] other, and more largely advertised, agencies for good—was of an extraordinary character.

Mere lists of names do not convey much, and yet, in an archive such as this, I suppose some indication—at any rate—must be given of those who were present, or, unable themselves to be there, were keenly interested in the great thing that had come to pass.

Among those names which will still have an interest for the readers, I may mention the Duke of Westminster, Duchess of Westminster, Earl of Aberdeen, Lord Mount Temple, Lord and Lady Cameron, Lord Justice Fry, The Lord Mayor, Lady Alexander, Lady Augusta Montagu, Lady Victoria Buxton, Lady Aitchison, Lady Abercromby, Lady Harrowby, Sir R. Owen, Sir W. Bowman, Sir J. Coods, Sir E. Colehart, General W. Hill, Bishop of London, Canon Mason, Rev. Webb-Peploe, Rev. J. T. Wigner, Rev. H. A. Mason, Rev. Hugh Price Hughes, Rev. A. J. Robinson, Rev. F. Hastings, Rev. W. Glenny Crory, Dr. Armitage, Dr. Adler (Chief Rabbi), Dr. A. Grant, Mrs. Henry Fawcett, Miss Robinson (Portsmouth), John Hilton.

Mr. Charrington, having asked for silence, announced that Mr. John Cory (the well-known millionaire colliery proprietor) would take the chair, and face the enormous crowd of jubilant people that thronged the mighty hall to its utmost capacity.

Lord Radstock engaged in prayer, and then the chairman began his address.

He said—

"I have received some letters since I have been[175] in the hall, and I will give you an extract from one, as it may interest you, and especially the workers. It is addressed from St. George's Infirmary, and the writer says: 'Three years ago I gave myself to the Lord in the old Great Assembly Hall. On the opening of the new structure, in which you are engaged to-night, my heart goes out with love and sympathy to all the workers there. Would that I were among you to-night.'

"God bless that good man. It is an encouragement to the workers here to know of one such who has received blessing on this spot. I do not intend to detain you long. We have eloquent speakers on the platform, whom you wish to hear, but I would remark that I only express the feeling of my friend Mr. Charrington, and of all the workers here, in saying that we have to lament to-night the absence of one who took a hearty interest in this Mission, and who would no doubt, if the Lord had spared his life, have occupied the position that I have the honour to occupy to-night. I refer to the Earl of Shaftesbury. (Applause.) We can quite imagine, by the words our late president spoke at the laying of the foundation stone of the frontage, how delighted he would have been to inaugurate the opening of this beautiful and splendid hall, and I would like to remind you of his words. He said: 'Mr. Charrington has said that he desires a larger building, and so do we desire it, and so let every one desire it, and pray for it heartily, and do what in him lies to get it. I trust you will have that building.'

"We have now to thank God we have this large building, which has been prayed for so long, and[176] was so much desired by our esteemed and good friend, Lord Shaftesbury. This splendid building will, I am sure, always remind us that we must not despise the day of small things.

"Mr. Charrington commenced this glorious and self-sacrificing work about seventeen years ago in a night-school, and afterwards in a hayloft. Then in a large upper room, next an iron hall, later on in a tent, again in a bigger tent, to seat 1500, and finally he purchased the present site at a cost of £8000. I can well remember the time that my friend came down to Wales, many years ago, in great ecstasy of delight, having bought this land, and with the idea of putting up a large Assembly Hall upon it. And now he has his heart's desire! On this site, I understand, he erected a temporary building, to hold about 2000 people.

"Even this place was not large enough, and he rented a music-hall to seat 3000 on Sunday evenings, the temporary hall being open every night for seven years. This temporary building, being condemned, was taken down, and then comes this last effort—the erection of this magnificent hall to seat 5000 people. I am sure that our united prayer will be to ask the Lord that thousands of souls may be saved in this place.

"I am delighted to find the splendid frontage building consisting of the Coffee Palace, without intoxicating drinks, and the Book Saloon, where pure literature is sold, with various club rooms, Young Men's Christian Association and Young Women's Christian Association Rooms, besides three fine entrances.

"I must say that the sums which have been[177] subscribed towards this building I feel have been a very good investment, and I am exceedingly pleased with the whole undertaking.

"But I feel more than thankful to God to-night, and I am sure every one will join in the thanksgiving offered by Lord Radstock, and I am more than satisfied when I remember the hundreds, nay, I may say thousands, of souls that have been saved through the instrumentality of my friend Mr. Charrington, and his helpers. The good that has been accomplished here, of course, no one can tell, and I rejoice to know that the same gospel—the old, old story—will be continued to be preached here. But Mr. Charrington not only offers salvation to the sinner, for he has undertaken operations on a large scale, in periods of distress, to feed the famishing and the starving; and I observe that in a short season of six weeks six hundred pounds were spent in bread and cocoa. Blessed is he that considereth the poor. (Applause.) What the late Earl of Shaftesbury said at the laying of the foundation stone fully expresses my feeling.

"Take, then, for your motto, 'Forward, in the name of the Lord,' and with energy, perseverance, and unflinching reliance on the promise, 'I am with you,' go and seek each one in his own place, each one in his own sphere, and also by united action, to win sinners for Jesus. Remember that in the East End of London, with its million of inhabitants, there is room—not only for this large hall, but for many more.

"I say, then, 'Forward, in the name of the Lord,' and continue, as hitherto, to rescue the perishing. Duty demands it. The strength for your labour[178] the Lord will provide. I have now to declare this hall open, and may the Lord bless the workers, and everybody connected with it."

It is getting on for thirty years now since those stirring words were spoken, and still the Great Assembly Hall stands in the Mile End Road, close by the old brewery, and is the greatest centre of Christian work in the whole of East London. From its first building until the present time, the work that has gone on there has never diminished in power for good, the energy of the workers has never flagged. The ramifications have been enormous. The Assembly Hall has become, as it were, the hub of a great wheel, with spokes extending in every direction, and I now propose to give an epitomised account of some of these stupendous activities, to present the Great Assembly Hall to my readers as it was and as it is.

From accounts of its beginnings in the earlier days I have gathered many quaint and even amusing stories.

One of the preachers whom Mr. Charrington enlisted under his banner was known as "Hellfire Tom." This man was an engine-driver on the Brighton line, a skilful mechanic, and, at the same time, a great drunkard. Upon one occasion, when driving his engine at full speed, he was so drunk that he missed a warning signal, and dashed through two gates upon a level crossing, thus endangering his own life and those of all the passengers in the train. He was tried for the offence, and, very rightly, received a sentence of three months' hard labour. However, he was converted, and became[179] a strict teetotaler, an earnest preacher for Christ, and would relate his experiences with a rough-and-ready eloquence that touched many hearts and led others to find the salvation that he himself had found. In connection with this man there is a curious story, which seems singularly à propos to tell here, when, as one reads, certain alterations in the Burial Service of the Church of England are proposed, and it is suggested that a modified form of the beautiful words of committal should be used in the case of evil-livers—thus constituting the officiating clergyman a sort of judge-in-advance of a person who has departed this life, and whom he may be called upon to bury. This man, "Hellfire Tom," lived before his conversion in a house of ill-fame. He related that one of the poor girls there died, and two or three of her friends attended her wretched funeral. These girls had no good influence whatever in their lives, Christ was little more than a name to them, but one of them came back to Hellfire Tom, and said that "it was all right with Sal, as the parson had said she had sure and certain hope of everlasting life"—words which seemed to comfort the poor creatures very much.

Another man who addressed Mr. Charrington's congregations in the earlier days was a certain Harvey Teasdale in private life. In public he rejoiced in the proud distinction of being the "Chief Man Monkey of London." He earned his bread by leaping and climbing round the galleries of Sadler's Wells Theatre, and was, it seems, a most disreputable character until he came under the influence of the gospel and definitely embraced a Christian life. He became one of the preachers[180] at the hall, and numbers came to hear him who had known him in his theatrical days.

Yet the most remarkable of all the preachers of this period was Henry Holloway. He was a convicted burglar who had spent seven years in the hulks at Gibraltar. In connection with the Mission he was always announced as "A voice from the convict cell," or as "The returned convict," and was naturally the means of reaching an enormous number of the criminal classes. On one occasion Mr. Charrington found a crowd of rough-looking men at the door of the new hall, waiting to gain admission. They at once said, "Oh, Mr. Charrington, you must let us in. We are all returned convicts and do want to hear Henry Holloway." The evangelist managed to take them round to the back of the hall, and let them in by a side entrance.

All these preachers were converted to the gospel before Mr. Charrington first knew them. He used them as the instruments of his work.

And what will my readers say when I tell them that, on several occasions, an old and extraordinary looking man in picturesque clothes, and with a strongly marked face, like a grotesque caricature, was in the habit of giving temperance addresses, and was none other than the great George Cruikshank himself, the most famous caricaturist perhaps that England has ever known? This, of course, was in the quite early period, but I like to think of the odd trio I have mentioned—and, did space allow, there are many, many others equally as strange—as testifying to the power of God upon them under the auspices of the evangelist.

[181]As I am speaking of personalities, it will not be out of place here to quote the testimony of a well-known preacher as to what Mr. Charrington did for him.

This gentleman is a personal friend of mine, and he preaches constantly at the Great Assembly Hall to-day. His name will be known to many of my readers. I give it here, and print his story in his own words, at his own request. It is his own wish that his name should appear, and I can but bow to it, and myself point out the personal self-sacrifice his decision must have entailed.

But it was ever thus—any one whom Frederick Charrington has influenced for good has always been ready to come forward at the hour of need and testify to what he has done for them.

In the chapter entitled the "Battle of the Music Halls," you will remember another instance of this loyal readiness, this time on the part of two poor girls who had been rescued from a horrible life, and restored to health and to respectable society by Mr. Charrington.

Mr. J. B. Wookey said to me, and my secretary took his words down in shorthand exactly as they appear here: "I was at one time Senior Deputation Secretary to Dr. Barnardo. It was while I was in the midst of that work, often suffering from strain of voice and nerves, that I began to take a little intoxicating drink to produce sleep. Then I was frequently the guest of people who pressed drink upon me, and slowly but surely it gained a terrible hold. I really could not do without it. I had to be stimulated by this means for work. Up to that time I had never publicly made a fool[182] of myself. But it became necessary to keep on increasing the dose. Well, about that time my mother, who was a member of the Society of Friends, was taken sick, and ultimately died. To her I was very passionately attached, and being left alone in the room looking at her dear, dead face, I asked myself, if she could speak, what would she be likely to make as a last request? I knew too well what she would say. I procured a sheet of notepaper, and wrote on it a most solemn vow that I would never again touch the intoxicating cup. I folded the paper and placed it in her dead hand, where it now remains in the grave. And yet, within a week, so strong had the appetite for drink taken hold of me, that I broke that most solemn vow. Then it appeared as if all was over. 'There came a mist within the weeping rain, and life was never the same again.' From that time onwards my descent was rapid. My good friend Dr. Barnardo died. I felt that there was only one thing for it, and that was to put the Atlantic Ocean between myself and my past; which I did. Then a terrible domestic calamity made it imperative that I should return to this country, and after months of anxiety of mind which no words of mine can describe, I felt that I was utterly lost, body and soul. I purposely avoided everybody I had ever known, and buried myself in a neighbourhood to which I had hitherto been a complete stranger. I could open the Bible, but could not read. Did often kneel, but could not pray. Could sit down to food, but could not eat. There seemed to be one thing and one thing only that could calm a guilty conscience, and give me sleep of mind, body and[183] soul, and that was drink. In the midst of saner moments I often prayed that I might die, and yet I knew too well I was not worthy. One day, however, I was most anxious to see Mr. Charrington's secretary, and having reason to believe that my old friend Mr. Charrington, whom I had known intimately for nearly thirty years, was out of town, I ventured to call at his house. To my utter amazement, Mr. Charrington himself opened the door. The very sight of him who knew all my troubles almost paralysed me. He, however, insisted on my coming inside. He preached no sermon, asked me to read no tract, but gave me a warm grip of the hand, offered me a seat at his table, treating me with the utmost possible brotherliness and kindness, and spoke words of hope and good cheer. He took me down to his beautiful home on Osea Island as his guest for a few weeks. I came and remained nearly eighteen months without a break. During that time I regained my mental balance, and once more felt the tight and loving grip of my Saviour and my God. I feel now that the old enemy has been finally conquered, and that all that is left for me to do to work out my own salvation, is to obey the sacred injunction to 'watch and pray.' Out of the last thirteen months I have been preaching for five months at the Great Assembly Hall, and although it has cost me something to open my old wounds, I have been able to do it for the sake of other victims of strong drink, and I have been privileged to see hundreds of men sign the pledge of total abstinence and yield themselves to God. I have also visited other centres of Christian work,[184] and hope to give the remainder of whatever time is left me to do all that in me lies to dethrone the drink fiend, and to draw lost ones to the Saviour who came to seek and to save them."

And while I am still dealing with people, I must quote the words of Dr. Waldo, the well-known American missionary, who for some years now has crossed the Atlantic to hold a short mission season at the hall. I had many interesting conversations with him about Mr. Charrington and his work, and shall not easily forget his genial and masterful personality. His words are deeply interesting, and show how much America is in sympathy with the work at the Great Assembly Hall.

"The first thing I felt when I entered the Great Assembly Hall was a sense of the immensity of the building. Mr. Joe Clarke, who was then a missioner, and burning with enthusiasm, showed me through the building, and particularly took me straight to the pulpit, and said, 'Every big building has a key, and you must receive the key of the Great Assembly Hall.' He went to the extreme end, and I read from the Book, and from this key I have preached for eleven successive years in the Great Assembly Hall. The next gentleman I saw was Mr. Charrington, who, in his hearty way, received me into his home at 41 Stepney Green. That was eleven years ago. His hearty reception, the cordiality and good-will beaming from his bright and searching eyes, made a profound impression upon me as he asked me to take a seat in his simple home.

"After preaching my first sermon on the word 'Sympathy,' Mr. Charrington said that his pulpit[185] was free to me to preach anything that I wished. The thought of preaching in a hall capable of holding five thousand people made me feel somewhat timid, and I shrank from the responsibility of facing the congregation in the greatest evangelistic centre in the world. But after attending the Saturday-night prayer meeting that has been famous all over the East End of London as the centre of its spiritual life, as I heard the new and old converts lift their hearts in grateful prayer to God, and heard the petitions offered on my behalf, soon the feeling of timidity lifted, and a courage filled my being that enabled me to be inspired with the thought of the great Apostle of olden days who said that 'I am not ashamed of the Gospel of Christ, for it is the power of God, and salvation to every one that believeth.'

"The morning service at eleven was largely attended, and the old fear of the multitude left me. I was caught up in the spirit of devotion that seemed to pervade the entire company. Then came the evening service when the congregation of between four and five thousand people assembled to hear the first message from me, the young American who hailed from Chicago.

"The service, which was a sample of the whole of the services held in this magnificent centre, left a profound impression on my mind. First I was conducted to the vestry, where a score of deacons and others met for a word of prayer, led by the hon. superintendent, Mr. Charrington, who asked that God's blessing might rest upon the multitudes, and upon the speaker. Whilst engaged in prayer, the music burst forth from the tremendous[186] audience, led by Mr. Winter. He sat at the vast, pealing organ, directing the enormous waves of sound. Led by a huge choir, all joined in the magnificent hymn, 'Sinners Jesus will receive,' which gave the cue to the entire service, and, in fact, every service in the great hall. We soon found ourselves upon the top platform. Behind us were a hundred voices, male and female. The deacons and lay preachers were on the platform, and Mr. Charrington sat in front on the one side, and myself on the other. A spirited service of wonderful power began, and when the time came for the message of the evening, as I looked at the sea of faces stretched out before me, I was thrilled in the extreme, and realised that I was there, listening and facing the greatest opportunity of my life, in speaking to these people.

"The text of the evening was, 'God forbid that I should glory, save in the Lord Jesus Christ.' The message came free, as if directed by the Spirit of God in answer to the prayer of the people. It was easy to preach. The surroundings demanded the best that was in a man, and the occasion furnished ample opportunity to make a profound impression.

"After the message was delivered, Mr. Charrington followed in his magnificent way, and in a voice that was heard in every corner of the great hall, and out into the street, he made his tremendous appeal for all to meet the preacher and workers in the inquiry room, where the opportunity would be given to sign the pledge of total abstinence, to yield themselves to God, and receive a higher and a grander life. Dozens that night surrendered[187] themselves. Even after the service was over, the religious work was not done. Three or four bodies of workers were on the Mile End Waste preaching the gospel.

"During every summer Americans have visited this Mission, having heard of it in their own country from me and from others, particularly the *Ram's Horn*, of Chicago, and several other noted papers of America which have "written up" this work of Mr. Charrington's, and brought it close to the hearts of the leading philanthropists throughout the entire Republic. On one occasion fifteen school teachers from Cleveland visited the hall with a well-known educationalist in charge, and were so enthusiastic about it, and with the service, that, in spite of the fact that dinner was waiting for them at the Hotel Cecil, they would not fulfil their engagements, but lingered to see the East End Londoners in devotion in the Great Hall, and in the streets. The universal testimony of these travellers, who had visited ten different nations of the world in their travels, was that they had never met anything in all the world like the work of the Great Assembly Hall of the East End of London.

"On one occasion, Mr. Charles Herrendeen, of Chicago, with his wife and son, came to the hall. He is a well-known millionaire and philanthropist. They sat upon the platform during the entire service! A handful of gold was afterwards found in the collection plate, which was rather unusual. He was a personal friend of mine, having been trustee of a church of which I was pastor in Chicago. He was perfectly amazed with the enormity of the[188] work, and said that he believed that 'God was nearer to the work of the Great Assembly Hall than any portion of His work throughout the kingdom.'

"Another time, J. L. Campbell, another famous preacher, visited the hall during the evening of the day on which King Edward was crowned, and listened to the discourse that was delivered by his friend. He sat upon the platform with his face beaming with joy. He said as he left, that he believed 'God Almighty smiled as much upon that service as He did upon that which was held in Westminster Abbey at the coronation of the king.'

"At another time, Mr. Brown, the great wholesale bootmaker, who resides in St. Louis, became greatly interested in the whole work, and particularly with the boy Jack Cook, who held several missions in the great hall. He adopted him and sent him to a school, and generally fitted him out for his life's work. When he had attended his first service and listened to all the enthusiasm that emanated from the lips of Mr. Charrington and the boy preacher of the evening, he said, 'Surely the Lord is in this place. Surely this is the gate of Heaven!'

"I remember one night that a man, who was a great drunkard, came in at the request of Mr. Charrington, and promised that he would come back again the next night, which he did. Finally, after his conversion, through his zeal and eagerness he became one of the leading officials of the mission, and chairman of the Board of Deacons. He bore the testimony that it was not anything that he had[189] *heard* at that meeting that made the profound impression upon him, but the extraordinary *personality of Mr. Charrington*, who took him by the hand, and led him to the place of worship, and to the Saviour of the world. He said, 'I shall never forget the handshake of the great man of God, who invited me to prayer with him.'

"Another millionaire from America, in attending service at the Great Assembly Hall recently, said, 'We have most of the biggest things in the world in America, but we have got no place anywhere in our country for the benefit of humanity like this.'

"Yet another American visited the hall when I was conducting my yearly mission, and took the march through the streets, and witnessed the seven hundred poor enjoying a bountiful meal, and remained to the evening service. Upon leaving, he said, 'I have travelled into different parts of the world, and I confess I have never seen anything like this at home, or abroad. It is a great need handled in a Christly way.'

"And I myself have for twelve successive summers preached during the month of August, and I have no hesitation in saying that this is the greatest field I know of on earth for sociological study, and for Christian service. Here sin is rampant, and here Grace is having the victory, 'For where sin abounds, Grace doth much more abound.'"

There have been very many preachers, of course, during the long life of the Great Assembly Hall. It would be almost impossible to mention them by name, and perhaps invidious also. But Mr.[190] Charrington has been, especially of late years, much indebted to the Evangelisation Society, who have sent him many of their most powerful preachers.

All these preachers have given due testimony in their time and place, not only to the good that they are able to do to others by their mission under Mr. Charrington's direction, but also to the spiritual good that has resulted to themselves, and to that feeling of "home," that sense of companionship and union, which will never leave them when they think of the vast building, and those who worked there so nobly and so long.

It is absolutely impossible, and it is outside the scope of this book, to go into any details of the thousands and thousands of people, living and dead, who have been led from a life of wretchedness and sin to happiness and peace. Of the thousands and thousands of people who have been *materially* assisted, I can only speak, generally, a little later on. These facts, however, are evident in every line of this biography. What I have not hitherto insisted upon, but which, nevertheless, is a curious and interesting fact, is that the Tower Hamlets Mission, which centres in the Great Assembly Hall, has always been an *aristocratic* Mission.

Charrington himself has never sought publicity. He has lived a very humble and quiet life, scarcely known personally outside the East End of London, and even during late years, since the beautiful island of Osea has passed into his possession and he has a noble country house there, he has by no means lived constantly upon the Island. He is firm as ever in his devotion to the East End, and his visits to Osea are only occasional. And yet,[191] though Mr. Charrington is so little personally known, his institution of "The Great Assembly Hall" is known the world over. He is known by his works, "his works do follow him." He has never gone beyond his work.

This is an undoubted fact. And yet, throughout his whole labours, he has been supported by some of the leading people of the country. Except in cases of very rare and intimate friendship, such as that with the Hon. Ion Keith-Falconer, and the Earl of Kintore, his father—with a few others—Mr. Charrington has always refused to enter into the *social* life of the great people who have shared his *Christian* life and helped in his *Christian* work. One memorable visit to "Broadlands," the seat of Lord Mount Temple near Romsey, deserves mention. Among the guests were the great Lord Shaftesbury and the late Mr. Wyndham Portal, then Chairman of the South Eastern Railway. Mr. Portal told Mr. Charrington that he had often played billiards with Lord Palmerston, who on returning from the House of Lords—generally at a very late hour—always played a game.

The billiard room at "Broadlands" was preserved exactly as Lord Palmerston had left it when he played his last game there. This, of course, was a private visit, but Mr. Charrington afterwards attended a religious conference held at the house. Men of all shades of opinion were present, and Mr. Charrington spoke on the same day as Canon Body.

He is not unsocial, however—you have a pen-picture of the man as he is in the last chapter of this book. It is simply that he cannot, *will* not,[192] spare a minute from active good works in the East End. Yet it would be wrong of me, as his biographer, if I did not draw attention to the support he has had, and this is a fitting place in which to do it.

I certainly ought to mention the late Lady Ashburton. This lady, famous in her lifetime for her good deeds, was always a patron of Mr. Charrington's work. In 1881 she paid the whole expense of taking two thousand five hundred members and friends of the Great Assembly Hall to Southend-on-Sea, and at the time of the Battle of the Music Halls she bore all the expense of the Rescue Home for Girls, besides giving large donations to the work.

It was when present at the opening of a beautiful hall which Lady Ashburton built at Canning Town, that Mr. Charrington first met the late Duchess of Teck. After the proceedings, the Duchess turned to the Marquis of Northampton, and said, in that breezy and genial way, for which she was so well known, "But where is Mr. Charrington? No one has introduced me to Mr. Charrington! I *must* see Mr. Charrington. Please bring him to me."

Mr. Charrington had the honour of being presented to the Duchess, who was accompanied by the then Princess May, now Queen of England, and had a most interesting conversation with the royal couple.

Subsequently the Duchess and the Princess visited the Great Assembly Hall, accompanied by Lord Dorchester, and were shown over that noble building.

It is interesting to note that our beloved Queen[193] Mary has herself stood in that great East End centre of sweetness and life. It is more interesting still to record that King George himself gave the first of those regular "feedings of the hungry," which have continued without intermission every Sunday for so many years, and have literally saved people from actual starvation, time after time.

A good deal has been said in this book about the late Earl of Shaftesbury—the good Earl, as he was known to every one. The present Earl of Shaftesbury, Chamberlain to the Queen, has continued his predecessor's interest in the work of the Great Assembly Hall. As many people know, Lord Shaftesbury has a very beautiful voice—indeed, an enterprising American syndicate once offered him a thousand pounds a night to go to the United States and sing in public!! It is needless to say that this offer was refused, but in interesting contrast to it is the fact that Lord Shaftesbury one night came to the Great Assembly Hall from the West End during a furious tempest which would have deterred nine men out of ten, and sang "The Star of Bethlehem," and an excerpt from "Elijah," to the poor people who were being fed at the time.

I wish I could recount the innumerable incidents which have occurred when great or famous people have visited the hall. It is impossible to do so, however, for they in themselves would make another book. But, as showing the extent of the help Mr. Charrington has been able to command, I will at least give a list of famous names—a list for which I recently wrote to the secretary of the Mission, Mr. Edwin H. Kerwin.

[194]Such names as these have a definite weight, which is the sole reason why I give them.

H.R.H. Princess Mary, Duchess of Teck; H.R.H. Princess May, Duchess of York (now Queen Mary); The Duchess of Bedford, The Duchess of Sutherland, The Rt. Hon. the Earl of Shaftesbury; Louisa, Lady Ashburton; Lord Radstock, Lady Radstock, The Hon. Ion Keith-Falconer, Lady Hobart, Hon. Hamilton Tollemache, The Earl of Kintore, Hon. Granville Waldegrave, Lady Beauchamp, Lady Blanche Keith-Falconer, Sir R. Beauchamp, The Earl of Aberdeen, Lady Rosslyn, The Hon. E. Waldegrave, Princess Lina and Olga Galitzin, The Countess of Warwick, Lady Eva Grenville, Hon. A. Ayrton, Count A. Bernstorff (Berlin), Princess Alexander Paschkoff, The Duke and Duchess of Westminster, Prince Oscar of Sweden and Norway, The Baroness Burdett-Coutts, The Countess of Seafield (Georgina), Lady Henry Somerset, Baroness Langenan, Lord Esme Gordon, Prince Galitzin, Lady Hope, Lord and Lady Carrington, The Earl of Westmoreland, Hon. G. Kinnaird, Hon. Emily Kinnaird, Hon. Elizabeth Kinnaird, Lord Kinnaird, Hon. Mary Waldegrave, Sir Arthur Blackwood, The Earl and the Countess of Dudley, The Countess Amherst, The Countess of Portsmouth, Sir George Williams, Lady Algernon Gordon-Lennox, The Marchioness of Ripon, Lady Gray, Sir George Cooper, Bart., Julia, Marchioness of Tweedale, Dowager Countess of Warwick, The Hon. Harry Lawson, Lady Cooper, Lady Rookwood, Lady Brownlow Cecil, The Viscountess Dupplin, The Hon. Randolph Adderley, Lord Brabazon, Lord Rosebery, K.G., Lady Macnaughton, Lady Warren, Lord Rothschild, Lord Beresford, Lord Coleridge, Q.C.; Lady Pullar, Lady Ernestine Bruce, Lady Mary Lawson, Count Paschoff (Berlin), Sir James Whitehead, Bart., Sir Wilfred Lawson, Bart., Sir[195] James Anderson, Bart.; The Hon. Montagu Waldegrave, The Hon. F. Bridgeman, M.P.; Sir John Pullar, Major-Lieut. Sir Charles Warren, Rev. Canon Wilberforce.

I will also add that one of the most munificent of Mr. Charrington's millionaire supporters was the late Mr. John Cory. He gave Mr. Charrington two hundred a year as a regular thing. In addition to that, from time to time he bestowed large sums upon the Mission entirely independent of his yearly subscription. Shortly before his death he sent Mr. Charrington a cheque for a thousand pounds to cover the expense of the village hall on Osea Island, and, when recently staying with Sir Clifford Cory, Bart., Mr. Charrington ascertained from him the fact that his father gave away in charity nearly a thousand pounds each week!

Yet Mr. Charrington has found that the millionaires of to-day are not nearly so ready with their cheques as those of the past. The great growth of material comfort, the increasing love of magnificence and splendour, seems indeed to have deafened the ears of the very rich to the piteous cry of the starving poor in the East End. If only this book awakens some of those so abundantly blessed with riches to what has been done, and is being done, by Mr. Charrington, then its publication will indeed be blessed.

Did not the late Lord Shaftesbury say—and is it not true to-day?—"This is a great and mighty work. I can only say that I rejoice to think that such a work as this is to be extended, and well does our friend Charrington deserve it. No man living, in my estimation, is more worthy of success for[196] the devotion of his heart, the perseverance of his character, the magnificence of his object, and the way in which he has laboured, by day and night, until he has completed this great issue."

I went, a few weeks ago, during the time of the great dock strike of this year—1912—to see the actual feeding of the hungry in Mr. Charrington's hall. I wish I could have taken with me a dozen of the richest men in England. I defy the most flinty-hearted Dives in existence to see what I saw, and remain untouched.

And, remember, that what I saw has gone on regularly for a long space of time.

I arrived at the Great Assembly Hall just after lunch upon a Sunday. Outside the hall a uniformed band was gathering, and by it stood a large, portable hoarding, mounted upon a handcart, bearing the words, "The Great Assembly Hall," and inviting all and sundry to visit the hall that evening and attend the service.

Even at that early hour—the "feeding" was not to take place till two hours later—along the railings which border the small ornamental garden which forms an oasis in the roaring Mile End Road, and are immediately in front of the hall, a crowd of patient, silent men had formed a *queue*, extending for many yards, and shepherded by a couple of watching policemen. There they stood in line, men of all ages, from the very old to the mere lad, the faces of each one of them pinched and gashed with hunger. The eyes had a dull, hopeless stare, the weary figures in their rags expressed the utmost dejection in every curve.

THE GREAT ASSEMBLY HALL
Feeding thousands of London's poor
[To face p. 196.

The band started a stirring march, Mr. Charrington[197] and I at its head, together with various other workers of the Mission, who distributed handbills of the evening service as we went along.

We marched a little way down the Mile End Road, and then we turned into some of the narrowest and most dreadful slums of London. In some of these slums the policemen have to patrol in couples for fear of aggression. At every door, at every window of these rookeries, were dozens upon dozens of faces, with the marks of drink and deep poverty upon them. Children swarmed everywhere like bees in a hive. And yet, among all that misery and destitution, it was most pathetic to see how many of them—the little girls especially—were as neatly dressed as their parents could manage, and how their shining hair was brushed and tied up with odds and ends of ribbons.

We passed a large group of young men openly gambling upon the pavement. We passed a little house where, not so very long before, two young men had entered at seven o'clock in the morning, and murdered an old woman who lived there for the sake of a few shillings. We passed innumerable drunken men, some of them fighting and quarrelling among themselves, and more than one drunken woman leaned, leering and nodding, against the wall of her house.

And yet, not a word was said against us. In no single instance, during that two hours' progress, was even an insult hurled at Mr. Charrington or his friends. On the contrary, people waved cheerily to him from upper windows, and he brandished the inevitable umbrella, which he carries as a sort of baton upon these occasions, with[198] a merry greeting. The little children ran to him and hung to the tails of his frock-coat, proud to hold his hand, and to march with him at the head of the music. In streets where at least half of the population were known to the police, and were of the definitely criminal classes, there was nothing but welcome for the evangelist and his music. There was no preaching whatever. Now and again, where two or three foul, dark streets converged, the band stopped and played, very touchingly and sweetly, for it is composed of first-class instrumentalists, that beautiful hymn, "Lead, Kindly Light." That was all, though on all hands the eager helpers were distributing handbills and inviting everyone to come to the Great Hall in the evening.

We had started upon the last part of our march, after one of these halts, when a very drunken man came up to me, and thrust his arm through mine. He had not lost the power of his legs—at any rate with my assistance—and for half an hour or more he insisted on walking thus with me, by Mr. Charrington's side and at the head of the band, pouring out praises of the evangelist in a thick, but sufficiently intelligible voice! It was a curious experience—to me, at least—but it did not seem anything out of the way to my new friends. Suddenly the head of an old man protruded from an upper window, and a voice hailed Mr. Charrington in loud and friendly greeting.

"Who's your friend?" I asked, and when the answer came I looked with added interest, for every one who reads newspapers has heard of the old gentleman known as "Bill Onions,"—that[199] writer of curious doggerel verse, who has been imprisoned something like 480 times for drunkenness, and who, for many years now, has been a convinced teetotaler, and every year attends at the police court of his last conviction to receive the congratulations of the magistrate!

When we got back to the Great Assembly Hall the crowd of the hungry had enormously increased, as also had the attendant policemen. The gates leading into the smaller hall, where the feeding takes place, were opened, and the men filed in, shepherded by the policemen, and delivered their cards of admission.

I stood outside and watched, and it was explained to me that only a certain number of men—and women, in another hall which I did not see on this occasion—were able to feed each Sunday. I think the number is somewhat over seven hundred. But it always happens that a certain number of the tickets which have been distributed on the previous Sunday are not used. There are generally about twenty. The recipients may have got work, may have left London in search of it, or may, alas, have succumbed to their privations, and be where hunger can tear them no more, as was the case with one poor woman who came to the hall on a Sunday, and had her first meal for that day. On the following Monday and Tuesday it was afterwards ascertained that she had nothing whatever, and she died on the Wednesday.

This is known, and, in consequence, a large number of poor outcasts join the *queue* in the hope that there will be room for them.

When all the regular ticket-holders had been[200] admitted, the tickets were counted, and, upon this occasion, it was found that some seventeen more invitations were available.

Seventeen men were counted off from the *queue*, their faces brightening with an inexpressible relief as they marched into the hall. But I never saw, in all my life, anything like the hopeless despair that came upon the faces of the large number of men who were left, who had waited for hours upon this single chance of a meal, and who must now disperse unsatisfied. It touched the very spring of tears, and stabbed the heart with a pain that cannot be forgotten. It was my first experience of anything of the sort, and it was at that moment that I began to realise—though only dimly, then—what Mr. Charrington was doing, and had been doing, for forty long years. The excellent lunch I had just had at my club in the West End seemed to turn to stone within me.

I have little space to devote to the actual meal. I shared it—it was good and sufficient. I sat upon the platform and saw the ravenous eagerness with which these poor men ate what they could. Many of them saved a crust or two and wrapped it in their handkerchiefs to make another meal later on. At the conclusion of the tea, a very short speech was made by a gentleman connected with the Mission, who had, in the past, nearly ruined himself with drink, but is now a happy and prosperous Christian, helping to uplift others. It was not a sensational speech, the emotions of the hungry were not worked up by rhetoric. It was a simple, heartfelt statement.

At the conclusion, more than twenty men of [201] their own accord walked up to a little side table and signed the pledge. This goes on day by day in the Great Assembly Hall, and the percentage of those who keep their promise has been investigated! It is well over fifty per cent.!

Upon the evening of the next Sunday I attended the service in the great hall itself.

The enormous place was packed with people. The upper gallery of all was absolutely crowded by men, many of them in the last stages of destitution, all of them quiet, reverent, and attentive. I was told that a large number of them admitted, to use their own words, that they had "done time." Of the service itself I will say little. I have already quoted other opinions of such services. But, to me personally, who had never been present in my life at anything of the sort, the impression was wholly satisfying. The music was perfect. The singing was by a vast trained choir, the finest that can be heard in the East End of London. The enormous organ was assisted by a band as well as the singers. There was absolutely nothing sensational, *nothing bizarre, nothing vulgar or in bad taste.*

The gospel and the gospel only was preached. Any shibboleths would—personally—have repelled me. Nothing but the story of Jesus and His love for humanity was told. Mr. Charrington himself presided. The preacher was my friend Mr. James B. Wookey, whose testimony to the work accomplished by the evangelist's powers is given in another part of this book.

I was sitting just behind him upon the high [202] platform, surrounded by the Deacons and Choir. I could not see the preacher's face, but his voice, which went pealing out into the great Hall before me, reached my mind as well as my ears with every inflection and change of note. It was an occasion which I shall not easily forget. Here was a man preaching to an enormous number of people in the first place. No ordinary church would hold such a concourse. In the second place the congregation was unique. There were well-dressed and prosperous people not only upon the platform, but in the body of the Hall and first gallery, and stretching right away to the roof were hundreds upon hundreds of outcasts, the men and women for whom Society has no place—the down-trodden and despised.

To these Mr. Wookey addressed an appeal, couched in very simple language, yet it was his use of English which drove home in an extraordinary way.

If we think of it, the greatest effect in all appeals to the heart have been got by the use and arrangement of simple words. If one takes that triumph of the English language, Milton's Lycidas, it is extraordinary to notice how in the most tender and most beautiful lines the monosyllable predominates.

It was just that fact which the preacher of this night thoroughly understood. It was strong nervous English, capable of being comprehended by the meanest individual in the Hall, and yet it was tensely living English also. I confess to extreme surprise. In a minute or two, however, my point of view was changed. I was touched, and deeply touched by the intense pathos of an appeal such as I have seldom heard. I was caught up, as [203] many other members of the congregation were also, by the almost painful driving force, the tremendous earnestness behind the words. I watched the faces in the gallery, row after row; I saw the tense and almost breathless interest upon every one of them. Nobody moved or stirred. The congregation was frozen into attention.

The subject of the sermon was simple enough. We were asked to give up our sins, we were entreated almost with tears to give up strong drink, and come to Jesus. Not simply in the hope of personal happiness and future salvation—though this was, of course, implied—but because every evil act we commit gives personal pain to the Saviour who died for us. It was an intensely moving sermon, and it must have knocked at the hearts of very many of us. There was a dead silence, and in tones faltering with emotion, the preacher concluded by quoting the well-known couplets—

"He died that we might be forgiven, He died to make us good, That we might go at last to Heaven, Saved by His Precious Blood."

Afterwards, in a large room under the hall, I saw many fallen men and women kneeling quietly with one or other of the helpers and confessing all their sin and troubles to Him who alone can heal and pardon.

Strange experiences have been the lot of Mr. Charrington during this part of the work. On one occasion a young man was about to commit suicide, and had a bottle of poison in his pocket. Mr. Charrington wrestled with him upon the floor [204] of the room and took the bottle from him by force, thus saving his life.

So much for my own experiences. Let me conclude this necessarily circumscribed account of the living, burning activities of the Great Assembly Hall at this day, by telling my readers that upon Lord Mayor's Day, when the Chief Magistrate of London holds his Civic State in the grand old hall in the city, two or three thousand of the very poorest are also entertained at the Great Assembly Hall by Mr. Charrington and his co-workers, on behalf of the Lord Mayor, the Sheriffs, and the City Companies.

The poor have enjoyed this banquet for twenty-six years in succession, and I take a typical account of one of these feasts from the columns of a daily paper published in 1902.

"There was a pleasing though pathetic scene witnessed last night in the Great Assembly Hall, Mile End Road, when a large number of London's destitute poor were entertained to supper. As the people of all ages trooped in to take their seats at the long benches laden with good things, many a wan face brightened, as it had probably never brightened before, at the prospect of a good and nourishing meal. For the most part the people came with freshly washed faces, and nicely combed hair, and to one who did not know the vast metropolis and its slums, it would be impossible to believe that these were the people—or at least, many of them—who practically lived in the streets, and helped to augment their own and their parents' incomes by selling matches, flowers, and other articles along the kerbside. There were about two thousand guests, and when they once 'fell to' there was almost a silence. This gradually[205] increased into a murmur, then into a general clatter of tongues as the good fare began to warm them. Then, here and there, came a merry peal of laughter. By the time the meal was finished, every one was gay and happy; each was in a veritable fairyland, and quite oblivious of the life of the morrow. But even such a momentary ray of sunshine into the lives of toil and trouble may help to fashion a character and teach not a few of them what can be done by kindness and well-dispensed generosity, while those who were responsible for the feast were amply recompensed.

"This annual gathering was begun in the year 1887, when three to four hundred people were fed, and from that time onward, owing to the flow of contributions, for which the Lord Mayors of London and their Sheriffs have been in a large degree responsible, the number of people provided for at this annual gathering has reached upwards of two thousand. The task of finding out the most deserving has been left to the clergymen, ministers, mission workers, city missionaries and others. No distinction of sect is made. Each recipient received a meat pie, a cake, two apples, and a loaf, while tea was plentifully supplied. At the conclusion of the meal, a very amusing entertainment was provided. The following telegram was sent to the Lord Mayor: 'Two thousand guests send greetings and thanks to Lord Mayor, Lady Mayoress, and Sheriffs.'"

The reply came speedily, and was as follows—

"Lord Mayor, Lady Mayoress, Sheriffs, and Ladies, greet the guests at Assembly Hall, and thank them for telegram which will be read by Lord Mayor to company at Guildhall. Lord Mayor hopes guests are spending pleasant evening, and regrets he cannot personally greet them.

"Lord Mayor."

[206]"Shortly after nine o'clock these happy people for a while went out into the Mile End Road and sought their squalid homes, after threading their way through London's murky streets on a typical November night. Who is responsible? What is responsible? How shall the sufferings of the poor of the East End of London be alleviated?"

The following appeared in the *Daily Graphic*, November 11, 1902—

THE OTHER BANQUET

"In the East End, when people speak of the Lord Mayor's Banquet, they do not refer to the affair at the Guildhall, but to the meal which has now been provided at the Assembly Hall, Mile End Road, on sixteen consecutive Lord Mayor's Days. Mr. Charrington is responsible for the organisation of this treat to the East End poor—a treat which is doled out to any who are deserving of it and need it, irrespective of their nationality or religious belief. Two thousand invitations were issued for the banquet held last night. The tickets were given for distribution to any responsible men and women who applied for them. All the two thousand invitations were accepted, but, in addition to these, a very few guests were invited at very short notice; in fact, they came to the doors—hundreds of them—and clamoured for admission. They had but one excuse to offer for their behaviour—they were hungry. Some of them were brought inside the gates and as many as could be fed, were fed, but there were hundreds who had to be persuaded by the police to go away. They came back to the doors again—and again—and again. For what? A cup or two of hot tea, and a paper bag containing a pork pie, a pound cake,[207] a roll, and two apples. After the meal there was some music by the students' orchestral band, a few speeches, and a display of animated photographs given by Mr. Luscombe Toms. The guests were welcomed by Mr. Charrington, in the name of the Lord Mayor, and a telegram of thanks and congratulation was sent to the Lord Mayor and the Sheriffs. The Lord Mayor had contributed twenty guineas towards the expenses, the Sheriffs ten guineas each, Sir Horace Marshall twenty guineas, and donations had also been received from several City Companies, and members of the Common Council. When the banquet and entertainment were over, all the paper bags had gone, and the urns, which had contained three hundred and fifty gallons of tea, were empty. Outside there was a hungry, envious crowd."

There has always been a great Banquet at Christmas also, in addition to that provided by the Lord Mayor upon his day.

It is interesting to remember that last year before King George left these shores to proceed to the Great Durbar, he not only took thought for the high business of State, but also for the needs of his poorer subjects. He sent a cheque for ten pounds from Buckingham Palace to aid the Tower Hamlets Mission in its work of feeding the East End poor at Christmas. Mr. Charrington announced the fact to the guests and intimated that the present was the third occasion on which King George had sent a cheque for the purpose.

An enormous work has been done among the children of the East End in connection with the Great Assembly Hall. There is the largest Sunday school in London, there are many agencies for [208] giving the little ones holidays away from their sordid surroundings.

Quite adjacent to the Great Assembly Hall is another Hall capable of seating 1000, known as the Children's Hall. It is used exclusively for Christian and Temperance work amongst the children of the neighbourhood, and is under the control of Mr. Edward H. Mason, who is also Superintendent of the Sunday School, which is probably one of the largest in the Metropolis.

Much attention is devoted to music. Complete Oratorios, and also Gems from the Oratorios are frequently given, the large Choir and Orchestra being composed entirely of the working people of the neighbourhood, and have been brought to a high state of perfection by the Musical Director of the Mission, Mr. G. Day Winter.

The Temperance work—Mr. Charrington's life-work—is unceasing. I have thought it just to sum up all that the evangelist has done for the cause of Temperance in another chapter, so I need not refer to it further in this.

But I must certainly mention the emigration work which has been carried on in connection with the Hall with great success. One of the principal helpers in this work was Captain Hamilton, a retired Army Captain, who for many years took an unceasing interest in the emigration problem in connection with the Tower Hamlets Mission. Four thousand people were sent out to Canada from the Hall, and finally, by a curious turn of fate, Captain Hamilton himself emigrated to British Columbia.

My endeavour in writing of the Great Assembly [209] Hall is rather to give a vivid picture of all that goes on there, without a multiplicity of detail. But if this account leads any one to wish for further information—as I pray that it may lead many people—a postcard to Mr. Edwin H. Kerwin, the secretary, will immediately bring them all the information he or she may wish to obtain.

"He who giveth to the poor, lendeth to the Lord."

[210]

CHAPTER IX
THE APOSTLE OF TEMPERANCE

Mr. Charrington's name is, of course, indissolubly linked with the Temperance cause. His work for Temperance has been the most strenuous of all his efforts. His hatred of strong drink, begun so many years ago when he gave up the great fortune that was made from beer, persists to-day with undiminished force.

Throughout the whole of this book the evangelistic Temperance work is very evident, but in this chapter I gather up a few special instances connected with his lifelong anti-drink crusades.

Of his earlier days, I have gathered a great deal of information from Mr. Richardson—Mr. Charrington's old and valued friend, who is referred to elsewhere in this book.

Here is one story of this time taken down in shorthand exactly as Mr. Richardson told it me.

"A large meeting was held in the East End for the support of certain candidates for the London School Board. The three great brewers, Edward North Buxton, Sir Edmund Hay-Currie, who is now the secretary of the Hospital Sunday Fund, and Mr. William Hoare were present.

"Mr. Bryant, of the celebrated match-makers' firm, was in the chair. Mr. Charrington went to this meeting, and took some few men with him. [211] Before starting, he said to them, 'We are pretty sure to get some bones broken, so do not come unless you are willing to run the risk. We must keep near the door, and look out for our heads. We shall very likely be thrown down the stone staircase.'

"They went to the meeting, and just got in the back of the hall of the Bow and Bromley Institute. There were nearly two thousand people there. Mr. Hoare, the brewer, was speaking. He was a very hesitating speaker, and was just saying, 'And we must do something for those wretched, ragged little children that roam about our streets and are not gathered into the schools.'

"Mr. Charrington thought that as he hesitated for another sentence, it was a good opportunity to break in, and he said at once, before Mr. Hoare could speak again, 'Why, it is you, Mr. Hoare, with your beer, and you, Mr. Buxton, and you, Sir Edmund Hay-Currie, with your gin, who are causing these wretched, ragged children to be roaming about our streets. It is you who are ruining and blasting the homes of the working classes, and I am ashamed to see you clergymen and ministers supporting these brewers and distillers upon this platform here to-night.'

'Mr. Charrington had only gone, in the first instance, to make a protest, not a speech, and expected to be thrust out of the place every moment. He hesitated for a moment, and there was a death-like silence. The proverbial pin could have been heard (if it had been dropped). Then amidst the silence a voice said faintly, 'Why, it's young Charrington! It's young Charrington!' [212] And then another one said a little louder, 'Well done, Charrington! Well done, Charrington! Go it, let 'em have it, let 'em have it!'

"These publicans were going against their own people because their houses were all tied ones. Then followed a scene of indescribable excitement. The language used was unprintable. Mr. Charrington suddenly found himself in the most extraordinary manner the champion of the people. They took him up in the most enthusiastic fashion, shouting out for a speech, delighted with him for personally opposing the brewers, and denouncing them to their faces. They cursed and swore at them, calling them everything imaginable. During all this there were ladies upon the platform. All the people were shouting, 'Make way for him! Make way for him!'

"They pushed one another aside, and somehow made a little alley for him right up to the platform at the other end of the hall, and cheering him on as one would a fireman going up a ladder. He walked forward amid the deafening cheers of the people, mingled with the awful curses on the brewers and the distillers upon the platform.

"When he got as far as the platform, those on it did all they could to keep him off. However, he managed to get on to a chair, laid hold of the rail, and swung himself on to the platform. As he did so the supporters of the brewers thrust their fists at him and tried to beat him off.

"Mr. Charrington just got his footing, and threw himself head first at the stomach of the gentleman standing just in front of him. He recovered himself, and then jerked his elbow into the stomach of[213] the gentleman on his right, and then his other elbow into the gentleman on his left. There was a grand piano standing at one side of the platform, and he climbed on to this and ran along it, and managed to drop into a chair just beside the chairman.

"All this time the people were yelling and getting frantic with delight, as they saw him on the platform at last. And then clergymen on the one side, and Nonconformist ministers on the other, began to abuse him, saying that his conduct was disgraceful. He said that, on the contrary, their being there at all was disgraceful. It was criminal for Christian ministers to be supporting brewers and distillers.

"The chairman rose and tried to get a hearing. 'Whenever he was chairman,' he said, 'he always tried to act justly and see that justice was done to all sides. As it was a public meeting, Mr. Charrington had just as much right to speak as any one else. If he would kindly wait until Mr. Hoare had finished his speech, he would then call upon Mr. Charrington for his.'

"The people present invited Miss Hastings, a lady of good family, to become the candidate in opposition to the brewers and distillers. Mr. Charrington proceeded to advocate her cause, and pleaded with the electors to vote for the lady candidate instead of the brewers and distillers. The result of it all was that Edward North Buxton only got in by four votes, and Miss Hastings was returned at the head of the poll. Mr. Hoare was turned out."

On another occasion, when Mr. Charrington was[214] member for Mile End on the London County Council, a licensing debate was held at which he was present. It was decided that the licenses of public houses then closed should drop, so as to reduce the number of public houses in London. Mr. F. C. Carr-Gonn, a great property owner in South London, was another member, and was also present on this occasion.

On the subject of the Temperance question Mr. Charrington used some illustrations of the evil effects of drink, and said, "Only recently we have had a case of a young man who was otherwise a respectable young fellow enough until he got intoxicated. Although the facts of the case were scarcely known, because he was alone with his mother at the time, it was said by the doctor afterwards that he had kicked his mother to death. He must have kicked her for nearly an hour, and her head was battered to a pulp, and he had kicked out all her teeth. She was most horribly disfigured. All this was through the effect of strong drink. He was a very affectionate son otherwise."

Just then, Mr. Carr-Gonn, in a state of great excitement, rose.

The chairman on that occasion was Lord Rosebery. It had been decided a short time ago that the chairman was always to be addressed as "Mr. Chairman," regardless of his title.

Mr. Carr-Gonn, being in a very excited condition, hardly knew what he was saying. He cried, "Mr. Rosebery! No, I mean my Lord Chairman! No! no! I mean Mr. Rosebery! My Lord Chairman, will you stop him! will you stop him!"

Lord Rosebery rose and said, "I am sorry, Mr.[215] Carr-Gonn, but I must rule that Mr. Charrington is perfectly in order, and if he likes to illustrate the subject, he is at liberty to do so. I cannot interfere. Please proceed with your speech, Mr. Charrington."

At this, Mr. Charrington went on to tell another story of a poor Irish couple who lived in a very dark little alley in the East End of London. They were a respectable and loving couple. The husband, however, would generally get drunk on Saturday nights. One Saturday night he came home drunk as usual, but his wife had made a point of never nagging him, and always spoke kindly to him when he was like that. She got him to rest on the bed on this particular occasion, saying, "Lie down for a little and sleep. You will be better when you wake up."

When he woke up, she said kindly to him, "Oh, Tim, Tim, do give up the drink; it will be better for us all." His only reply was to pick up a bar of iron that was lying on the fender, and did duty for a poker, and with one blow smash in her skull. She never spoke again. He had killed her on the spot. And when Mr. Charrington heard of this, he said, "Well, he stopped her voice, but so long as I have got breath in my body, she being dead, shall go on speaking through me—I will repeat her words: 'Give up the drink; it will be better for us all.' It will be better for the nation, it will be better for the families, it will be better for us all to give up this cursed, damning drink."

We know that all this started the temperance policy of the L.C.C.

I now come to an incident in Frederick Charrington's[216] splendid work for Temperance which shows, as clearly as anything can show, the enormous stir that his determined opposition to the liquor traffic made in London at the time of which I speak.

The brewing interest, and the publicans, held a meeting in Trafalgar Square. It was to have been a mass meeting, and indeed it was largely attended, though not so largely as was anticipated by the originators.

A counter temperance demonstration was organised, and in the result the brewers' meeting was completely spoilt and broken up.

Now with this counter demonstration Mr. Charrington had nothing whatever to do—as it happened. His name, however, was so widely identified with the Temperance cause, that the opposition had no doubt in their own minds that their meeting had been disturbed by him.

They determined, therefore, to "get even" with him, and the method selected was to smash up everything at the next meeting in the hall.

Mr. Charrington had issued invitations for six o'clock, but at four-thirty the Mile End Waste was alive with a huge crowd, numbering among its members some of the most sinister-looking ruffians in London. They were there with a definite and avowed purpose of retaliation.

In a lane by the side of the hall, so seriously was the situation viewed, a hundred and fifty mounted police were waiting.

The crowd clamoured for admission, and surged forward, making the most violent efforts to enter at different points.

In the event, the people became so numerous and[217] threatening, that the authorities of the hall were simply compelled to throw the doors open and admit them.

The hall was filled in an incredibly short space of time, and it was filled by the worst elements in the crowd—the hired bullies who were to wreak the vengeance of the liquor lords upon Mr. Charrington and his supporters. Each man of this crowd had been provided with a bottle of whisky, and many of them had bludgeons in addition.

A great rush was made to the platform, and a yelling fury of drunken men endeavoured to storm it, the stewards literally fighting for their lives to protect it.

I am informed that the *mêlée* passed description, and that many of those who were in it had to be removed to the nearest hospital that night.

The police rushed in and linked arms three deep to hold the assailed platform, upon which Mr. Charrington was sitting, calmly surveying the tumult.

Even after some semblance of order was restored by the police—that is to say, after the actual fight ceased—the subsequent proceedings were all in dumb show. Huge blackboards were produced, resolutions written upon them, and declared carried with drunken roars of approval. Sir Wilfrid Lawson was to have spoken at this meeting, but he remained in a committee room, and was not allowed to show his face at all, as the resentment of the crowd was specially directed against him—though not more so than against Mr. Charrington.

When the whole affair was over, many credible[218] witnesses saw the hired bullies being paid half-a-crown each at the entrance of the hall, by men with bags of silver coin, who had organised this disgraceful riot.

I must now deal with one of the most curious coincidences that has ever come across my notice.

Sir Walter Besant, as I said in the first chapter of this book, drew his character of "Miss Messenger" from Mr. Charrington, and his action in regard to the paternal brewery. As a result of Sir Walter's book—*All Sorts and Conditions of Men*—the People's Palace definitely grew into being, and was about to be erected. Frederick Charrington, on two memorable occasions, was brought into direct conflict with the controlling authorities upon the ever burning question of drink.

The first instance when this occurred created a tremendous sensation in the Press.

Summoned by the then Lord Mayor (Sir John Staple), who presided, a largely attended meeting was held in the Mansion House, in connection with the Beaumont Trust scheme for the establishment of the People's Palace for East London. Besides numerous supporters of the movement there were present a large number of persons who were desirous of eliciting the views of the trustees as to their intentions with respect to Sunday opening and selling intoxicating drink, and it was evident that there were many who believed that the trustees had already decided to open on Sundays and to sell liquor, although no declaration had been made to the effect.

A CARTOON WHICH APPEARED IN FUN DURING THE PEOPLE'S PALACE AGITATION
[To face p. 219.

The Lord Mayor explained that before the money in hand could be made available it was necessary[219] that further sums should be received. Having dwelt upon the desirability of technical training, one of the objects of the scheme, his lordship said certain questions had been put with reference to the proposed opening of the People's Palace on Sundays, and to the sale of alcoholic beverages.

Sir E. Currie then made a statement as to the position of the scheme, and announced that his Royal Highness the Prince of Wales had written regretting his inability to be present, and expressing his unabated interest in it. Similar letters had been received from Lord Salisbury, the Duke of Westminster, and others. The Queen's Hall now building would be ready for opening early next summer.

Mr. F. R. Jennings, Master of the Drapers' Company, then moved, "That the efforts of the trustees who are promoting the establishment of the People's Palace for East London merit the sympathetic and practical support of the community."

General Sir D. Lysons seconded.

Before the resolution was put to the meeting Mr. F. N. Charrington rose to make some observations, and in reply to the Lord Mayor, who intimated that Mr. Ritchie, M.P., and Sir R. Temple would not be able to stop, declined to postpone his remarks, as they applied to the first resolution only. A great many persons on both sides were anxious, he said, that the principles should be settled before the details were discussed, and one lady, who represented many others, had declared she would not give a sixpence until it was settled whether the People's Palace would be opened on [220] Sundays or not, and whether intoxicating drink would be sold there.

The Lord Mayor, interposing, read the resolution and added, that, as chairman of the meeting, he considered the question raised did not effect the motion.

Mr. Charrington rose and said, "I beg leave to say that it is impossible to say whether the efforts of the trustees do merit our sympathy and support until we know whether the Palace is to be opened on the Lord's Day or not, and whether a license is to be applied for."

The Lord Mayor replied, "I should be very unwilling to prevent any gentleman from speaking, but if you persist, I must rule you out of order. I should be very sorry to do so."

Mr. Charrington bowed. "Then it is impossible for us to give an opinion until the question is settled," he said. "We ask: Is strong drink going to be sold or not, and is the Palace to be opened on the Lord's Day? We only want these two questions answered. Both sides want to know whether these questions are to be answered or not."

A scene of great disorder immediately ensued, and the Lord Mayor sternly said, "I must ask you to resume your seat."

Mr. Charrington was quite unmoved. He said, "I contend that my two questions are entirely legal. We are cursed enough with strong drink without having any more introduced into this Palace, which is intended for the benefit of the public."

"You are out of order altogether," was the Lord Mayor's rejoinder.

[221] "There is beer and gin enough already," said Mr. Charrington.

The Lord Mayor: "I must ask you to leave the hall. I will not allow this to continue."

Mr. Charrington: "Is this place to be opened on Sunday or not?"

The Lord Mayor: "Sir, if you persist in interrupting the meeting when I have declared you to be out of order, I shall have you removed." (Loud cheers and counter-cheers. Cries of "Bravo, Charrington!")

Mr. Charrington: "I have a legal right to speak."

The Lord Mayor: "I will take all the responsibility upon myself, and if you don't sit down, I will order the police to remove you."

Mr. Charrington still persisting, Sir E. H. Currie left the platform and swore at Mr. Charrington, who replied, "We've had enough of your gin shops; go back to the platform," which he did. A police officer having been sent for, he was directed to remove Mr. Charrington. Accordingly, the evangelist, who was loudly cheered, left the hall amidst great excitement, exclaiming at every step, "The curse of strong drink!"

This action of Mr. Charrington's created an enormous sensation throughout England. It was felt, and, I think, very rightly felt, that such a courageous action, in such a celebrated place, would further the Temperance cause and give it a new impetus.

I have records of nearly the whole of the religious Press at that time, and their praise and support of Mr. Charrington's action was unanimous.

[222] The interruption was much criticised, of course, but mark the result. Within two or three weeks the trustees wrote officially to the *Times* to say that the decision arrived at was that intoxicating drinks should *not* be sold. As a consequence of this all the polytechnics inserted a clause to the same effect in their trust deeds. Mr. Charrington contends, therefore, that by standing on a chair for five minutes he accomplished—and for nothing—what would have cost a couple of thousand pounds to advertise and ventilate in the Press!

How right, how inevitably right he was, is amply proved by the story which I am about to tell of what actually occurred at the People's Palace during the next year. The passengers along the Mile End Road one Saturday evening in November, between ten and eleven o'clock, were amazed to cross the path, at almost every few yards, of a solitary drunken man, and groups of three and four men in a similar condition, in volunteer uniform, reeling about, shouting, singing, swearing, and otherwise conducting themselves in a lawless and riotous manner. Every one was curious to discover the cause of the unusual scene, and it was soon whispered abroad that the intoxicated volunteers were issuing from the People's Palace, where they had been treated to a Jubilee supper. A ragged little urchin, who had been chaffing several volunteers, who were sprawling about in the mud together, not far from the Lycett Memorial Chapel, in characteristic fashion, replied to the inquiry of a friend of mine, "'They've been 'olding the Jubilee, sir, at the expense o' Charrington; not the Assembly 'All one, ye know, but the one 't's got [223] the brewery. Ain't they tight, sir? Charrington's beer bin too strong for 'em."

The supper was a complimentary "Jubilee" one, given by Mr. Spencer Charrington, M.P., of Mile End, one of the leading partners in the brewery firm of Charrington, Head & Co., and treasurer of the People's

Palace, to the 2nd Tower Hamlets Rifle Volunteers. The guests numbered about a thousand men of the regiment, with thirty-two officers and many civilians, among these being the President of the Local Government Board, and half a dozen East End clergymen. When we consider the amount of liquor which was given to each man—since intoxicants could not now be sold in the Palace—it is not difficult to understand this truly disgusting form of celebrating the Jubilee of our gracious Queen. Of the thousand volunteers at the supper, it was authoritatively stated that no fewer than six hundred were the worse for drink. On leaving the scene of their evening's debauchery, and coming into the night air, some of the volunteers became nothing better than madmen. They rushed into the shops of tradesmen in the Mile End Road, smashed their weighing machinery, and otherwise caused considerable damage. They grossly insulted respectable women and girls, and in various other ways annoyed and terrified the lieges. Some were picked up in the gutter lying dead drunk, and bespattered from head to foot with mud, not only in the Mile End Road, but in various other parts of the East End. Others were lifted into cabs by friends, and in some cases by policemen, and sent home.

Is it to be wondered at, after what has been mentioned,[224] that a portion of the 2nd Tower Hamlets Rifle Volunteers have acquired for themselves the appellation of the drunken "six hundred"?

The scandal created by this affair was enormous, more particularly in the East End, where the People's Palace stood and was a prominent centre in the people's lives.

Mr. Charrington was determined upon a course of action which should prevent such a disgraceful scene recurring for ever and a day.

He accordingly drafted and sent a memorial to the late Queen Victoria, which ran as follows—

"To the Queen's Most Excellent Majesty.

"MADAM—

"In approaching the Throne, we desire to bring to the notice of your most Gracious Majesty the fact that the People's Palace, Mile End Road, which on the occasion of its opening was honoured by your Royal presence, has been used for purposes for which it was never designed, and which we are assured Your Majesty could not and will not approve.

"Mr. Spencer Charrington, M.P. for the Mile End Division of the Tower Hamlets, invited, on Saturday, the 5th inst., six hundred of your Majesty's loyal (Tower Hamlets) Volunteers to dinner.

"Not content with the provision of a substantial repast, Mr. Charrington, who is one of the firm of brewers bearing that name, caused to be introduced into the noble hall of the People's Palace no less than ten 36-gallon barrels of ale, and[225] enormous quantity of whisky, besides gin and other spirits, etc.

"These liquors were distributed during the evening to your Majesty's Tower Hamlets Volunteers, with results which have seriously compromised their character, discipline and honour. The fact is that inside the building scores of Volunteers were seen in every stage of intoxication, and that from 10.30 p.m. until 11.30 p.m. the whole roadway in front of the People's Palace was the scene of the most degrading intemperance. Large numbers of young men, members of the Volunteer corps referred to, came out of the Palace reeling about in every stage of drunkenness.

"Their conduct was shameful and abominable, and what is truthfully described in a leading article in the *Eastern Post and City Chronicle* as 'The Orgy at the People's Palace,' disgraced the whole neighbourhood. Mr. Charrington is a large brewer, and a Member of the House of Commons, and it would appear that his great influence has sufficed to keep out of the London daily Press any notice or criticism of this great disgrace to a large public institution. Therefore we have taken the opportunity of bringing the facts before the notice of Your Most Gracious Majesty. Mr. Charrington is one of the principal Trustees, and the Treasurer of the People's Palace. It is humbly submitted to Your Gracious Majesty that this gentleman is not at liberty to use this Institution for scenes as those described on the corresponding page of this memorial.

"We are simply expressing the desire of large numbers of Your Majesty's dutiful subjects, when[226] we humbly and respectfully ask that Your Majesty will be graciously pleased to cause such inquiries to be made as may be desirable to ascertain the facts as set forth in this letter, and that Your Majesty's powerful influence may be exercised to prevent such demoralising scenes being again witnessed at the People's Palace. This institution was designed to further the instruction and social elevation of Your Majesty's subjects residing in the East End of the metropolis, and it was never contemplated that it should be used to foster intemperance amongst Your Most Gracious Majesty's loyal volunteers.

"We remain, with profound respect, Your Majesty's most dutiful subjects,

"FRED. N. CHARRINGTON,Great Assembly Hall, Mile End, E."HENRY VARLEY,48, Elgin Crescent, W."EDWIN H. KERWIN,31, Mile End Road, E."

A reply was received from Sir Henry Ponsonby as follows—

"Balmoral,
"November 20, 1887.

"SIR,

"I am commanded by the Queen to acknowledge the receipt of your letter of the 16th instant, and to inform you that it has been referred to the Trustees of the People's Palace.

"I have the honour to be, Sir,
"Your obedient servant,
"HENRY F. PONSONBY."

[227]On the 14th of December of that year Mr. Charrington had the gratification of knowing that his efforts had been crowned with success. He again received a letter from Sir Henry Ponsonby, which ran as follows—

"*Windsor Castle.*
"*December 13, 1887.*

"SIR,
"Your letter of the 16th November was duly forwarded by the Queen's command to the Trustees of the People's Palace. The Trustees have passed a resolution that in future no intoxicating liquors will be allowed upon the premises of the People's Palace.

"I have the honour to be, Sir,
"Your obedient servant,
"H. F. PONSONBY."

This was a signal success for temperance, a success entirely due to Frederick Charrington's personal efforts. His energy has always been extraordinary, and one is really lost in amazement as one thinks of those days. He interrupts, throws into utter confusion, an important meeting at the Mansion House. He risks his life over and over again in his temperance crusades. Determined to stamp out the abuse of drink, he not only memorialises the Queen of England, but achieves his purpose in so doing. It is an astonishing record.

In one of the debates in the Houses of Parliament, the question of compensation for the closing of public houses occurred, and one of the greatest[228] demonstrations ever held was held in connection with this, and entitled "The No Compensation Demonstration." It is supposed to have been the largest gathering of people that ever came together in Hyde Park.

A meeting of leading temperance workers was held in Lord Kinnaird's private house in town on this subject. Mr. Charrington happened to be away at the time, and so was not present at this meeting. When he returned, he found that they had come to the conclusion that the Government was too strong for them to make any opposition to their proposals to compensate the publicans. Mr. Charrington said, "Oh, but this will never do. We must have a great demonstration." He then and there determined to start it on his own responsibility. He first of all paid a visit to the lobby of the House of Commons, and interviewed all the members he could who were in favour of temperance. He informed them that a demonstration was going to be held, despite the resolution taken at Lord Kinnaird's meeting, and that being the case, would they join in and help in it? They all agreed to give their time or their money for the project. After that Mr. Charrington went round to the temperance societies, telling them that he had arranged for the demonstration to be held, and asking them if they would join in with his scheme?

They all agreed to help. Thereupon Mr. Charrington called in the assistance of well-known temperance workers, and started on his own part. The various churches in the metropolis and the temperance societies all entered into the scheme, with the exception of the Salvation Army, who[229] would not join as a body. Mr. Charrington's warmest supporter was Cardinal Manning, who brought all his people with their bands and consecrated banners.

This was shortly before the Cardinal's death, and Mr. Charrington often recalls with great interest the visit that he paid to the Cardinal in relation to this matter.

One of Mr. Charrington's honorary secretaries, Mr. Samuel Insull, accompanied him to the residence, and, not knowing that Mr. Charrington was already very intimate with the Cardinal, he said, "Do you know Mr. Charrington, Your Eminence?" who replied, "I should think I did know Mr. Charrington," and, laying his wasted hand upon Mr. Charrington's shoulder, he said "God bless him!"

It is sufficient to say here that the whole demonstration turned out to be the greatest success ever accomplished in the temperance cause. So great were the numbers attending, that when, at the close of the meeting, people were passing out from the gates, the end of the procession was still coming in at the other end of the park. It is calculated that there were at least over two hundred thousand people assembled.

Mr. George Nokes, familiarly known as the Bishop of Whitechapel, has for long years been one of Mr. Charrington's most trusty lieutenants in conducting the total abstinence propaganda amongst the poor, with whom he is a great favourite.

The more I write of this biography—and my pleasant labours are now coming to a pleasant conclusion—the more I marvel at the unequal way in which honours are bestowed in this country.

[230]We all know the famous joke made by "Punch" when that satirical journal coined the word "beerage" as a substitute for "peerage." Sir Wilfred Lawson, himself a great friend and earnest supporter of Mr. Charrington, commented upon this fact over and over again. In all his public speeches he drove it home, and in light verse, for which he had a pretty talent, he again pointed the moral. I have in my possession a book lent me by Mr. Charrington, consisting of cartoons by Sir Frank Carruthers Gould, of the *Westminster Gazette*, and Sir Wilfred Lawson, who supplied the accompanying verses. The book was published some years ago by Mr. Fisher

Unwin, and was entitled *Cartoons in Rhyme and Verse*. Upon the title page there was a characteristic note "to the reader," by Sir Wilfred, who said,

"If any one thinks that these verses are 'rot,'I'm the very last person to say they are not."

Despite Sir Wilfred's humbleness, I have no hesitation in saying that if the verses in question have no literary form, they nevertheless go straight to the point.

I will quote two of them.

"THE BREWER'S POWER. Who to the heathen far away,Send Christian men to preach and pray,And bring them to a brighter day?My Brewer.

Who, when aloud the poor have cried,And poverty is raging wide,Has means of charity supplied?My Brewer.

Who fills his pocket with the sale[231]Of porter, beer, and generous ale,Which crowd the workhouse and the gaol?My Brewer.

Who fills our slums with waifs and strays?Who havoc with our nation plays,And brings disgrace on all our ways?My Brewer.

Who is it bosses all the show,As through this curious world we go,And dominates both high and low?My Brewer."

And again,

"THE BISHOP AND THE BREWER Said the Bishop to the Brewer, 'Sir, I very greatly fear,From all that I have heard, that you adulterate your beer.

Said the Brewer to the Bishop, 'Nay, that really is not true;Who told you such a story? I insist on knowing who.'

But the Bishop he was silent as to what they put in beer,He didn't seem to have, in fact, the very least idea.

For in all his great researches, both in pamphlet and in 'vol.,'It never really struck him that it must be alcohol.

Sir William Gull has told us how the world by this is cursed,That alcohol of all bad things is just the very worst.

But the Bishop—dear, good man!—he still has got a strong idea,That there's something very charming in the purity of beer.

Oh! these Bishops and these Brewers, I really greatly fear,They will never, never solve this point about what's in the beer.

But the land is full of sorrow, and there's little hope of cure,Unless these wise men hit upon a beer that's really 'pure.'

Then let us set to work, boys, with heart, and hope, and cheer,And help them all we can to get 'The Purity of Beer.'[232]

'Tis beer which keeps in comfort—as by every one is known,The Brewer in his mansion, and the Bishop on his throne.

The British Constitution, and all we value here—Church, Army, Navy, Parliament—it's corner-stone is beer."

The brewer, because he amasses a large fortune out of beer, is ennobled.

The ex-brewer—Frederick Charrington, for instance—who gives up an enormous sum for conscience' sake, and an enormous sum again made from beer, remains unhonoured, save by the love and adherence of his own people in the East End. If Frederick Charrington had mixed up an active political propaganda with his Christian work, by now he would have received a baronetcy or at least a knighthood. If he had been merely a paid secretary of some philanthropic organisation, he might yet have been knighted—as more than one recent ennoblement shows. But because he gave up everything, and worked for his Master, without pandering to this or that political party—though in politics he is a Liberal—the *accolade* has never come in his way. From his own point of view I know such an honour would count as nothing. It is for other, and unworldly honours, that he has lived his life. But, as a recognition of his self-sacrifice and devotion, surely some public acknowledgment from the throne would be a very proper thing?

The poor people are not snobbish. It matters nothing to Mr. Charrington's million or so of humble friends whether he is "Mr." or "Sir." But—and of this fact I am thoroughly persuaded—they would regard any honour which His Majesty might be pleased to confer upon him as not only well-merited,[233] but in some sort a fitting recompense for a life of work and devotion almost unequalled in the annals of our time.

I will conclude this chapter of special reference to temperance work by quoting a poem dealing directly with Frederick Charrington, and which has had a very considerable success.

I take it from the *Gordon League Ballads*, written by "Jim's Wife," who in reality is Mrs. Clement Nugent Jackson. The book is entitled *More Gordon League Ballads*, and was published by Skeffington & Son last year.

The first series of these ballads sold in many thousands, and as dramatic stories in verse for reading or reciting at temperance meetings, they can hardly be surpassed. Nearly all of them are founded on fact, as is "A Brave Man," which I give below.

I make no apology for the inclusion of this verse. It is thoroughly representative of what is publicly thought about Frederick Charrington by his innumerable friends and admirers.

A BRAVE MAN

Brave men—I say it humble,Are common on English ground;Common as spires and chimneysWhenever you walk around;But the man of whom I'm thinking was brave with a bravery rare—Ah! a hundred times rarer than rubies—in England or anywhere.I am thinking of a Brewer.This may take you by surprise!But the tale has fact to rest on,And is not a pack of lies.He was rolling rich and generous—generous to every one.A Brewer and a Gentleman, John Sidney Donaldson.

He sent big cheques to Hospitals,[234]And for Children's Holidays,And to Unemployed Relief Funds,And Homes for Waifs and Strays.He was kind to all poor people and meant to do 'em good!Though he knew but precious little about the neighbourhoodIn which the greatest number of his licensed houses stood!'Twas the poorest part of London,Drink-riddled through and through,But his agents worked the business,And all John Donaldson knewWas how it looked on paperAnd the dividends he drew.He was Member for a County that was like a garden ground,For blossom and for beauty and for orchards smiling round.And you always found him willing,To open his Manor gatesFor Band of Hope rejoicings,And Sports, and Temperance Fêtes.

When Parliament was sitting,It happened, one spring day,He visited his brewery.And strolling up that way—Alone, and sort of curious to see what he would meet—As he passed a gorgeous public, gilded and tiled complete,He saw a tipsy woman flung out into the street.The man who flung her savage,Went back inside the place;She fell upon the curb-stoneAnd cut her head and face.And she wasn't more than thirty. 'I'll give that man in charge!Says John Donaldson a-blazing, for his heart was big and large,Too large to hurt a woman—And then he went across'To lift the tipsy creature,And I've heard him say—a ForceLike twenty batteries struck him, and made his eyes see fire!For painted on the house-front was—DONALDSON'S ENTIRE!He looked up at the sign-board.The house was his own tied house. A new one—not long opened—And called 'The Running Grouse.'He'd meant to call that man out. He'd meant to make a row.And send for a policeman—but he couldn't do it now.Something rose up and held him. The crowd that ran to stare,Said the woman's home was handy, so he helped to take her there,

And a wretched hole he found it!...[235]A man was up the stairs,Trying to cook his dinner,And give five children theirs.Just home from his work—poor devil!He looked up with a frownWhen he saw what they were bringing—'Ah!' he says, 'Chuck 'er down.If you'd brought 'er in 'er coffin!I'd 'ave tipped yer 'arf-a-crown.'

'Your wife is hurt and bleeding,'John Sidney Donaldson said.'My wife,' groans the husband bitter,'I wish she was yourn instead!'And he picks up his yelling baby,And crams its mouth with bread.'Tain't the fust time she's a-bleedin'. 'Ere's a 'appy 'ome,' says he.'That's the mother of my children! an' she don't get drunk on tea!Bright and 'appy, ain't we, guv'nor?I dunno who you are,But "The Running Grouse" 'ave done it—With its dirty Private Bar!'He shook his fist out of the window—'We don't want it 'ere.My wife was a sober woman, and it's ruined her in a year!A curse on the 'ouse, an' the landlord!An' I'll say it till I'm dead....'

John Donaldson gave him a sovereign,And went out with a hanging head.

. . . . .

He haunted that part of LondonFor three whole months and more;And he saw what Brewers seldom see,What he'd never faced before.He saw the truth stark naked—not glossed or veiled or hid,He saw with his own eye open that harm that his own beer did.

He saw for himself—John Sidney,Wherever his Houses stood,A Force that worked for evil,That did not work for good.

He saw—he was bound to see it—in the slums the drink-shops made,Christ's flag torn down and trampled by the brute heel of the Trade.He saw, laid bare as murder[236]Done in the broad daylight,The base and ceaseless temptingThat goes on day and night.The tempting of men and women already weak in will,And poor enough in pocket, to be poorer and weaker still.

'We didn't want it 'ere!'... No!And they didn't want it there!Yet here it was, and there it was,For ever! Everywhere!The Tied House in the open,The Hidden Drinking lair,The Spirit Vault, the Cellars, the Private Bar and seat,Calling from every corner and tempting from every street!

The cries, the blows, the curses,Entered into his ears.He saw his golden profitsBlackened with blood and tears.He saw—as angels see them—the facts of what has grownThe saddest money-making the world has ever known.And when he'd seen it fairly,He didn't turn and run!In a hurry to forget it!As many would have done.He wasn't built that way,John Sidney Donaldson.He took and thought for over half a year.And then he made his mind up—steady and firm and clear—To sacrifice his fortune and say good-bye to Beer!

'You're a fool,' said brother Brewers.'And mad!' said the world outside.'I've seen ... *and I can't unsee it*,'John Donaldson replied.'There are other ways of business that are happier ways and higher,And I won't make another shilling out of DONALDSON'S ENTIRE!'

. . . . .

I don't say he turned pauper,And slept upon the boards!But instead of a man with millionsHeading straight for the House of Lords,

He dropped to a man with hundreds—just heading for nothing at all[237]But the prize that falls to the conscience which has answered a noble call.He is living now in London,Careless of blame or praise.Working to help the PeopleIn a hundred splendid ways.Pledged to the cause of TemperanceTo the ending of his days.What he did may be forgotten, or labelled a mistake!But the sacrifice of riches is a mighty one to make.I'm proud of this little Island that gave John Donaldson birthAnd I place him right in the forefront of the bravest men on earth!"

Since I am quoting a few verses in this chapter, I may perhaps give, as a final specimen, a few sternly vigorous lines which were handed to me by my friend the other day. They express, he told me, his whole sentiments upon the drink question in a nut-shell. They are not in the least my own, but that is not the point—their interest lies in the fact that they represent Frederick Charrington's unalterable convictions in a succinct form.

"LICENSED—TO DO WHAT? Licensed *to make* the strong man weak;Licensed *to lay* the wise man low;Licensed a wife's fond heart *to break*,And *make* her children's tears to flow.Licensed *to do* thy neighbour harm;Licensed *to kindle* hate and strife;Licensed *to nerve* the robber's arm;Licensed *to whet* the murderer's knife.Licensed thy neighbour's purse *to drain*,And *rob* him of his very last;Licensed *to heat* his feverish brain,Till madness crown *thy* work at last.Licensed, like a spider for a fly,*To spread* thy nets for man, *thy* prey;*To mock* his struggles—*suck him* dry,Then cast the worthless hulk away.

Licensed, where peace and quiet dwell,[238]*To bring* disease, and want, and woe;Licensed *to make this world a hell*,And *fit* man for a hell below."

"Call up the dead from their cold, cold gravesAnd summon up memory's link,And see if human tongue can tell,The millions damned through drink."

To sum up and crystallise his great temperance efforts, Mr. Charrington has invented a concrete symbol of them. The initials B.R.O.T.A. stand for "The Blue Ring of Total Abstinence," which is entirely Mr. Charrington's idea, and serves as a badge that unites abstainers throughout the whole world.

This ring is made of metal and blue enamel, bearing the aforesaid initials. It can be had in cheap metal, while for richer people it is manufactured in gold set with diamonds. In itself it is a beautiful and decorative thing. As a symbol, as a cementing of the great brotherhood of abstainers formed by Mr. Charrington, it is unique. Mr. Charrington invariably wears one of these rings himself, and from the farthest parts of the world applications for them are daily received.

We now pass to the final chapter of this book, where we see Frederick Charrington in an entirely new setting.

[239]

THE LAST CHAPTER
LORD OF THE MANOR OF OSEA

You have seen the subject of this memoir under very many changing circumstances, the central figure in one lurid scene after another, but there is a side to Frederick Charrington's life as strangely contrasted as possible to nearly all I have hitherto written.

My readers will not have accompanied me so far without realising that in Mr. Charrington is an unique personality. No one has done what he has done, and the originality of temperament has always been curiously aided and abetted by originality and strangeness of circumstance. I venture to think that this chapter illustrates not the least interesting of the great missioner's activities. Certainly he again appears against a background without parallel in English life to-day.

A few years ago—many people will remember it—the press of Great Britain was full of articles upon Osea Island.

Mr. Charrington, it was announced, had purchased this island, lock, stock, and barrel, and was about to develop it as a seaside and health resort, while at the same time carrying out the great temperance scheme.

The whole of the island was to be let or sold under express conditions that no license of any kind[240] whatever would be permitted, or clubs for the sale of intoxicating drink.

Osea was to be, in short, a Temperance Island, and as such was to stand alone in the United Kingdom.

The announcements which appeared at the time of which I am speaking created an extraordinary amount of interest.

THE PIER, OSEA ISLAND, WITH MR. CHARRINGTON'S STEAMER, THE "ANNIE," APPROACHING
THE SALTINGS, OSEA ISLAND
[*To face p.* 240

The *Spectator* said—

"Mr. F. N. Charrington is about to try a most interesting experiment—the effect of total prohibition under fair conditions. He has purchased the well-wooded island of Osea, on the coast of Essex, and intends to turn it into a seaside resort in which the manufacture, sale, and consumption of alcohol will be absolutely prohibited. No license of any kind will be granted, and stringent conditions as to intoxicants will be inserted in all the leases. The island, in fact, will be a large sanatorium conducted on strict temperance principles, and will, it is probable, be in the first place a resort for the great number of persons who wish to break themselves finally of the habit of excess in drinking. The evidence which will gradually accumulate will, we hope, be sifted with much care, and will help to settle three disputed points. Will total abstinence for a time eradicate the desire for drink?—a question upon which the evidence of prisoners is by no means hopeful. Does total abstinence develop, as many affirm, a tendency to the use of drugs such as opium and ether?—a doubt suggested by the mass of experience acquired in the East. Has total abstinence any effect in diminishing working energy? Teetotalers declare with one[241] voice that this question is already answered in the negative; but none of the Northern races as yet show themselves convinced, though there is an approach to the conviction manifest in Canada."

Nearly every paper of any importance in the kingdom devoted considerable space to Mr. Charrington's new scheme.

Near New York there is another island where no intoxicants can be obtained, and it was hearing of this that first gave Mr. Charrington his idea as to the purchase of Osea.

The thought of a drink-barred domain arose in his mind as a logical outcome of his forty years experience in dealing with the miseries and vices of the poor in East London. The work for temperance naturally brought Mr. Charrington into contact with all sorts and conditions of people, and it was not only the slaves of the fiend alcohol in the lower classes—he saw many members of the upper classes going down to their destruction no less surely than their poorer brethren.

He made inquiries, and thought over the whole problem with sustained and earnest attention.

He found that while there were several sanatoria for well-to-do inebriates scattered up and down the country, yet, in nearly every case, such retreats were in proximity to the public-house. No one knew better than he to what lengths the inebriate will go when the craving is upon him, and he found that the unhappy victims who were confined in grounds often very limited in extent would either cunningly or violently break away and secure alcohol.

It was then, while meditating upon the best[242] methods to adopt in rescuing inebriates, that Mr. Charrington noticed a report of the fact that a New York temperance society had purchased an island for a retreat or a sanatorium. Here, it seemed to him, was a thoroughly admirable solution of the problem. Proprietorship of an island precluded the incoming of drink across the silver streak of sea, and at the same time, the domain was large enough in extent to make living upon it perfectly pleasant and without any sense of confinement.

One cannot, however, go to Whiteley's and order an island, and there was still the problem of finding one which should be suitable for the purpose. It was solved at last by the purchase of Osea.

Nothing could have been more convenient. The island is a *real* island. It is always surrounded by deep water on three sides, while on the other the mainland is reached by a road called "The Hard" about a mile long, and only uncovered at low tide.

Shortly after the acquisition of Osea Mr. Charrington stated his plans to an interviewer. How these plans have been extended I shall proceed to say, but meanwhile it is interesting to read the proprietor's views at the time, when the island had only just become his own.

The interviewer of *Household Words* wrote—

"I had noted in a contemporary: 'Mr. Charrington has long been a power in the East End, where his name is a household word,' and I thought it would be in the eternal fitness of things if I interviewed him for *Household Words*. As Honorary Superintendent of the Tower Hamlets Mission he is naturally a very busy man, and as soon as he[243] could give me a few moments I put the question to him—

"'What is the main idea of this new scheme of yours of a teetotal island?'

"'It is not altogether new,' was the reply, 'for the same idea has been carried out on various properties owned by temperance landowners of not allowing drink licenses on any part of their property, as is the case with the Corbett estates; but the good work has been rendered ineffectual by drink being obtainable on adjoining property.'

"'Drink would not be obtainable in inebriate homes,' I suggested.

"'Inebriate homes situated in ordinary neighbourhoods experience the same difficulty,' he exclaimed. 'Inmates afflicted with the accursed craving will scale high walls and walk miles to obtain drink. You would not credit the trouble they would take, the fatigue they would undergo, and the risks to life and limb they would run to procure alcohol. It is only a man who has spent a lifetime in a practical study of the question who can realise its difficulties.'

"'And you anticipate much good from the acquisition of Osea?'

"'In many ways, yes. As a retreat for those whose removal from all chance of temptation is a necessity it will be perfect. Instead of being confined within four walls, like being in a prison, they will be able to roam at large for four miles. Already I have had applications from persons wishing to buy building plots for inebriate homes, convalescent homes, and from one lady M.D., who desires to erect a house for her patients suffering from nerve trouble, and to whom the quiet will be invaluable.'

"'Will it be populated entirely by invalids and inebriates?'

"'Oh, dear, no! Yachting men have applied[244] for sites for bungalows, and can have them on agreeing to the non-intoxicant clause. It will be a very delightful temperance seaside resort. The island is well wooded, with high elms running in single lines north and south and east and west, the trees being in centre of avenues, and by planting young trees on either side we shall get double avenues, as in Chicago and Berlin.'

"'Have you commenced to build yet?'

"'Only workmen's cottages for the builders' men to live in, and these will be picturesque, half-timbered dwellings, similar to those in the city of Chester.'

"'And you anticipate a commercial success for your philanthropic investment?'

"'Most decidedly. Since I acquired Osea at a remarkably moderate cost, I have seen two other islands offered for sale for the same purpose, one near Tenby, and one in Scotland, at £28,000 and £18,000 respectively, which figures are a great contrast to mine, and Osea has the great attraction of being the nearest seaside resort to London.'

"'How do you reach it?'

"'By Great Eastern Railway to Maldon in Essex, and thence by a steamer which has been purchased, which now runs twice a day, the distance being only five miles.'

"'And Osea is not a desert island?'

"'It never has been since the Conquest. In the Doomsday Survey Book (1086) there had always previously been on the island three serfs, one fisherman, and pasture for sixty sheep. If needed there would be room for 10,000 people. Osea has many natural attractions. It abounds with most curious marine plants and shrubs, and is so wild that some of the sea-gulls, the tuke, the stone-runner, and the bar-goose have taken to breeding on the shore.'

"To be able to enjoy life on an island within[245] forty miles of the metropolis, including sea-bathing, fishing and shooting, has the wonderful charm of novelty, to say nothing of its freedom from the pandemonium created by drinking trippers. This of itself ought to draw all London holiday-makers, and we wish Mr. Charrington success in his noble efforts to promote temperance amongst the people, and trust he may have the gratification of seeing his most sanguine hopes realised and his self-sacrificing labours truly and thoroughly appreciated."

In a book such as this, which purports to be a comprehensive history of Frederick Charrington's life, and which will be the only lengthy biography of him ever written with his sanction, it is necessary that I should give some account of the island with which his name will always be associated.

I propose, in the first instance, to tell the history of the island from the very earliest times, and afterwards to describe it in detail and to say something of my life with Mr. Charrington there. It may have struck some of my readers that up to the present I have said little or nothing about the great evangelist's personality. When I began this book I decided to leave this intimate part of the biography to the very last chapter. I designed to draw a pen picture of the man as he is to-day, as he lives upon the island which is his home among the simple things of nature.

In the first place, to the history of Osea. This has been compiled by his friend Mr. Rupert Scott for an excellent little publication issued by Messrs. Partridge, which is in itself a complete guide to the island.

Mr. Scott tells us that before the Norman Conquest[246] the name of this jewel of the Blackwater was Uvesia, and later Ovesey or Osey.

"During the reign of Edward the Confessor (1042-1066) it was owned by one Turbert, who was Lord of the district.

"At the time of the Norman Conquest it was in the possession of one Hamo Dapifer, nephew to William the Conqueror. He held it as a manor, and four hides of land, and there resided on it one bordar or resident. According to the Doomsday survey book (1086), there had always previously been on the island three serfs, one fisherman, and pasture for sixty sheep, and at the time of the survey belonged to the Bouchier family, afterwards created Earls of Essex; and was included in the Capital Manor, or Parish of Great Totham.

"During the reign of Henry II (1154-1189), it was held by Henry Malache, from the king, as one knight's fee. This is found in a MS. of the time of Henry VIII, viz.: 'Totham Magne cum Ovesem, alias Ovesey.' It is not known how this Henry Malache was related to the Bouchier family.

"In the reign of Edward II (1315), the Island of Osea was owned by Gilbert de Clare, Earl of Gloucester, and then came into the possession of Bartholomew de Bouchier and his wife, who retained it from 1410-1411 under Henry VI.

"Its next owner was Sir Hugh Stafford, who married Elizabeth, daughter of Bartholomew, Lord Bouchier, who died in 1420, and was held 'by him as the Manor of Oveseye from King Henry V, as the Honor of Bologne, by the service of half a knight's fee.'

"The island next came into the hands of one[247] Ludovic Robbesart, and Elizabeth his wife, in 1431, during the reign of Henry V, and upon their death for the following two years was held by Anne, widow of the Earl of March.

"The next possessor of Ovesey Island was Henry Bouchier, created first Earl of Essex, and he held the manor of Totham-Oveseye from King Edward VI, and died in 1483.

"He was followed by Anne Bouchier, Marchioness of Northampton, who brought the island to her husband under the title of 'Manor or Isle of Ovesey, with free fishery, free warren, and wrec of the sea.' She died in 1570, during Queen Elizabeth's reign. Her husband forfeited his estates for espousing the cause of Lady Jane Grey, but this Manor of Ovesey was returned to him by a letter patent from the Queen dated August 8, 1558, for his maintenance.

"On the death of the above Anne Bouchier, Marchioness of Northampton, this manor descended to the heir-at-law, one Walter Devereux, who was the first Earl of Essex of that name; but in order to carry on his warfare in Ireland he mortgaged and sold his estates in Essex, including 'Ovesey Island,' which was purchased by a Mr. Thomas Wiseman, of Great Waltham, as, or 'in the name of one tenement, isle, or land surrounded with water in Great Totham' and called 'Awsey,' otherwise 'Ovesey.' Mr. Wiseman held it of Queen Elizabeth by a Knight's service. He died July 15, 1584, without issue.

"It then came into the possession of his two sisters, Elizabeth, wife of Richard Jennings, and Dorothy Wiseman.

[248]"Osea Island was purchased by a Mr. Charles Coe, of Maldon, but it is not known from whom, and it was still owned by him at the time of his death in 1786, and afterwards was conveyed to the Pigott family, who were evidently related to him, because on the south wall of St. Peter's Church at Maldon there is a mural monument to 'John Coe Pigott,' and dated March, 1802.

"'The next owner of the island known was Mrs. Pigott, who married Henry Coape, and was succeeded by his son, Henry Coe Coape, who, through troubles, had to make it over to his brother."

Few spots of only a comparatively small acreage have so well-defined and localised a history as this, and the knowledge of what Osea was, no less than what it is, adds a unique interest to Mr. Charrington's possession.

I arrived at Osea Island, where nearly the whole of this book has been written, upon a bright afternoon in June. The run from Liverpool Street to Maldon is quite a short one, and on descending from the train at the little old-world Essex station, it was difficult to believe that the island of which I had heard so much, and on which, as it has turned out, I was to spend so many happy days, was really within reach.

I drove through Maldon, and came out into an ordinary country road fringed with dust-powdered hedges and high trees. It was ordinary enough, and if any country lane upon a June afternoon can be lacking in the picturesque, the lanes through which I was driven were so. It was all rather flat[249] and monotonous, and the sense of anticipation was a little dulled.

After a drive of about two and a half miles, however, the coachman of my carriage turned to me, and pointing with his whip, said, "That is Osea."

I craned my neck forward, but could see nothing but a distant clump of what were evidently very large trees, cutting into the horizon in a silhouette of dark green. There seemed to be no trace of island whatever, and even when I stood up in the carriage I could see nothing but an adjacent sea-wall, and the red sails of some great sea-going barge, moving, apparently, among the corn-fields.

The suggestion was curiously Dutch, and reminded me of a journey I once made down the great ship canal which runs from Holland to Ghent. A few minutes afterwards the carriage took a sharp turn to the right. The fields changed their character. Coarse pasture-land took the place of corn, and we were running upon a well-kept road bordered by wire fences, which seemed to lead directly to the estuary itself. And then, in a moment more, I got what was my first real glimpse of Osea. The carriage climbed a gentle eminence, and there, spread below me, for the first time I saw the wide salt marshes and the long, curving ribbon of road, submerged twelve hours in the day under fifteen feet of water, which is the only approach to Osea by land.

Beyond was the Island.

One saw at once, and this was the first and prevailing impression, that this was a real island. On either side beyond it was a stretch of gleaming[250] sea, the Island forming the centre of the picture. Just below the road proper ended, and what is locally known as "The Hard" took its place.

The horse began to go more slowly, and in forty seconds we had left all cultivated lands behind and were travelling at a slow trot upon one of the most curious and interesting highways—for "The Hard" can claim to be that—in England.

It was dead low water, but this strange roadway was still covered here and there with little marine pools through which the horse—well accustomed to the journey—ploughed his way manfully. A long row of stakes, at an interval of every ten or twelve feet or so, showed the course of the road, and separated its firmness from the vast expanses of mud on either side. The stakes were all hung with brilliantly-coloured sea-weed, and decorated with arabesques of barnacles. Everywhere, here and there, were sullen tidal creeks, or rather lakes in the mud, which the receding tide had still left full of water. The word "mud" is an unpleasant one, and it suggests something very different from what I saw. Even the more technical and correct phrase, "saltings," hardly gives a reader who has not seen this peculiar and interesting feature of our English landscape, any adequate idea of the scene.

I have already spoken of the long stretches of water, now touched to red and gold by the rays of the afternoon sun, but all round them the whole of the "mud" was covered with the marsh zostera, or widgeon-weed, in every variety of delicate greens and yellows. It looked firm enough to the eye, and yet I knew well that a few steps away from the good, firm passage of "The Hard"[251] would mean frightful danger. Once in the mud a man would sink well up to his waist. He would sink no farther, probably, for the saltings are not quicksands, but he would be held in a grip as firm as steel, and, unless rescued, would remain until the "cruel, crawling foam" crept up and engulfed him.

As we covered the first few hundred yards of the last stage of our journey I realised with a thrill that we had indeed left the confines of ordinary landscape, usual experience, very far behind. The plovers were circling and calling all around us with their slow, graceful flight, a colour symphony in dark black-green with flashes of white. Everywhere they called to each other with their melancholy voices and seemed quite unafraid of man. I could have shot half-a-dozen in the first three hundred yards from the carriage, had I been bent on slaughter.

The strange calls of the marsh-birds—not strange to me, however, who had spent many winters wild-fowling in various parts of the United Kingdom—were heard on either side. With flute-like tremolo the red-shanks—dove-coloured and white—pirouetted in quartettes over the marsh. I saw at least two varieties of the rarer gulls, and then, greatest excitement of all, not a hundred and fifty yards away stood three great herons, full three feet tall, standing like sable sentinels against the green.

And now, at last, we were actually a few yards from the island itself. A well-made road, bordered on one side by a sea-wall, grown over with thick grass and brilliant with wild flowers, ran inland.[252] Upon the other side were smiling cornfields, and everywhere among the fields rose great elms.

From where the sea-road touches the Island, up to Mr. Charrington's home, the "Manor House," is exactly a chain mile. After the fields, the road turns sharply to the right, and proceeds along a fine avenue of shady trees until the "village" is reached.

For several years in succession parties of the Unemployed have been sent to Osea by the Mansion House Committee, the *Daily Telegraph* fund, and other agencies, and it is partly by means of their work that roads were made, sewers laid in the village, and the costly sea-walls strengthened.

There are quite a lot of people who can hardly conceive a picturesque village without, as its central adornment, a village inn. Personally—though, no doubt, there are such places—I have never seen an English village without a public-house. Certainly in any novel dealing with country life the village inn is always mentioned, and frequently plays a spectacular part in the story, while upon the stage a village scene is never complete without the rustic public-house.

Not so at Osea, though I defy any one to find a more picturesque little spot than this tiny settlement in the heart of the Island.

Apart from the one that I have just mentioned, there are other features about the village that make it unique.

In the first place, it is incredibly small at present. In the second, the buildings form a most astonishingly picturesque blend of old and new.

There is an old, flower-covered cottage as one[253] enters, beyond it is the village shop, where every necessary can be obtained. The farmer who farms the cultivated land of the island lives there in a charming old house. Close by in the little village square are enormous elm trees with seats built round their trunks, affording a most grateful shade upon a hot day. There are a few other quaint houses of considerable age, and two of the prettiest and most artistic little bungalows that I have ever seen. These are but the beginning of a whole series of these charming little residences, and are already occupied. With their red roofs, white walls, and green-painted windows, they are as neat and dainty as one of those delicate models of chalets that one buys in Switzerland.

But the principal building in the village is the convalescent home, to which it is intended to bring some of the sick and suffering poor who come under the sheltering care of the Great Assembly Hall workers. This home is nearly finished. The interior alone remains incomplete, and the sum of about a thousand pounds is yet required before it can be opened. I am concerned now, however, merely with its picturesque aspect, and I remember well how struck I was by my first view of the beautiful gabled house with its tall white Tudor chimneys, its Elizabethan woodwork, its true peace. The great bow windows are filled with leaded glass, the high-pitched roofs are of red tiles, and when at length the necessary money is forthcoming I can well conceive what a Paradise this Island Palace of Rest will seem to those who come to it from festering alley and fœtid slum.

There is another very interesting building in the[254] village, though perhaps this can hardly be called picturesque.

This is known as the "Village Hall," and is a large structure of corrugated iron, the money, £1000, for which was the last gift of the late Mr. John Cory to Mr. Charrington for his Osea Island scheme. In his letter enclosing the cheque Mr. Cory said he hoped others would follow his example.

I may perhaps be unduly prejudiced in favour of things Osean, but even this corrugated iron structure, with its background of trees, has mellowed and weathered itself into harmony with its surroundings.

The interior is panelled throughout, and lighted by lofty windows. There is an excellent stage for concerts, and three extra rooms in addition to the large hall. There is a billiard table there for the men working on the estate, and for the use of the many camping parties and others to whom I shall presently refer. In wet weather badminton is played there, and the floor is arranged for roller-skating—let those who think that Osea is without indoor attractions owing to the absence of gin-shop or the theatre, pause!

Of course, upon my first drive to Osea I only took in a single eyeful, as it were, for the carriage left the village and proceeded up a firm, gravelled road to the "Manor House," Mr. Charrington's large and beautiful home.

Another man than Frederick Charrington might well have said to himself, when he purchased such a place as Osea, that he would build a retreat from the harassing work of rescue upon which he was always engaged. He might well have allowed[255] himself to enjoy a little peace now and then undisturbed by those cares for others which he has sustained so nobly throughout his life. But there is nothing of the sentiment uttered by the cultured man in Tennyson's poem. Mr. Charrington had no thought of building himself "a lordly pleasure-house, in which alone to dwell."

Osea was not only to be the one prohibition island in England. It was not only to be an example and encouragement to others in this respect, but it was also to be a means of helping and rescuing other and very differently placed slaves to the Fiend Alcohol than those of the East End. The "Manor House" was not from the first, is not now, merely the great philanthropist's charming country house. It is also a retreat for those members of the upper classes who have fallen into the drink habit. Here they may come if they wish and live a quiet, well-ordered life in a mansion which presents no essential differences either in its appointments or way of life from the comfort of their own homes. There is no restriction of any sort. Victims of drink or of drugs are not kept within the imprisoning walls of some large garden misnamed a "park." They have a whole kingdom of their own in which to enjoy every form of healthy outdoor pursuit, they have a perfectly appointed house in which to live.

The "Manor House" is a large building with many windows looking out over the sea, charming octagonal rooms in two turrets with steep-pointed roofs in the style of an old French chateau, a beautiful lounge with large, open fireplace, where every one foregathers at all hours of the day, a[256] billiard room, dainty private sitting-rooms—all that the most exigeant could possibly desire. Nor is the hospitality of this delightful house offered only to sufferers from self-poisoning. Many people requiring absolute mental rest and perfect quiet, both men and women, make Osea Island their home for a time. And this leaven of the outside world makes the life of the guests at the Manor a singularly bright and cheerful one. I only know of the life in the regular inebriate "homes" from hearsay. But from what those who have confided in me have said, even the best of such places are invested with gloom—a sense of the locked door, of being set apart from the world, which is never absent.

TREE POINT, OSEA ISLAND
[To face p. 256.

In Mr. Charrington's country house there is nothing of the sort. I myself have stayed there to write the greater part of this book—*experto crede*. All sorts and conditions of men, in addition to the more regular inhabitants, who remain for a period of not less than nine months, have passed in and out of the hospitable doors of the Manor House during the weeks I have been there. The experiences which Dr. Waldo, the famous American evangelist, gave me of his work under Mr. Charrington's banner, were told me in my private study at the Manor House, while the tall, handsome man with the twinkling eyes of merriment was staying in the mansion. I have watched one of the most famous painters of the day, of international renown, making sketches of the island, and chatted with him over an after-dinner cigar upon the ethics of Art. At dinner, a week or two ago, out of the ten men present, eight were members of famous[257] public schools, four of the great Universities, one an officer of high rank in the army.

It will be seen, therefore, that not only has Mr. Charrington provided perhaps the truest and best means of escaping from bad habits that can be found in Great Britain, but that he also lives, when upon the island, in an environment no less suited to his personality than that other and greater environment in which his whole life has been spent.

For, now that I come to speak of the man personally—as I know him—the first thing that I wish to say is that he is a very many-sided man.

I have told you in an earlier chapter of what he is in that supreme Lighthouse of the East End, the Great Assembly Hall. You have accompanied him with me into the foulest slums of the Mile End Road district, but in his quiet country home upon the island he is quite as much a part, and always a central part, of the picture, as he is in London.

Frederick Charrington is essentially a man who is never "out of drawing." Whether he is chaffing the son of a peer at Rivermere, sitting in grave conference with some of the greatest men in England, or walking through some slum with a little girl hanging to each hand, he is always adequate, always at his ease.

Only the other day, for example, I heard in a roundabout fashion that the little daughter of an East End tradesman who is a valued worker at the Mission returned home for her birthday after a visit to a relative in the country. Hearing that his little friend was coming home, Mr. Charrington ordered a birthday cake for the child, with the words "Welcome Ivydene" upon it in sugar.[258] And not only this, but he himself went to the little tea party and partook of his own cake.

I suppose, in common with every one else, there must have been moments of deep depression in his life. I am equally sure that very few people have been allowed to see them. He is always merry, though never exuberantly so. His humour is quiet, but very real. There is nothing of the dry or "pawky" order about it. It is simply an intense, an almost childlike love of what is humorous. There is nearly always a twinkle in his eye, and the racy stories of his experiences, told in that low, musical voice of everyday life—which, nevertheless, has rung with such a clarion call in so many great assemblies—would fill a larger book than this.

There is a little humorous twitch of the mouth beneath the moustache, the eyes light up, and then come the invariable words, "Oh, this was rather a funny thing."...

I have never been much of a believer in photographs as being able to convey any real idea of personality. Lots of people will differ from me, but that is my own opinion. The portraits I have chosen to illustrate this book are all excellent ones, as far as portraits go. But to me, at any rate, they are only sketches and shadows of the real Charrington. There is a painting of him when he was a very young man, which hangs in his dining-room, and that does indeed catch something of his spirit, and must represent him with considerable fidelity as he was many years ago.

It was made by Edward Clifford, the fashionable portrait painter of three decades ago, who also drew the pencil sketch which is the first illustration[259] in this volume. For nearly ten years this celebrated and successful painter devoted his week-ends to helping at the Mission.

Unfortunately there is not, to my knowledge, a really good painting of Frederick Charrington as he is to-day. Mr. Nicholson or Mr. Sargent could do him justice, and, in passing, I would ask why there is no authentic portrait of value? I know Frederick Charrington far too well to suppose that he would for a moment spend—or, as he would say, waste—the money necessary for a picture by a well-known artist, but—and may these lines bear fruit!—surely there are hundreds of people who would gladly join a movement which would result in some such picture being obtained and placed in its natural home, the Great Assembly Hall. As there is no such picture, and as photographs are inadequate, I must do the best I can in a few words of prose, though it is always a difficult thing to describe the appearance of any one with whom one has lived and been in communion with for some considerable time.

I think one would describe him as a tall, though not as a very tall man. He is broad shouldered, but slender. Despite his sixty-two years—and it is almost impossible to believe in his age when one sees him—there is hardly a grey hair in his head. His hair, of a dark brown, grows thickly. He wears moustaches and a very small imperial. The eyes are of a deep steadfast blue, and have an extraordinary power of penetration. I have met few people who look you so firmly and directly in the face as Frederick Charrington. It is a steady, kindly, unwavering regard, from the eyes of a man who has nothing to conceal, and everything to[260] give. The nose is straight and Grecian, the lips tender and humorous—a singularly handsome man, in short. But the fact that he has been blessed with good looks rather above the average contributes only slightly to the sum of his extraordinary personality.

And yet, reading what I have written—a mere catalogue of features—I realise how inadequate it is to present the man.

There is nothing in a mask, after all, whether it be made of painted pasteboard or flesh. It is true that, in the case of the human countenance, gross vices leave their marks upon it and nobility of soul and rectitude of life inform it with a hint, a shadow, of the soul within.

But that is when one sees a face with one's own eyes, hears a voice, listen to the words. Nor is it always true even then.

I knew a man—he died last year—who had the face of an angel. It was so pure and beautiful that many spotless women of the most refined perceptions and the loftiest minds, made this man their friend. His open life was kindly, polished, cultured, and blameless. He *was* kindly and cultured. But beneath it all, as very few people ever knew, as very few people ever will know, this man lived a life of such black shame that one can only hope and pray that his stained soul has not gone to swell the red quadrilles of Hell.

No! It is in the living, breathing man that one discerns the truth, and his face is only an index—a finger pointing towards it.

I have spoken of Frederick Charrington's personal appearance, of his sense of humour, and of his voice. But there is still much to be said.

[261]One impression he gives me, and the testimony of all those who have known him far more intimately than I have, and who have been with him for many years, only confirms it. I would say that he is a man pre-eminently born to lead, to *rule*.

I am entirely convinced that in whatever station of life he found himself he would, as if of right, rise to the head. He is the least conceited man I have ever met. He thinks nothing whatever about himself. But there is a certain inward force, an unconscious conviction, in him, which makes him naturally assume the generalship, and so stand in the forefront of the battle.

The kindliest, quietest, most gentle-spoken of men, there is nevertheless, underlying it all, a temperamental dignity, a determination, rather than a desire, to be obeyed, which is the backbone of the whole man. It has made him what he is—the most self-sacrificing and practical philanthropist of his day. He impressed the message of his personal renunciation upon his family when he was little more than a lad. He went his own way, regardless of opposition, and he did this, not because of any innate stubbornness or self-will, but simply because he was absolutely certain and convinced that God was leading him by the hand, that to him there was indeed a cloud by day and a pillar of fire by night.

There is something paradoxical about him, and yet, as I said once before in one of my novels, after all, paradox is only truth standing on its head to attract attention. And the particular paradox in regard to my friend is this: Himself the humblest-minded servant of God who ever fought in the Great War, a subordinate position would [262] have been of no use to him, I do not mean to say that he would not have accepted it. He would have done so if his duty had seemed to him to lie that way, but he would certainly have been a failure.

It must be remembered that this type of character is extremely rare. It is perhaps the rarest of all—and therefore it is frequently the most misunderstood. But there are certain temperaments so inherently royal in their nature, so born to kingship, that if circumstance denies them action, they are never heard of and a great force is lost to the world.

There are thousands upon thousands of men and women this day who may thank God Almighty that the man who has rescued them from an utter overwhelming of body and soul has been given the opportunity of exercising the temperament with which he was born.

But, like all leaders, Frederick Charrington is adored by his subordinates. He must lead, but he cannot be tyrannical. A kinder and more considerate man never breathed. All sorts of little details in my own pleasant friendship with him, not less than those things which men who have known him for thirty and forty years have told me, go to prove the indubitable fact.

As a novelist one is, first and foremost, intensely interested in temperament and the psychology of the mind. I came to Osea Island to study this man of whom I have been writing. I have done so to the best of my ability, and I think that very little about him has escaped me.

I once saw him in a rage royal.

I cannot detail the circumstances, it would not be fair to the other party concerned. It is sufficient [263] to say that a young man of good society was behaving himself in a thoroughly indefensible way. If this young fellow had done what he proposed to do, and it was something which Mr. Charrington had no legal right to restrain him from doing, the result would have been disastrous.

The young man defied the elder one. Several people were present at the scene, and the situation was becoming one of great tension.

As a man of the world I knew what nine out of ten men would have done at the beginning of the incident.

I saw Frederick Charrington's face change to an almost steely hardness. The provocation was enormous, be it remembered. His eyes gleamed with a blue fire. The strong jaw set, the hands clenched themselves—and then as suddenly unclenched. None of us knew what was going to happen.

What did happen was this: Mr. Charrington, still in the quiet, persuasive voice that he had used throughout, conquered by sheer weight of moral force. He is a strong and athletic man himself. I knew, as certainly as that I am writing this, that the natural Adam in him would have simply rejoiced in the swift blow, the physical rejoinder. Nothing of the sort happened, and a quarter of an hour afterwards, as I was sitting with him in his motor-boat and we were slipping over the dancing waves of the Blackwater, he was quietly lighting his pipe and laughing over the whole incident. Not a great thing, perhaps, you will say, but an indication of the man....

The greatest characteristic, indeed, of Frederick Charrington is his courage.

[264] That he possesses physical courage in a marked degree no one who has read this life will be disposed to deny. Physical courage is a high and noble quality, but it can be overrated. It is well for the protection of society, and for the well-being of the social order, that we decorate the soldier with the V.C., or the man who descends into the burning mine with the medal. But at the same time, that moral, or should we not call it *spiritual* courage, for which there is no decoration in this world, is surely a far rarer, far higher quality? When the two are combined, welded and fused into one, as is the case with Frederick Charrington, then, indeed, we meet with a Michael of this world!

I suppose it is a fault in a biographer to be too enthusiastic. I can even remember, some years ago, reviewing a certain biography in which I felt constrained to point out that the writer had quite lost his sense of proportion in admiration of his hero. I think, now, that probably the writer was correct, and that it was only my prejudice against the subject of the biography which led me to say what I did at the time.

Yet, believe me, having met many good and eminent men, in many cities, in many parts of the world—*I write with a glow!*

And it is not only because I *should* not, but that I *could* not, if my words did not come straight from my conviction.

Thus Frederick Charrington as I see him in daily life.

I will say something of my stay on Osea Island, because it will complete the picture of Mr. Charrington in his kingdom, and will also give me the opportunity of completing my sketch.

[265] I have hinted before of pleasant companionship, and the visits of well-known people. But there is another side. The peace and calm which falls upon the soul in this remote place, which, at the same time, is so astonishingly near to London, is a thing incommunicable by words. The only sounds I hear from my study window are the calls of the birds, and the *lap, lap* of the tide. The air is extraordinary.

Every one has his own pet watering-place. Every one supposes that the air *there* is finer than the air anywhere else. As a matter of fact, I am inclined to think that from the mouth of the Thames as far as Hull the air of East-coast watering-places is precisely alike—wonderfully invigorating, full of the salt freshness it has gathered in its progress over the German Ocean, with real healing upon its wings.

And, just like any one else, I have *my* own peculiar and particular love. That is the air of Osea.

Let me proceed to prove to you why the air at Osea is better than air anywhere else. It is because of the "saltings." Just as the sea itself around the island is more salt than the sea of the free ocean owing to the deposits left upon the mud at low tide, so the air is more heavily charged with ozone. The other day an artist on the staff of *Punch* visited me at Osea in his yacht, and spent a few hours on the island. As he was getting into his dinghy in the evening, he said, "I do not know Charrington, and he must be an odd sort of crank not to allow any drinks here. Still, I suppose he justifies himself upon the principle that his own private air is like champagne—it certainly is marvellous!"

I am not puffing Osea as a residential quarter,[266] but it is worth while recording another tribute to this life-giving air, which I shall be so sorry to leave for a time, when I have written the imminent last words of this biography. The head of a great City company has been staying here recently. He came down, in search of peace, at the end of the London season. He told me, upon the night of his arrival, that he had been unable to sleep for weeks, unable to eat properly, was thoroughly unnerved. Two days afterwards, as we were walking upon the pier, he turned to me in a transport of enthusiasm. "By Jove!" he said, "I have never met anything like it in my life!"—and the man I refer to is one of the best travelled persons of his day.

The silence, the huge arc of sky, the life-giving breezes, the perfect and tranquil beauty—what more can the heart of man desire? Very little, I think, and yet there is even more to be said about Osea.

Situated as it is in the middle of the Blackwater, it is naturally a great yachting centre. At week-ends, moored off the island, there are innumerable boats, from the little yawl with a single cabin and a crew of two, to the stately cutter of a hundred tons, with its auxiliary motor, and its spruce sailors.

There is a pier of about a hundred yards long stretching out into the tideway, where there is always a vast stretch of deep water, and to this pier twice or three times a day, from Maldon, comes Mr. Charrington's own steamer, which runs for the convenience of the island inhabitants and also of excursionists. Day by day this boat, with its hundred or more people, makes a circuit of the island, and proceeds onwards to the German Ocean.

Osea itself is well supplied with boats belonging[267] to the Manor House. There is a large motor-boat, which runs in and out at the disposal of any one. There are sailing-boats, rowing-boats, fishing-boats, to suit every taste, every accident of tide or weather.

Sea fishing can be had all the year round. I have not tried it, personally, nor has Mr. Charrington himself much time to devote to this form of sport, but the islanders assure me that all is as it should be. In the official Maldon guide to Osea I read, and from it I reproduce, as follows—

"Spruling, or handline fishing, is the method most in vogue, using the common log- or lugworm for bait; this fine fellow lives in the sandy mud along the shore, but it is not easily dug by the amateur, although in many spots it is abundant; their local price is generally half-a-crown per quart. The best time for fishing is autumn and spring, but it is only for about two hours before and after low tide that it is possible to hold ground, the tide running too strong before and after; by spruling sufficient fish can often be caught; a party of four has caught as many as 400 good fish in about two hours. These are mostly dabs, plaice, whiting, codling, and the large-mouthed, voracious little father-lasher, locally called 'bull-rout,' which often gives good sport, but is otherwise very little use; occasionally a weaver, with its poisonous fin, or a red gurnard may be caught. A more successful method of fishing is by hoop-netting, baiting with the small shore-crab, but this is not permitted upon the ground of the Tollesbury and Mersea Oyster Fishery Co., which is well marked by the large beacons on each shore; the upper edge of the oyster ground is a very good spot for sport. Dabs, plaice, and similar flatfish are known as market-fish, scantlings and hoppers, according to size, the latter being the smallest; soles as soles, slips and tongues.

[268]"Spruling is best by night, especially in September and October for codling and whiting, and when lying quietly at anchor, possibly waiting for the tide to get slack enough to fish, we are sure to notice the tide leaving the mud, and then the drain heads, as they are called locally, make a noise like the tail of a mill when the wheel is in motion, or like the hum of a distant railway train. This is always especially noticeable just at dusk.

"The variety of sport to be derived from sea-fishing is great, and its votaries will not need them to be particularised, while the amateur can learn best by following the instructions of his fellow-sportsmen. Bass are frequently caught up to 10 lb. in weight. Grey mullet are almost as big, but they are very agile and wary, jumping like hares over a peternet when shooting the creeks. Garfish are taken in plenty in early summer; they swim on the top of the water, and when present are sure to be seen in the sun jumping out and playing on the surface; when cooked, these little-known, long-nosed fish much resemble mackerel, but they are sweeter; a foolish prejudice exists against them because their bones are grass-green. It seems almost impossible to hook the wily and soft-mouthed mullet, but bass, garfish and other summer species may be taken by drift lines. Eels, which are abundant, but not so large as they used to be, are taken in quantities, but generally by the professional by babbing; this is practised from a punt in shallow water, by threading a bunch of logworms on worsted and sinking this to the bottom on a short line, with a six- to eight-foot rod. Anchor or moor the punt so that it does not sheer about with the tide. A bite is quickly felt, as the eel tugs very strongly, but to catch them all requires practice; flounders are often caught with the eels. Eel shearing or spearing on the mud, either when walking on splatches (flat boards tied on to the soles of your boots) or from a punt or boat, is[269] seldom profitable to the amateur. Eel trawling with a very fine-meshed net, a most destructive operation, was first discovered by John Heard, of Tollesbury, when trawling for prawns on Mersea shore. To catch the eels it is necessary to have a tunnel in the trawl to prevent them coming back and escaping; they travel backwards.

"The various kinds of net-fishing are too numerous to mention, but there are several of the Maldon fishermen who can be prevailed upon for a consideration to take a passenger or two for a day's trawling, if he be not too particular as to the luxury of his accommodation. The known fish fauna of the Blackwater is a rich one, and the occurrence of almost any British species in this fine estuary is possible. Salmon and trout are frequently taken."

There is a little shooting, but not much—I except always wildfowl. For several years in the past the shooting has been let, but Mr. Charrington has given up disposing of his rights, and in the season such game as there is upon the island is always at the disposal of sportsmen who are living there. Still, I think that fifty brace of partridges would mean a very good year upon Osea.

I am tempted to catalogue the wild flowers, though I know nothing about the details, except that all is beautiful. There are printed authorities to consult upon the floral delights of Osea. And the descriptive writer is too apt to catalogue the gutter, and think he is writing of the street. Let all those things go. Let me rather tell in a few final words of gentle evenings, August nights, and silver dawns, in which I have talked of deep things with my host.

A world of physical and material beauty has its way in inducing high and beautiful thoughts in[270] the human mind. Charrington and I have sat in the garden of the Manor House when a great round, red moon has hung in a sky of black velvet, and the kissing night-breezes have filled us with health and thrilled the blood. But it has not been only æsthetic enjoyment of material perfection that irradiated the night. It has been the stories he has told me in his low voice, while the red end of his cigar—for, like Spurgeon, he is a great smoker—has pulsed and glowed in the blackness—that have brought one's thoughts nearer and nearer to the heavenly mysteries that dark and dawn have curtained from the human sense.

I have listened to that slow, reminiscent voice, mingled with the little breezes and the noise of the tide. I have heard, "Now, Thorne, this is a little incident" ... or, "I expect this will strike you as being rather funny" ... and the whole pathos of human life has become part of the night.

I have turned towards my companion and said ... "Go on, tell me some more."

And ever the subdued organ voice has continued, speaking of the great work in the East End.

The whole gamut of life in its most revolting, and yet, sometimes, its sweetest and noblest aspect, has been put before me through the quiet hours of night in a series of flashing vivid pictures, which have raised the soul to higher hope, have filled the heart and eyes with tears, and have made one even more conscious of the certain presence of God in the world than the summer night could show.

And all this without a note, without a single touch of self, on the part of the narrator. It has all come out quite naturally and simply. I have abstained from journalistic questionings. When[271] he would be silent I have not urged him to speak. When the mood was on him to talk to me, I have listened.

All his life he has enjoyed good health, though living in the congested East of London. Two serious illnesses alone have to be mentioned: typhoid at one time—when it was touch-and-go with him, another time serious influenza with some lung complication. His doctors ordered him a year's travel, and he visited Australia, Egypt and South Africa. He has, indeed, travelled very extensively.

He has never married. In early life, as I have said elsewhere, he became convinced that his work would be better served if he remained single. I think, however, that his somewhat monastic theories have been softened by Time. At least I have heard him say that he does not advise any one to follow his example!

There are a little cluster of us—I refer to people in the literary and artistic world—who have come together and who are thinking of building ourselves homes upon the shores of the island. I hope this, for my friends and for myself, will soon come about.

Be that as it may, I shall never forget the days and nights I have spent with Frederick Charrington when I have been endeavouring, faithfully and without prejudice, to present his life as it has been, and to show him to my readers through the medium of my mind.

I may have made a thousand mistakes in my view—I hope not. All I know is, that I have tried to do my best.

All that I am certain is, that I have been privileged to tell the story of a great spiritual force of this era.

[272]In everything that he has done throughout his life he has always proved himself a Christian and a Gentleman. Upon that day—many years distant I hope and believe—when he is gathered up to be with Jesus, he will leave behind him a legacy of good works, an inspiration to other missionaries and evangelists of Christ, which will not easily be forgotten.

Who of us can say that in our youth we turned away from all this world has to offer and renounced enormous fortune and high place?

Who of us can say that since such a day we have lived wholly and entirely for others, among the most appalling surroundings, with the greatest courage?

To have held up the standard of our Lord in the very forefront of the battle, never to have swerved so much as a hair's breadth from the very thickest of the fight. To have kept the Faith always....

I will say no more.

The life of a good man, surveyed in its entirety, hushes the voice, and stills the moving pen.

You, who have travelled with me thus far, if it seems good to you, and for the sake of Jesus, and this man who has fought for Him so valiantly and so long, *help him in his work*.

I bid you good-bye, as my friend also.

In the last words of this memoir, I like to think of him walking, as I saw him not long ago, through horrible slums upon a certain Sunday afternoon.

Clinging to each hand, trotting eagerly beside him, were two little girls with eager, upturned faces and bright golden hair.

Printed in Great Britain
by Amazon

40667499R00046